THREE SHOT BURST

The Foggy Moscowitz series

Phillip DePoy

severn
House

This first world edition published 2016
in Great Britain and 2017 in the USA by
SEVERN HOUSE PUBLISHERS LTD of
19 Cedar Road, Sutton, Surrey, England, SM2 5DA.
Trade paperback edition first published
in Great Britain and the USA 2017 by
SEVERN HOUSE PUBLISHERS LTD

British Library Cataloguing in Publication Data
A CIP catalogue record for this title is available from the British Library.

ISBN-13: 978-0-7278-8663-7 (cased)
ISBN-13: 978-1-84751-766-1 (trade paper)
ISBN-13: 978-1-78010-833-9 (e-book)

Typeset by Palimpsest Book Production Ltd.,
Falkirk, Stirlingshire, Scotland.

ONE

Florida, 1975

David Waters ordered a gin martini, no olives, at Mary's Shallow Grave, just after six in the evening. He said he needed to calm his nerves. Anyone who knew David would have agreed, he was a very nervous person – if by *nervous* you actually meant *crazy*. He saw a kid named Lena in a corner booth, sipping a Coca-Cola. He sauntered over, leaned in, and said something to her. Without a word, Lena stood up and shot him three times in the chest. David was lying next to a mess of broken glass and blood when I came in, and he was just about as dead as he was going to get. No one seemed concerned for him at all. Everyone had gathered around Lena to make sure she was all right. That's because Lena had no parents, no fixed abode, and she was fourteen years old.

That's why they called me.

'Foggy,' Detective Baxter said when he saw me push through the door. 'Good.'

'You rang?' I mumbled.

He lifted his head in the direction of the kid. She was still sitting in the booth; Mary, the proprietress, was sitting beside her. They weren't talking.

I sauntered over and Mary stood up.

'You want anything?' she asked softly, headed back toward the bar.

'No, thanks,' I told her, eyes on Lena.

I sat down across from the kid. She was dressed in a tee shirt that said 'Ennui' on it, a loose-fitting pair of ratty jeans, and slick black cowboy boots. I was dressed in a nice mohair suit, a smart black tie, and Florsheims. We doubtless made something of an odd pair in Fry's Bay, Florida, home of the slowest moving cultural evolution in the Western Hemisphere.

Mary's Shallow Grave, all dark wood and stained floors,

was at least fifty years old and looked a hundred. The size of a very large living room, it had been built in the 1920s when Fry's Bay was little more than a private deep sea fishing destination for the bloated swells – guys who subsequently lost everything when the stock market crashed. The crash landed hard on Fry's Bay, and the town had never recovered. By 1974, it was the best example of hopelessness I ever wanted to know.

'I'm Foggy Moscowitz,' I began.

'I know who you are,' Lena told me calmly. 'You're from something called *Child Protective Services*. They told me you were coming. Apparently they think I'm a child who needs protection. We can skip ahead. I have a tested IQ of 157, and I carry a gun because I have no parents. I'm fourteen years old, and I've already graduated high school. If I had any cash at all, I'd be in college already. I'm not bragging. I just want you to know who you're talking to.'

'Got it. I'm talking to a brainy Dead End Kid.'

She blinked. 'A what?'

'Oh,' I said, eyes wide, 'so I guess Miss I-have-a-tested-IQ-of-157 doesn't know everything. It just so happens that Leo Gorcey was a sort of hero of mine.'

'Who?' She leaned forward.

'Leo Gorcey was the leader of the Dead End Kids,' I said. 'They were tough guys in a bunch of old movies. I saw them on Saturday mornings at the local cinema where I grew up.'

'Tough guys,' she repeated.

'The toughest,' I confirmed. 'Like you.'

'Damn straight.' She leaned back. 'So what were you doing out at the movies on Shabbat?'

'You assume because my name is Moscowitz and I have a New York accent that I'm a Jew?'

'Partly,' she admitted, 'but mostly my clue was when you came in and Mary said, "There he is, he'll take care of you. He's a Jew but he's nice."'

I glanced over at Mary disapprovingly.

'So you see what I have to put up with around here,' I said.

'You don't have to tell me,' she commiserated. 'I grew up smart. The last thing you want to be in a small town is *smart*.'

'Well.' I narrowed my eyes. 'You shot David Waters. That wasn't especially smart.'

'No choice.' She said it cold as ice.

'You shot him three times.'

'I pulled once, the *gun* shot him three times. It's a Heckler and Koch VP70. Anyway, the cops have it now.'

The VP70 was a 9mm machine pistol with the three shot burst system and a polymer frame. It had just come out recently, in 1970, and she was right: a single pump would have fired three rounds. But it was a strange weapon for a kid to have, especially since it was double action only, which made the trigger pull fairly heavy.

Nevertheless, I decided to play along with her supposition that she was the brightest bulb in the joint, so rather than quiz her about it, I tried a little interpersonal psychology.

'You know that the VP stands for *Volkspistole*,' I said, 'which is German. It means—'

'The people's pistol,' she interrupted. 'Like Volkswagen is the people's car.'

'Perhaps you can imagine my discomfort with the German industrial system in general,' I allowed, 'given that you've already surmised my ethnicity.'

'Would you like me better if I told you that I took it off a Neo-Nazi?'

'I like you just fine as it is,' I said, 'but I probably *would* like you better if you hadn't killed a member of the top oil-rich Seminole family in the state. No matter what gun you used.'

'I said I didn't have a choice,' she snapped. 'He was drunk out of his mind, and I was scared.'

'You don't look scared to me,' I assessed.

She glanced over at the dead body. 'I'm not *now*.'

'Yeah, well – right. Now he's dead.'

'He threatened me, and I feared for my life,' she intoned, like she'd heard it on television.

'Uh huh,' I said, elbows on the table, 'that's pretty much what Detective Baxter told me when he called. I just wanted to hear about it from you.'

'Why?'

'So I could see the look in your eye when you said it,' I told her.

'And?' she asked, her chin jutted my direction in a clear display of defiance.

'And I found out what I needed to know.' I stood. 'Come on.'

She resisted.

'Come on where?' She stuck to her seat. 'What did you find out?'

'You're not scared of anything,' I answered, glancing down at the dead body. 'Least of all that drunken rich kid. You plugged him because of something he said to you. I just have to find out what that was. Until I do, you're coming with me.'

'I'm *not* coming with you, in fact,' she insisted, grabbing the edge of the table in front of her.

'You can't stay here in the bar,' I reasoned, 'and I don't want Officer Baxter to take you to jail. We have no appropriate juvenile facility here in our little corner of paradise, so you're coming with me. You can come kicking and screaming, or you can come laughing and singing. But you're going to come with me.'

She took in a fairly deep breath.

'Well,' she told me philosophically, 'that's life, that's fate, that's the ordained way. Your path is your path no matter what you do.'

'I'm not sure what you're talking about,' I told her, 'but if it makes it any easier for me to get you to walk a couple of blocks to my place, I'm all for it.'

'I'm reading the Alan Watts book on Zen,' she allowed, easing herself out of the booth. 'This might be a sort of object lesson for me in that regard.'

'Once again, no idea,' I assured her. 'But I'm happy to see at least the illusion of cooperation.'

'"The illusion of cooperation,"' she repeated. 'You know, Foggy. This could be the beginning of a beautiful friendship.'

I glanced down at her. 'Are you quoting *Casablanca* to me?'

'I am.'

'And *you're* Bogart?'

'Yes.'

I smiled. 'OK. Just so I know where I stand. Claude Raines is pretty great, too, you know.'

'He was perfect in *The Invisible Man*.'

'Agreed.' I caught Baxter's eye. 'Let's go speak with the local constabulary.'

I headed toward the policeman by the front door; Lena followed.

'I'm going to take the kid to my place for tonight,' I said to Baxter. 'We'll figure out where to go after that – in the morning, right?'

He shrugged. 'OK, but you understand what kind of monster storm there's going to be in the morning when David's father hears about this.'

'There's not a person within a hundred miles of where we're standing,' I responded, 'who doesn't think David Waters got what was coming to him one way or another.'

Baxter looked over at the dead body. 'Yeah. But when it's family – you know.'

'Rich Seminole family, you mean,' I grumbled.

'Yes,' he insisted, a little too heartily. '*Rich* family.'

'Isn't the phrase "rich Seminole" an oxymoron?' Lena interjected.

'The Waters family members all have oil, land, and money,' I explained, 'as long as this new outfit Exxon doesn't manage to take it away from them.'

'My money's on the corporation,' Lena mumbled. 'Those bastards usually get everything, don't they? In the end?'

I caught Baxter's eye and said, 'She's a tough guy.'

'I'm a Dead End Kid,' she corrected.

'A what?' Baxter asked.

Lena gave me a smile. 'You see what I have to put up with around here?'

Then, from out of nowhere, Mary growled, 'Where you taking that kid, Foggy?'

I turned around to see her standing behind the bar, hair piled on top of her head like a dingy mop. The circles under her eyes, in that light, were darker than her bruised plum eye shadow, and the Kool dangling from her thin lips was more ash than tobacco.

'It's OK, Mary,' I assured her. 'She's coming to my place tonight.'

Mary closed her eyes for a second, then she took the smoke out of her mouth and crushed it into an ash tray on the bar.

'Good,' she said softly. 'Because she ain't about to go to jail.'

'No,' I assured her, 'she's not.'

'You a good man, Foggy,' she told me.

That settled, Lena and I took off. We found ourselves outside just as the December sun was beginning to set over the ocean. There was a preponderance of mauve.

'Pretty,' I said, nodding toward nature's beauty.

'Yeah,' Lena mumbled, 'you know what makes those colors so intense? Air pollution. In thirty or forty years it'll be so bad that you'll need scuba gear to take a walk on the street in this town.'

'I see.' I looked down at her. 'But what I want you to know is that even out of something awful in life, you can still get a little beauty, like this sunset.'

'And what I want you to know,' she said, eyes narrow, 'is that life stinks, no matter how you light it up.'

TWO

My place in Fry's Bay is not so bad. It's a quiet apartment in a 1940s building. There are only three other apartments. Two are owned by the relatively wealthy, and they call them condos, although they are in no way different from my month-to-month rental. And they're almost always empty. The fourth place is occupied by the building's owner, Evelyn. She's a very nice ninety-year-old dame who bought it when it was new and never let go. The front of the building faces a nice garden, and you can always find Evelyn out there fussing with the flora. The back of the building looks out onto the ocean, and that's why the old girl never let go: it's beautiful. Very peaceful. A far cry from my Aunt Shayna's place in Brooklyn where I mostly lived until I absconded to Florida.

'Jesus, Foggy,' Lena said when I opened the front door and she got a load of the view, 'nice place!'

'Yes,' I agreed.

She skipped over to the sliding glass doors that opened onto the patio.

'You can see the ocean.'

'That I can. You hungry?'

'You cooking?'

'Don't sound so skeptical,' I told her. 'I scramble a mean egg.'

'I could have eggs.' She collapsed onto the sofa. 'This is my bed?'

'Right.' I headed for the kitchenette.

She bounced off the sofa and beat me to it. 'You're going to get your nice suit all messed up.'

'I'm very meticulous in the kitchen,' I asserted.

'Shove over,' she commanded. 'I'll make us an omelet.'

'Oh you will?'

She opened the fridge. 'You got onions, peppers – what is that? Havarti?'

'Get out of my refrigerator,' I told her.

'You get out of my kitchen,' she grinned. 'I'm trying to make an omelet here.'

'And just what would you know about making an omelet?' I demanded.

'Take a seat in the living room,' she said very compellingly, 'put your feet up, have a drink, and you'll find out. And you won't have to worry about your nice threads.'

'You're very bossy,' I observed.

'It's cute coming from a person my age,' she explained. 'I figure I have about three more years of that kind of cute before it gets to be annoying.'

'Then what, wise guy?'

'Then,' she said, shoving my arm to hasten my egress, 'I'll have to change my tune. Now go! Oh! Speaking of tunes, put on some music.'

I abandoned the kitchenette, took off my coat, put *Stardust* on the stereo, and sat on the sofa.

'You're a menace, you know?' I told her. 'You've caused a real mess in this town. And now I have to figure it out.'

'Yeah.' She smiled but didn't look up from what she was doing. 'I took to you right away also. I love this music.'

'Good.' I had to smile myself. 'Glad we got all that settled. So. Are you going to tell me what David Waters said to you tonight, or am I going to have to wait?'

'Don't spoil it, Sherlock,' she complained. 'Things were going so well. Hey! You have mushrooms. This is going to be a very tasty dish.'

I watched her turn back to the stove. She looked like she was enjoying herself. That's when I began to wonder what was wrong with a kid who could kill a man in cold blood and then make a nice egg dish. Me, I never killed a guy, and I was a little unnerved at the sight of all that blood and glass at the Shallow Grave. She seemed unrepentantly oblivious. Still, she liked *Stardust*, so she wasn't all wrong.

'You seem very comfortable in the kitchen,' I said, watching her easy way with a frying pan.

'I used to cook for my – I know my way around the kitchen, that's all,' she said, not looking at me.

I leaned back on the sofa. 'Now is about the time that I – sorry, but I have to ask about your parents. I should notify them.'

'They're dead.'

That was all she had to say on the subject. But my opinion was that keeping it short usually turned out to be the best way to lie.

'I'm very sorry to hear that,' I told her without a hint of sympathy. 'How'd it happen?'

'Look.' She stopped what she was doing and finally looked at me. 'The last thing in this world I want to talk about is my rotten parents, OK?'

'OK.' I smiled. 'But where are they really?'

'Oklahoma,' she snapped.

And that was the end of our banter. She clammed up. No matter what I said after that, she wouldn't respond.

She finished the omelets – they were superior in every way – and we dined in relative silence. It was about eight o'clock by then.

'Am I supposed to insist that you go to bed?' I asked her, clearing the dishes.

'To tell the truth,' she admitted, 'I'm pretty sleepy. I had a rough day. Even before I got to Mary's place.'

'Now that you mention it,' I told her from the kitchen, 'I wouldn't mind an early evening myself. You get the bathroom first. I'll fix the dishes.'

In no time at all, the kid was snoring on the sofa underneath a quilt. I figured I'd get farther in the question department after she'd had a good night's sleep.

I was just settling down on top of my bed, clothes on, when I heard the front door of my apartment explode. I jumped up. Three men the size of the Mighty Joe Young had materialized in my living room. My door had been knocked off its hinges by one of the apes.

I flew into the room only to find Lena holding the goons at bay with a very clean 1951 Beretta M. A semi-automatic, it was a pistol that had been created exclusively for the Italian military. It wasn't the same Beretta as James Bond used – it was bigger.

'I'm not even going to ask where you got that gun,' I said to Lena.

'Steady, boys,' she said to the big gents in my home. 'I shot David Waters a couple of hours ago, and I'm just as willing to shoot you.'

'Nobody's going to shoot anybody,' I said, taking a few steps forward.

Then, through what was left of my front door, there came the one person I would never have guessed I would see: a man named Mister Redhawk. His parents had actually named him 'Mister' so that there would be no mistake about how he should be addressed.

'Mister Redhawk,' I said. 'Long time no see.'

Redhawk was more or less the definition of a well-dressed man about town, decked out in a serious sharkskin suit with a tie that cost more than my car and a long braid down his back. He was a Seminole big shot, and no one messed with him on either side of town. I liked him mostly because liking him kept me from being afraid of him, which everyone else in the state was.

'Mr Moscowitz,' he said softly.

Then he glared at one of the goons.

'I said to knock *on* the door,' Redhawk growled, 'not knock *down* the door.'

'Oh.' The goon looked around at the mess and then over at me. 'Sorry.'

'It'll be fixed within the hour,' Redhawk assured me. 'Now.'

'You want to talk to Lena,' I surmised.

He nodded.

'You understand I can't let you take her away,' I went on. 'She has to stay here with me.'

Redhawk smiled. 'Not many people tell me what to do.'

'Yeah,' I agreed, 'I don't really like telling *anybody* what to do. The thing is—'

'The thing is,' Redhawk concluded, 'I could speak with the child right here. Would that be all right?'

'We really should ask the child,' Lena said. 'I don't mind shooting one of your gorillas, but I'd rather not because it might make the other one shoot at me and Dr Moscowitz.'

Redhawk's eyes lit up further. 'Foggy? Have you acquired an advanced degree since we last saw each other?'

'It's an honorific,' Lena answered. 'I've awarded him a doctorate in child psychology.'

'Fine,' Redhawk sighed. 'Let's get right to the point. Why did you kill David Waters?'

'He was no good,' Lena answered simply.

'I concur with your assessment,' Redhawk said quietly, 'but if you were to kill everyone in this town who's "no good," after a while there would be no one left at all.'

'I don't know,' she said. 'Foggy seems OK.'

You had to admit that the kid was one tough little biscuit.

'And yet,' he told her, 'you still have your gun pointed in my direction.'

'Maybe if your door-breaking friends waited outside,' she answered, 'you and I could actually have a little chat that would be mutually beneficial.'

It was the phrase 'mutually beneficial' that disturbed me.

Redhawk, as I had always heard was the case, made his decision instantly.

'Joseph, would you and your brother please wait in the car?' he said, his eyes still on Lena.

And without a single word, the goons evaporated.

'There,' Lena said, lowering her gun. 'Was that so hard?'

'What did David say to you that made you shoot him three times?' Redhawk asked, his patience obviously wearing thin.

'To be fair,' I interjected, 'the gun shot three times, not the girl. She only pulled the trigger once. Shot him with a Heckler and Koch VP70. Spits out a three shot burst.'

'Not the point,' Redhawk rightly objected. 'I want to know what David said that offended you enough to take his life.'

'Let me tell you a little something about your boy,' Lena said, leaning forward.

She still had the gun in her hand, the safety off.

'I know all about—' Redhawk began.

'He likes little girls,' Lena interrupted. 'He sits in the park and watches them. He has them sit on his lap. He gives them candy. Do you understand me?'

'He propositioned you,' Redhawk assumed.

'In the most disgusting and, by the way, illegal manner possible in the state of Florida,' she affirmed.

'Heinous,' Redhawk said without the slightest hint of emotion. 'But why kill him? Why not, for instance, shoot him in the leg with your considerable pistol?'

'I'm a little girl!' Lena blared out. 'Christ! Some greasy drunk leans over me in a threatening manner and makes a suggestion I can't possibly repeat out loud and you want me to be cool-headed and take a reasonable course of action? I pulled my gun and it went off. I didn't have any control over the moment or the pistol.'

'You seem fairly sophisticated for a person your age,' Redhawk observed. 'Your diction is quite adult.'

'Look,' she objected, 'lots of people say that kind of thing when they want to blame a kid for something that was actually an adult's fault. I don't care how sophisticated I sound, I'm fourteen years old. David Waters was an adult making illegal suggestions to a person who is, legally, a child. How were you at handling a crisis when you were my age?'

'You can't go by me,' Redhawk said in a dead voice. 'I've always been cool-headed.'

'Have you ever been a little girl afraid of what an older man was going to do to your body?' Lena demanded, clearly beginning to lose her grip.

'And how is it that you still have the gun that killed David?' Redhawk went on, ignoring Lena's question. 'The police didn't take it away from you?'

'They did,' she snapped. 'This was in my boot. That – what's his name?' She looked at me.

'Detective Baxter?' I guessed.

'Yeah, that guy,' she went on. 'He took my Heckler and Koch, put it in his suit coat pocket, and patted me on the head. Never checked my boot.'

'Look,' Redhawk said, a little louder than he had been speaking before, 'David Waters was a drunk and a – let's say *womanizer*. I've even heard of his penchant for the younger set, and it doesn't surprise me, given the rest of his degenerate life recently. My problem is that his father is a prominent member of our tribal council. The elder Waters is oil rich and – it's no secret – also mean as a snake. He doesn't care what his son did. He only wants a certain kind of old-fashioned justice.'

'He wants Lena dead,' I assumed.

Redhawk nodded.

'You're here – did you come here to kill her?' I asked, taking a step toward the kid.

'No. I came here to get answers. I got them, I suppose. I don't like them, but I believe they're true. So now I'm warning you: Waters will do his best to see that the girl is killed.'

'You're telling her, but you won't say that to the police,' I said, knowing the answer already.

'Correct. But I'm not just telling her. I'm telling you too, Dr Moscowitz.'

'You think I can protect her.'

'No.' He glanced toward the door. 'No one can protect her. I told you so that you would talk her into leaving town, getting adopted, changing her name, and anything else that you can think of that might save her life.'

'What makes you think I'd do that?' I asked.

He turned to leave. 'You're the one with the degree in child psychology.'

'It's *honorary*,' I said to his back.

THREE

Lena and I were at the police station bright and early the next morning, on about three hours' sleep apiece. Baxter listened to Lena's tale of harassment and reaction and to my story of the visit from Mister Redhawk.

'Jeez, what a mess,' Baxter said to himself.

'There's no way for you to win this,' I commiserated. 'No one in Fry's Bay liked David Waters. When they hear why the kid plugged him, they'll all be on her side. You know that.'

'But Ironstone Waters will wreck up the town,' Baxter lamented, 'politically and physically, if I don't arrest the kid and prosecute her.'

'I don't know,' I hedged. 'I think the father doesn't care what you do. I think he's already set on killing the kid.'

'Is there any chance you can arrange all that stuff the Redhawk suggested?' Baxter asked me. 'Get the kid out of town? Find her parents, or get her adopted, or something?'

'In six months, maybe,' I told him.

'Oh, I'd be dead *long* before that,' Lena said calmly.

'So what do we do?' Baxter asked me.

'You're the police detective.' I stared him down.

'Look,' he began, 'I'm one of three guys in the entire county that does murder investigations. I took the gig here in Fry's Bay because I banked on there not actually *being* any murders here. I have no idea what to do in a situation like this.'

There was a moment of silence in Baxter's office. I took advantage of it to look around the crummy room. A dirty linoleum floor was scratched and skidded beyond repair. The wall behind him hadn't been cleaned or painted since the Eisenhower era. Baxter had no pictures on the wall, or on his desk, which was absolutely overcome with paperwork. It was clear, upon such reflection, that he would never have any idea what to do in a situation like this.

'Let me go talk to David's father,' Lena said out of nowhere.

Baxter and I stared.

'Or I could just leave you in the ocean about three miles out,' I said. 'It's jellyfish season.'

'I have something to tell him,' she insisted.

'No, you don't,' I insisted.

'Is it something that you haven't told us?' Baxter asked.

'Foggy,' she said, 'you can talk to Redhawk. He could arrange it.'

'He won't do it,' I told her.

'He certainly won't do it if you don't ask him to,' she answered back.

I glared at Baxter. 'You're not going to do anything? Not even about my broken door?'

'I thought you said that Redhawk would fix it.'

'Yeah, he did already,' I confessed, 'but that was after he broke it. Isn't there some kind of "broken door" law around here?'

'What do you want me to do?'

'Foggy,' Lena insisted, 'get me to David's father. Seriously. He needs to hear what I have to say.'

'How about telling me and the ridiculously hapless Detective Baxter, here, what you have to say that could possibly make any difference.'

I waited.

'Sorry,' she said after a moment. 'David's father has to be the first one to hear it.'

Another half-hour's worth of cajoling did nothing to loosen her resolve. Baxter eventually chased us out of his office, and there we were, still too early in the morning and out on the street.

I'd always thought that Fry's Bay was pretty that time of day. You could see the sun making diamonds on the water, and there wasn't a cloud in the nearly white sky. There was a chill in the air, but I liked it.

I asked the kid if she wanted breakfast, but she sang the same old song she'd been grinding out.

'Let's go talk to Redhawk,' she whined, 'and get me to the elder Waters! Damn.'

'Well,' I surrendered, 'there is a place where one of his bodyguards, Philip, hangs out. He's usually there this time of the morning. It's just around the next block.'

Three minutes later we were walking into Pete's. It was like a lot of bars anywhere, I guess. The smell of stale beer, cooked onions, and too many cigarettes was overpowering. The floor was a little sticky, but it was old wood: dark and somehow dignified. The bar was on your right as you walked in, dining tables on your left. About halfway back, the bar and dining area ended and the rest of the place was littered with pool tables. Those tables were not in any particular order. The ceiling was twenty feet from the floor, but it was so dark that it was impossible to see. The bar had brightly colored, backless, spinning stools.

And, as luck would have it, one of those stools was occupied by Mister Redhawk's moose-like companion, Philip. He was decked out in his usual triple-extra-large Hawaiian shirt, waist-length hair loose down his back. His forearms were bigger around than my thighs.

'Hello, Foggy,' he said without turning around.

'Philip,' I acknowledged. 'Didn't see you last night.'

'You mean when Mister Redhawk paid you a visit.' He nodded. 'I begged off, account of we're friends, you and me. He understood.'

Philip turned around. He had a sweet face, not at all the kind of menacing gob a lot of muscle guys had.

'This must be the kid in question,' he continued. 'Hi.'

'Hi,' Lena said right back, offering up a smile that could knock a jockey off his horse.

'She wants to talk to Mister Redhawk right away,' I said, trying to seem calm about the proposal. 'She has new information.'

'She ought not to be here, Foggy,' Philip said. 'She ought to be gone by now.'

'I want to give myself up to Ironstone Waters,' she announced.

That shut me and Philip up for a second.

'Bad choice of words,' I admonished her.

'But telling him that will get his attention,' she said.

'I think you've already got his attention,' I told her. 'You've got that real good.'

'Please take me to him,' she said, managing to sound even younger than she was. 'Please!'

Like she was asking for cotton candy.

Philip sighed. 'Marty!'

Marty Craw, the owner of Pete's, was known as Fat Tuesday,

owing to the fact that he was from New Orleans and his name sounded like Mardi Gras if you said it fast enough. That's the sort of thing that people in Fry's Bay found clever.

Marty appeared, wordlessly.

'Phone,' Philip intoned.

The phone was produced. Philip made a call. The phone disappeared, along with Marty, who knew a touchy situation when he saw one.

'He's coming here,' Philip said, but he sounded worried about it.

'Why is he coming here?' I asked.

'Yeah,' Philip said carefully. 'Why indeed.'

'How long before he gets here?' I wanted to know.

Philip only shrugged.

'Grab a stool, Lena,' I told her. 'You want something?'

'Scotch, neat,' she answered.

'How about a root beer,' I countered. 'Have you ever actually had Scotch?'

'Not really,' she confessed. 'It just seemed like a cool thing to say.'

'It *was* kind of cool,' Philip acknowledged. 'A little *Sinatra*.'

I went around behind the bar, rummaged a root beer, reloaded Philip's glass with mescal, which I knew was in his glass, and fetched myself a cup of muddy coffee. The three of us waited, silently, for what seemed like an hour. But eventually Mister Redhawk sauntered in, accompanied by the gorillas from the previous night's escapade.

'This is very disappointing,' he said as he came through the door. 'I thought we were going to get this little girl out of town, Foggy.'

Lena was off the stool and headed toward Redhawk before I could stop her.

'I have a very important message from David Waters to his father,' she said in a rush, 'and I have to give it to him today. It was David's last request.'

That halted Redhawk.

I couldn't tell if the kid was bluffing or not. It sounded real.

'Why didn't you tell me this last night?' he asked.

'You can't be serious,' she objected, 'you bust in on me when

I'm asleep, along with two huge men with guns, and you want
me to trust you?'

'What's different now?' he wanted to know.

'Foggy told me I could trust you.'

I wanted to see where she was going, so I nodded.

'What is it you have to say to David's father?' he asked quietly.

'Tell me, and I'll tell him.'

She shook her head. 'Not the deal. David made me promise.
And whatever else I may be, I'm true to my word.'

Redhawk glanced my way. 'Are we absolutely certain that
this person is a fourteen-year-old kid and not some sort of thirty-
year-old dwarf?'

'Jury's still out, I'd say,' I answered.

'Serious as a crutch, Mister Redhawk,' she told him earnestly.
'I have to talk to David's dad today. You can come with if you
want to. You may remember that last night I said this would be
mutually beneficial.'

'Of course, I'll be accompanying her,' I said quickly. 'She's
legally my ward at the moment. I have to stick with her.'

Redhawk sighed. 'Wouldn't have it any other way.'

'I guess I'd like to ride along too,' Philip piped up. 'Now
I'm all curious. David Waters hated his father. I have to wonder
what his last words to the old man would be.'

Redhawk closed his eyes.

'He's thinking,' Philip whispered in my direction.

'I'm actually trying to will myself backward in time,' Redhawk
said, eyes still closed, 'so that I could leave town before any of
this happened.'

'That never works,' I told him. 'I've tried it myself. If it worked,
I'd still be living in Brooklyn.'

Lena gave me a look. 'Bet there's a story there.'

'Would everyone mind shutting up and coming with me?'
Redhawk asked us all politely.

Philip abandoned his barstool. Lena headed for the door. I
followed her.

Ten minutes later we were past the edge of town. Redhawk's
Mercedes limo was roomy, but two bodyguards in the front seat
and the four of us in back was a full load. The day was shaping
up nicely, but the swamp made me nervous, and we were headed

through the swamp and Seminole land. My opinion was that there were bad animals in the swamp, and every single one wanted to kill me. Still, there we were, rumbling down a dirt road in a packed car, bumping over ditches, and skidding in the occasional mud as the landscape turned all forest primeval.

Then Philip nudged my elbow with his.

'Ironstone Waters lives just up there,' he whispered.

I looked. A mansion the size of a baseball stadium loomed just off the road. It looked familiar, but I knew I'd never seen it.

'You're staring, Foggy,' Redhawk said. 'Never seen a palace before?'

'That's just it,' I told him. 'I feel like I *have* seen this joint before.'

Redhawk sat back and smiled.

'That's because it's modeled after the guy's house in *Citizen Kane*,' he told me. 'It's the owner's favorite movie.'

'Christ,' Lena mumbled.

I couldn't tell if she was impressed or disgusted. Maybe a little of both.

When we pulled up in front of the house, several conspicuously armed Seminole guards appeared.

'Everyone sit tight,' Redhawk told us.

He got out slowly.

'Hello, Thomas,' he said to one of the guards. 'This is very important. I have the girl who killed David. She's right here in my car. But I want everyone to understand that, for the moment, she's entirely under my protection. Do you understand that?'

The guard didn't respond. He seemed stupefied.

'If you're uncertain,' Redhawk said carefully, 'go inside, speak with Ironstone, tell him *exactly* what I said.'

The guard still didn't move.

Philip patted my forearm. 'Excuse me, Foggy.'

Without further ado he climbed over me and shoved himself out of the car and into the guard's face.

'Mister Redhawk wants you to go inside, Thomas,' Philip said sweetly, 'and tell Ironstone what he just said. If you don't, I'll break you in half, OK?'

Despite the fact that Thomas had a machine gun and two other guards at his side, he seemed pretty rattled by Philip's proposal.

'Sorry, Philip. Right. Sorry, Mister Redhawk.'

He turned immediately and went inside the house.

'That wasn't really necessary,' Redhawk said softly.

'You're welcome,' Philip answered.

After a tense couple of minutes, Ironstone Waters appeared in the doorway of the mansion.

I'd never seen him before, but the imposing figure frozen on the top step couldn't have been anyone else. He looked like he'd been carved out of granite, painted with berries, and baked in the sun. His grey hair was in two braids that ran down the sides of his face. He was dressed in a floor-length silk bathrobe and opera loafers. He had a pistol in his hand.

'Ironstone Waters,' Redhawk said, 'do you understand that this girl is under my protection for the time being?'

The old man's grip on the pistol tightened.

'She killed my boy,' he growled.

'She did,' Redhawk affirmed, 'but she also has a message for you. From him. You don't want to kill her before you hear your son's final words, do you?'

Ironstone squinted.

'You've heard the details of the event,' Redhawk went on.

Ironstone nodded.

'So you know that David said something to the girl before she shot him. She hasn't told anyone exactly what he said, yet. But she's here to tell you.'

'Who's that with you in the car?' he snarled. 'That skinny Jew who's supposed to protect children?'

'You know who he is,' Redhawk answered calmly. 'And you know that he does his job very well.'

'Is he under your protection too?' Ironstone wanted to know.

Before I could holler out that I didn't need protecting, Philip spoke up.

'Actually, he's a friend of mine, Uncle,' Philip said plainly.

Ironstone seemed to consider a multitude of options before pocketing his pistol and turning to go back into the house.

'Come on in, then,' he said over his shoulder.

Redhawk turned to the car.

'Foggy,' he said, 'you and the girl come with me. Everyone else will wait in the car.'

'I'd like to have a few more words with my uncle,' Philip said.

'Philip, please don't be difficult. You know this is a volatile situation.'

'You don't think I can stay calm?' Philip asked.

'I know you can stay calm,' Redhawk answered impatiently, 'but I need you out here. Do you see that?'

Philip looked around at the house and the remaining guards, and then he nodded.

'I see that,' he said softly.

I had no idea what was going on, but it was obvious that half of Redhawk's conversation – with both Ironstone and Philip – had been unspoken. There was more at work than I could understand, and it made me nervous. But I assumed Redhawk wanted Philip to wait outside in case we had to make a quick getaway. That assumption only made my nerves worse.

Redhawk leaned down and looked at me through the window. 'You don't have a gun on you, do you, Foggy?'

'Me? Never. I don't care for guns.'

I decided not to remind him that Lena was probably packing the same gun he'd seen the night before.

He stood back up. 'Let's go then.'

FOUR

The inside of the mansion was even more impressive than the outside. I couldn't speak for the rest of the place, but the great room was a dead ringer for the one in the movie, huge fireplace and all. The house was a little cold, but there was a fire blazing. It might have been the only heat in the house.

'Sit,' Ironstone commanded, his back to the fire.

Lena and I took a small sofa; Redhawk chose a very nice leather club chair.

Ironstone stared at Lena so hard I thought he might be trying to kill her with his mind.

At length he said, 'You're the monster who killed my son?'

Lena smiled. 'Let's not go throwing names around. Your son liked to go to the park and sit little girls on his lap, I assume you've heard that.'

It was bold. It could have made Ironstone back down or it just as easily might have exacerbated his ire.

All it actually did was stop him from talking for a second or two.

Lena used that to her advantage.

'That's why you disinherited him,' she said. 'He was a bad drunk and a child molester, and everybody knows it. Am I right?'

Ironstone's eyes flickered. 'What makes you say that I disinherited him?'

'Do you want to hear my story or not?' she fired back. 'Because I know a lot more than that about David Waters. A lot more.'

Anyone could tell from the sound of her voice that she meant what she said.

'You think you know more about my son than I do?' the old man asked, menace edging every syllable.

'No,' she answered calmly, 'but I do know more about his recent *activities* than you do.'

I couldn't see where the kid was going. What she was saying, and the way she was saying it, didn't add up, at least not to her moment of shock and murder in Mary's Shallow Grave. It added up to a more extended relationship with David Waters than she'd let on. It was increasingly obvious to me that she wasn't bluffing. She really had something to say, although I could not, in a million years, have guessed what it would be.

'Well?' the old man asked. 'Go on.'

'David left this very nice home about three years ago,' Lena said, leaning forward, 'something to do with a woman named Ellen Greenberg. She was a florist in Fry's Bay, I think.'

'I don't have any idea what you're talking about, but—' the old guy began.

'Bullshit!' she snapped. 'You got rid of the girl. I don't know how, but they say Mr Moscowitz here is pretty good at finding things out. He'll figure out if you shipped her out of town against her will – or had her killed.'

'Wait just a minute,' Ironstone said. 'I didn't get rid of—'

'That also doesn't matter at the moment,' Lena interrupted. 'I'm just laying out the background. David thought the girl ran off. He was drinking. He was going to the park and playing with children. He disgraced you. You knew all about what he was doing because you were having him watched. Like a hawk. Two guys on him all the time.'

'No,' Ironstone protested.

'Stop it,' Lena said. 'I saw them. They weren't exactly subtle. David saw them too; he just didn't care.'

'Look,' the old guy interjected.

'That's when David got in touch with me.' Lena sat back.

Everyone looked at her. Redhawk tried three times to say something. I was probably the most confused.

'You talked to David before last night?' I asked her.

'What are you saying?' Ironstone asked at the same time.

'Mr Waters,' Lena answered, very formally, 'I am what some people refer to as a *hit man*. As you can see, the title really doesn't fit me, but it's a quick way for me to go on with my story.'

'Lena,' I said to her slowly, 'I have no idea why you're saying this, but as your current custodian I'm telling you to shut up now, and we should go.'

'Here's what happened,' she went on, ignoring me. 'David

took out a life insurance policy a while ago, a big one, several million. I got the notification at – doesn't matter how I got it, but I have a copy of the policy.'

'No, you don't,' the old man mumbled. 'I'd know about it.'

'The policy was purchased in Miami. Didn't go local. Anyway, I found out about the policy – let's say through a mutual friend. I was perfect for his purposes, since his recent reputation as a pervert was so well established and I am, well, who I am. We talked on the phone. He made the arrangements. It was all set up in advance.'

I felt a little sick.

'You're saying that David took out a life insurance policy,' I interrupted, 'and then hired you to kill him?'

'Yes.'

'Why would he do that?' Redhawk asked, in spite of himself.

'What you didn't know,' Lena raced, on fire, 'is that this Ellen Greenberg was pregnant – with David's baby. A little girl, I'm told.'

'No.' Ironstone shook his head in disbelief. 'You're just saying all this to keep me from killing you right now. I would have known if David was having a child.'

'It's all documented,' Lena said casually. 'I have files in a safe deposit box. Foggy will get the key after I've gone. Because the thing is: last I heard, Ellen and the kid were still hiding out somewhere around here. Don't know why, but I think it's true.'

'The beneficiary of this life insurance policy,' I mumbled to myself, 'is David's daughter.'

Lena smiled. 'Nice work, Sherlock.'

Ironstone crumpled a little, and his face sagged.

'I would know if my son had a child,' the old man repeated, but most of the steam was gone.

'I'm guessing that Ellen Greenberg was terrified of you, terrified you'd find out about her relationship with David,' Lena said to Ironstone, no mercy in her voice. 'And about the baby.'

'That policy he took out – the money goes to that child.' Ironstone squinted, struggling to understand what was going on.

'Yes, to that child, you bastard,' Lena whispered.

Before I realized what was happening, Lena stood up, took

out her Beretta, and pointed it right where Ironstone's heart ought to have been.

'David didn't pay me for this one.' Her voice sounded like she was gargling staples. 'I'm doing this one all on my own.'

Redhawk was out of his seat, though it wasn't clear what he was going to do. Ironstone produced his own gun from the pocket of that silk robe and aimed right back at Lena.

Then, without a single thought, my most ridiculous instinct kicked in: I jumped in front of Lena.

Both guns went off – and I went out, down to the bottom of a very dark well.

FIVE

When I woke up in the hospital, the first thing I saw was Philip, gun in hand. Before I could panic, Lena shoved him out of the way and put her hand on my shoulder.

'You're awake,' she said.

'Maybe I am,' I responded.

'You took a bullet for me.' She seemed stunned.

'Yeah,' I acknowledged, 'but to be fair, if you'd gotten killed in my custody, I might have lost my job.'

'Nobody ever did that for me.' She looked away. 'And several people have had the opportunity, believe me.'

'I don't know *what* to believe about you,' I confessed. 'Is anything you said at the Waters manse true?'

'All of it,' she insisted.

'You're a hit man.'

'That's not the term I use.'

'You've done this before,' I pressed. 'Killed guys.'

'Since I was eleven. Mostly they were guys like David Waters: people who needed killing. Euthanasia deals. I figure I've got about three more years of that kind of business before it gets to be annoying and I'll have to change my tune. But by then I'll have enough money to go to college.'

'You're either the spookiest kid I ever heard of,' I told her, 'or the biggest liar.'

She smiled. 'Why couldn't I be both?'

'You're going to skip town before I can get out of this bed.'

She nodded.

'I figured. So I have about eight hundred and thirty-four questions for you.'

'How about three?' she said. 'I don't have much time. Philip's going to stay here and watch over you, though, so you're in safe hands.'

'Thanks, Philip,' I managed to say.

'I wanted to do it,' he told me, grinning, 'and Mister Redhawk's paying me. So . . .'

I turned back to Lena. 'So what happened after I went down?'

'Ironstone's goons were on me like monkeys on a banana,' she said, 'but Redhawk, he fixed everything. He's all right.'

'Agreed,' I said. 'Go on.'

'Ironstone's bullet hit you, mine went wild because you knocked my arm. I shouldn't have tried to kill the old man. I lost my head for a minute there. Very unprofessional of me. Anyway, Redhawk called the police and told them that a government employee had been shot in Ironstone's house. Ironstone didn't know what to do. I backed away. Philip brought you to Redhawk's car, stopped the bleeding, and here you are in this nice clean bed. The end.'

'No,' I insisted. 'Not the end. You said I could ask *three* questions.'

'All right.'

'What the hell did David Waters say to you that made you shoot him?' I had to know.

'Simple. You heard my story, right? He hired me to do it. But all the arrangements were over the phone. He told me to meet him at Mary's Shallow Grave, but I'd never met the guy in person. So when he came over to me and leaned in, all he said was, "I'm David Waters. Do it quick before I lose my nerve." So I obliged.'

I let go a pretty hefty sigh.

'The important point is,' she went on, 'some little kid around here stands to inherit some pretty substantial cash – the kid's mother, too. If they ever find her.'

'I'll find Ellen Greenberg, if she's alive,' I promised. 'And her kid.'

'I was pretty sure you'd feel that way,' she said softly. 'Last question. I really do have to go.'

'Where?' I asked. 'Where are you going?'

She patted my shoulder. 'Got a job. So long, Foggy. I'll be in touch.'

She headed for the door of my hospital room.

'You'll be in touch?' I called after her.

She stopped but didn't turn around.

'I might have figured something out about you and Ellen Greenberg, by the way,' I went on. 'Something that stirs up more questions than it answers.'

'Yeah, I thought you'd probably get to that once you start poking around.' She gave me a big grin and headed for the door. 'But you're right. Ellen Greenberg's my older sister.'

And then Lena was bay fog on a bright morning: gone.

Me? I went back to sleep.

The next thing I remember is Maggie Redhawk's big face so close to mine that it scared me.

Maggie Redhawk was a fifty-year-old nurse, a woman of what she called 'mixed ethnicity.' All that really meant was that she couldn't decide whether to write 'African-American' or 'Native American' on her employment form, because she was both.

She always told me that I looked more like a Seminole than she did. Maybe that's why she was always willing to help me when I needed it; why her brother had been so swell to me and Lena.

I stared into her eyes. 'What? Are you trying to kiss me?'

She grinned. 'If I wanted to kiss you, big boy, I wouldn't have to try.'

I looked around. We were alone.

'Where's Philip?' I asked. 'He was here a minute ago.'

She straightened up.

'A minute ago,' she repeated. 'I see.'

'What's going on?'

'You've been in a coma, genius,' she sighed. 'This is the first time you've opened your eyes in almost a week. And Philip's been here every day. I just sent him out for dinner.'

I tried to sit up. 'A week?'

'You were almost dead, kiddo.' She checked some tube or other and shook her head.

'And Lena's gone.'

'The kid from the place? Yeah, like, since the night you got here.'

'OK.' I struggled a little more to get up. 'When do I get out of here?'

'You don't, Foggy. Not anytime soon. Look.' She sighed and sat on the bed. 'You got shot through the heart. It wrecked one of your valves. You're lucky to be talking, now. Doesn't it hurt?'

'Now that you mention it,' I said.

'So you have to stay right here, get all knitted up.'

'No. I have to find Ellen Greenberg. And then I have to take care of her kid. And then I have to find Lena. I've got a full datebook. So give me a pill or something and get my suit.'

'No, Foggy,' Maggie said, a little irritated. 'You wrecked a heart valve! A whole entire heart valve!'

'OK, but I got three more, right? I once boosted a Dodge Dart that only had two cylinders working. Sounded like a sewing machine, but it got me all over Brooklyn.'

'Before it died,' she said.

'Well, yeah,' I admitted, 'but I got *three*!'

'You're not a car! Damn. Anything more strenuous than a jog to the beach and you're done.'

'I know you're exaggerating,' I told her, 'because you care about me.'

'I'm not exaggerating, and I don't care about you at all,' she countered. 'I just don't want to lose my job. I got benefits.'

'Bullshit,' I snapped. 'You get more benefit out of being a Seminole than you do being a nurse. And letting me die wouldn't kick you out of the tribe.'

'If you think that there's anything to be gained by being a Seminole woman in Florida, think again.'

'And if you think I'm going to lie here in bed while Ironstone's gang figures out what to do with Ellen Greenberg and her kid, *you'd* better think again! I got a job too, you understand!'

She stood. 'Yeah, about that. Child Protective Services shut down your office.'

I blinked. 'What?'

'You were in a coma, Foggy. And it was pretty much a one-man office since all that business this past February. So . . .'

'OK, but I'm going to reopen it now. First, there's a fourteen-year-old kid who needs my help, whether she knows it or not. And there's another kid somewhere around here who's about to be put on ice just for being the daughter of David Waters. So either tell me where my suit is, or have a look at my ass through the back of this gown as I exit the establishment.'

Maggie folded her arms.

'Here's what's going to happen,' she said. 'I'm going to give you a couple of bottles of pills. Whenever you get a certain feeling in your chest like that Dodge Dart, which will happen on a regular basis, you take the blue one. And if you can't breathe and your left arm goes numb, take the other one. And if neither one of them works, there's a third procedure.'

I sat all the way up. 'Such as?'

'Such as kiss your ass goodbye,' she said, 'because you're about to be dead.'

I shrugged. 'OK, good – long as there's a procedure. Now can you help me out of all these tubes?'

And then I fell right back to sleep.

That happened a lot for a few days – waking up and going right back to sleep – before I finally slipped out when no one was looking.

I think it was a Tuesday night. I was out on the street, headed for my office. I felt like I had the worst hangover in history and also like King Kong had done a Gene Kelly on my chest. To make matters worse, my suit was all rumpled.

I was lucky it was nighttime, late. Most of the citizens of Fry's Bay were home in bed. I didn't really feel like running into anyone. And it took a little longer for the old office building to come into view.

It was a cinderblock piece of crap with salt-air-peeled paint, pink. It was a two-story box with windows and a flat roof that leaked. My joint was on the second floor. The sign out front said, 'Child Protective ervices.' The S was missing.

Up the stairs and headed toward the office door, I actually started feeling better. I thought the walk was doing me good. I'd been in bed for a month, no wonder I was a little stiff. But the feeling didn't last.

The door was open. I could see that the place had been wrecked; most of the furniture was gone. And there was someone sitting at my desk going through my drawers.

I slowed down, stuck to the shadows, trying to see who was pilfering, but it was too dark.

If I'd had any sense, I would have backed away and gone to get Baxter or somebody, but apparently when you get shot, your brain takes a holiday. Instead, I stepped into the light.

'If you find my IRS form in there would you give it to me?' I sang out. 'I don't want to get in Dutch with the Feds. I got enough trouble.'

The man was startled but only enough to stop moving for a minute. I kept walking, headed right for him. Once I got a little closer, I could see that the man at my desk was one of the guys I'd seen at Ironstone's house.

He was up in the next second, gun in hand.

I stopped walking.

'I, like, *just* got out of the hospital,' I said to the guy. 'I really don't want to get shot again. I have no gun, no energy, and no malice, so there's absolutely no reason to shoot me.'

He lowered his gun.

'How'd you get out of the hospital?' he asked. 'They said you were in a coma.'

'I woke up. What are you doing in my office?'

'Ironstone Waters wants to find his grandchild.'

'Did you look in the left-hand drawer?' I said brightly.

The guy stood up and rounded the desk. He had on a shiny black suit with wide lapels, and a gray shirt with a lavender tie. The Natty Gangster look that was popular with a certain set.

'He knows that Lena gave you a key,' he told me. 'A key to a safe deposit box where all the information is. So just give me the key, and everything'll be all right.'

'I been in a coma, Igmo,' I said gently. 'I got no key.'

In fact, I really didn't have a key. I vaguely remembered Lena mentioning it, but she'd left town and I'd gone dark and no key had been proffered.

He kept coming anyway. I was just waiting until he got a little closer.

'It's not in your desk,' he went on. 'So I figure you got it on you.'

'I really don't,' I promised him, 'but you're welcome to look.'

I spread my arms wide. He got close enough that the tip of his pistol touched my lapel.

So I dropped, took a hold of his left ankle with both hands, and stood up again very suddenly. His foot came up, his head flew back, the gun went off, and he was down on his back in the next second.

I dropped his foot and went to grab his gun. I twisted it and it came loose right away. He was gasping, had the wind knocked out of him. I thought about jumping up and down on him a few times, just to teach him a lesson, but I had my heart to think about. Best not get too excited.

Instead I pointed the gun at his face.

'I'm going to shoot you in the eyeball now,' I told him, 'and explain to Officer Baxter how you were an intruder that shot at me first. You'll be dead, and he'll take me out to dinner.'

'Ironstone just wants to help the kid, his granddaughter,' the poor guy moaned.

'Well, he disowned his son, chased a perfectly nice florist out of town, and he shot me, so I'm not inclined to help him out.'

'You're not really going to shoot me in the eyeball.' He blinked.

'I'm not?'

'Not if I promise not to kill *you* – although, Ironstone wouldn't mind doing it.'

'Why?' I whined. 'What did I ever do to him?'

The guy shrugged. 'He just doesn't like you, I guess.'

I nodded. Most people took to me right away, but there was the occasional citizen who was immune to my charm.

'What happened to all of my furniture?' I asked him.

'Yeah,' he said, getting his breath back, 'I wondered about that myself.'

I reached out my hand and helped him up.

'Which one are you?' I asked him.

'What?' He was still a little dazed.

'What's your name?'

'Oh. Herbert.'

'Herbert is a Seminole name?'

He sighed. 'My mother was from London. I hate it.'

'What does it mean?'

I knew that Seminole names were supposed to mean something, and that my friend Philip hated his name because it meant 'lover of horses' and all the kids had made rude jokes about his sexual practices when he was little.

He hung his head. 'It's supposed to mean "bright army," but it's British slang for a dull, uninteresting person.'

'Did your mother know that?'

He nodded. 'She didn't like me very much. She got knocked up by a guy from our tribe out in the swamp.'

'That doesn't mean she didn't like you.'

'She used to say, "You're my little *Herbert*, aren't you, you bleeding bastard."'

I nodded. 'Sorry, kid. That's rough.'

Then I shoved his gun into my outside coat pocket, and when I did I felt something there that gave me pause. It felt very much like a key – say, the sort of key that might open a safe deposit box.

SIX

So nine o'clock the next morning I was standing at the front door of the Fry's Bay Savings and Loan, waiting for Sybil to let me in.

Sybil Blessing was thirty-two going on eighty, hair piled high, over-rouged cheeks, and a skirt one size smaller than comfortable. Eventually she clacked toward the big glass door on her wobbly high heels and winked at me.

'Hey, Foggy. Ain't seen you in a while. They said you was dead.'

'Yeah, I just been busy. Look what I got.'

I held up the key.

'Safe deposit.' She stared. 'Whose is it?'

'How do you know it's not mine?'

'Because you ain't got a box here is why,' she laughed.

'Well, as it happens,' I explained, slipping into the air conditioning, 'it belongs to a client.'

'Some kid?'

'That's right,' I assured her. 'She handed it over to me so I could help her out, you understand.'

She shrugged. 'I don't understand nothing these days, pal. But you got the key, I'll give you the box.'

I followed after her as she shambled toward the vault.

'This has to do with David Waters getting shot up over at Mary's, right?' she asked me, not turning around.

'What makes you say that?'

'They say it was a kid who shot him,' she said. 'Not that he didn't deserve it. What? Was he trying to get next to a little kid? Disgusting. I'm glad she shot him.'

We arrived at the vault and she had it open in no time. The inside was about the size of my living room, and there was a metal table with a single chair close to a floor-to-ceiling array of safe deposit boxes.

She went to the wall of boxes and held her hand out. I laid the key in it. She looked at the number, nodded, and worked her magic.

She drew out Lena's box and set it on the table. 'There you go. I got to leave you some privacy, see? So I'll be out there. You just holler when you're done.'

I nodded and sat in the chair. She clicked her way out. I opened the box.

There were two photos, one of Lena when she was a little bit younger, and another one of Lena much older, which I realized after a second was probably her sister, Ellen Greenberg. There were also three letters, some cash, several documents rolled up and tied with a blue ribbon, and a single spent bullet.

I pocketed everything except the cash and closed up the box. 'Sybil!'

'Already?' she sang back. 'I'll be right there.'

She appeared in the doorway to the vault.

'Got what I needed,' I told her.

'I doubt that,' she said, looking me up and down. 'What you need is a shave and a meal and a little sun. You look like a vagrant.'

'Thanks,' I said, 'now that you mention it, I am a little hungry.'

She shook her head disapprovingly as I walked by, headed for the door.

'I'm going to Yudda's,' I said without looking back, 'if anybody wants to know where I am.'

'Who's going to want to know?' she called after me.

'Baxter, Redhawk, and Ironstone Waters,' I told her.

She said something, but I was already through the door, so I was spared her critique of my situation.

Yudda was a sizeable Cajun, mid-forties, ridiculously misappropriated by Florida. It was a rare day when he didn't talk about how much he missed New Orleans – just not enough to go back and face his ex-wife.

He was also the best cook in the county: creative, daring, and not afraid of the occasional spectacular failure. On the creative side: gumbo fritters. No idea what was in them, except I could see the okra, but it was like you were eating a hush puppy and fiery gumbo at the same time. On the wrong side: monkfish crepes. Maybe it was bad monkfish, but it tasted like sulfur and week-old garbage.

As his place came into view, I felt my stomach leap up. If I'd really been out for a week or so, I probably had lost a little weight, and my stomach had shrunk. Better play it safe, I thought. Stick with a nice calm soup.

Yudda's was a shack, really, about the size of a railroad car. Tin roof, peeling paint, the smell of wood smoke, and way too hot inside, even in the cold months.

He wouldn't be open yet; it was too early in the morning. But I knew he'd be there, cooking, or thinking about cooking.

'Hey!' I called out. 'Yudda!'

There was a short moment of silence and then the great man appeared in his doorway.

'Foggy?' He stared. 'They said you was dead.'

'I been in the hospital.'

He stepped aside. 'Well I'm glad you ain't dead. Come on in. What can I do?'

'What's the soup?'

'I got a bouillabaisse that would kill your mother,' he said. 'Best I ever done.'

I shoved past him on my way to the last of three booths. 'Then I'd better have it.'

'What else?' He lowered his voice. 'I got some great Scotch.'

'Just water for me,' I said, 'and a little privacy. I got some stuff to look over.'

He shook his head. 'Work?'

'Yeah.'

'Just got out of the hospital,' he said to himself, 'and already working too hard.'

'Thanks, Yudda,' I called.

I sat in the booth facing the door and took out the rolled up documents. I untied the blue ribbon, but they stayed curled up, like they'd been in that position for a while. I flattened out the first one, it was a birth certificate: Baby Girl Ellen, March 23, 1958. The one under that belonged to Baby Girl Elena, September 27, 1961. The third one was a life insurance policy for a million dollars. The beneficiary was someone named Ester Greenberg Waters. I figured that was David's daughter.

The photo of Ellen would be helpful, but she looked so much like Lena that she wouldn't be hard to spot. The mystery was why I'd never seen her if she'd lived around Fry's Bay. Ironstone had done something to get rid of her. Lena said that David hadn't been able to find her for three years. Still, the photo would help when I was out and about.

All three letters were written on the same floral stationery – Chalet Suzanne in Lake Wales. I knew it. It was in the exact middle of Florida, if such a thing was possible. It had been called the Carleton Club, invented by James Kraft, the cheese man. It burned down in 1943, but they built it back using stuff from the horse stables and the chicken house, so it was a little odd.

Still, it had a modicum of swank, and the stationery was impressive.

All three letters were from Ellen to David. Love letters. Undated. Really sugary. I was a little embarrassed to read them, and I was about to stop when I got to the third paragraph of the first one. It began like this: 'The three of us, we make three. Telephones. Pens. How can they communicate how much I love you, in the same place?' Each of the three letters had that exact phrasing in the third paragraph. I considered myself as romantic as the next guy, but I had to observe that the diction left a little to be desired.

By the time Yudda brought me my silverware, I had concluded that at least part of each love letter was a code. I folded them back into their respective envelopes. I was in no condition to crack cypher.

Instead I studied the final item: the spent bullet. It had come from a Colt M1911A1, a heavy gun, about two and a half pounds. It was a single-action semi-automatic, never jammed, never misfired, and was pretty accurate even at three hundred feet. In short, I was pretty sure that the bullet hadn't come from any gun that Lena had ever used. It had too much weight and too little intimacy.

So what was it doing in Lena's memory box? In amongst the other important items, it had significance to her.

About that time Yudda lumbered over to my table with the bouillabaisse, a whole baguette, and a bottle of Cantillon Kriek, some kind of Belgian beer he loved. No idea where he got it, but it was pretty good.

I considered, and rejected, the idea of just going after Lena, wherever she was. My main gig was to find her sister, like I promised. I wasn't sure if having a birth certificate would help, but for some reason it seemed nice to have. The photo would be more helpful.

Then my stomach got the upper hand, and I dug into the bouillabaisse, which was the best I ever had. It was all I could think about for a while: the clams, the mussels, the whitefish, a hint of orange peel, hot pepper, and a broth that was made, I swear, from the tears of God.

I stopped about midway and mumbled something like, 'Yudda, what the hell? How does a mortal make something like this?'

Yudda was sitting on a stool by the door, reading the morning news. He shrugged. 'I'm from New Orleans.'

That seemed to be the entirety of his explanation, so I returned to destroying the rest of the bowl.

When it was empty, and the beer was gone, I sat back, a little clearer in my head. Ellen Greenberg had lived in Fry's Bay. I was still surprised that I'd never seen her, as our little blue heaven is fairly small, and Ellen had a kid, which was my business. But there would be other people in town who knew her. That was a nice place to start looking for her. And I could also pay a visit to the Chalet Suzanne in Lake Wales, see if anyone there remembered her or knew where she had gone.

I looked up.

'Hey, Yudda,' I called out, 'you ever see this kid?'

I held up Ellen's picture.

He squinted. Unable to make a complete assessment without closer scrutiny, he relieved the stool beneath him of his considerable weight and thundered toward me.

'Lemme see it.'

I handed him the photo. He really took his time, then handed it back.

'Nope. No idea.' He gave me back the photo. 'She got a kid that's in some kind of trouble?'

'Yeah,' I told him. 'You could say that.'

And there was my gig: Lena's sister Ellen had a kid who was in danger. A family member, one Ironstone Waters, the grandfather, was on their trail. I had to find the kid.

That's what the paperwork would say.

SEVEN

I showed Ellen's picture to everyone in town, even the drunks at the donut shop and a couple of stray dogs in the alley behind the abandoned bakery. No dice nowhere. By nightfall I figured if Lena's sister ever lived in town, she must have been invisible. It didn't make any sense. Fry's Bay was a very small town. Somebody should have recognized her.

By the end of the day I was pretty tired. Which was a surprise to me. You'd think after sleeping for a week I'd be pretty well rested up.

As I wended my weary way homeward, I suddenly remembered Lena saying something about David and kids in the park. I figured Lena meant Abiaka Park. It was small, close to the beach, very peaceful.

The Cherokee warrior Abiaka wasn't as well known to whites as Osceola, but he was probably just as important. He was a great spiritual leader, and he directed Seminole warriors in a couple of genius moves, especially in the Battle of Okeechobee. The park named after him was a very quiet place and always kept up – nice flowers, well-watered, that sort of thing. I figured it was tribally maintained. Maybe somebody who was taking care of the place had seen something. It didn't seem important enough to stop me from going home and lying down, but it would be something I'd get to sooner or later.

I made it to my front door about the time the moon was rising. Redhawk had made good on his promise to fix the door; it was new. But someone, probably Baxter, had festooned police tape across the entrance. I removed it.

The second I walked in, I felt like a flat tire. I think the sight of my bed must have had some sort of hypnotic effect on me. I wasn't sure I could get my coat off in time to collapse. Apparently being in a coma can take it out of you.

I was just about to lumber forward and fall like a tree when the phone in the kitchen rang. I made it to the offending machine, picked up the receiver, and parked at the kitchen table.

'What, exactly?' I muttered into the phone.

'Foggy?'

'Maybe.'

'It's Baxter. Christ. You're supposed to be in the hospital still.'

'Naw,' I assured him. 'I been all over town today, you know, working.'

'Well, Maggie said that's what you were doing, but I didn't believe her. You're an idiot.'

'Yes,' I agreed, 'but I'm an idiot for the *state*. I'm working a case. Ever hear of an Ellen Greenberg?'

He was silent for a moment.

'No.'

It was a suspicious *no* because Baxter was often the talkative type. But he was also a policeman, and I didn't like to accuse that sort of person since they can lock you up. I just got out of the hospital. Jail wouldn't do me any good at all.

'Right,' I said, 'so why did you call me? Just to tell me I'm an idiot?'

'Why did I call you?' He sounded sore. 'You don't get what ungodly hell transpired after you shot up Ironstone Waters's fabulous mansion?'

'There was hell?'

'Like you wouldn't believe. How much do you remember?'

'After I was shot?' I said. 'Nothing.'

Baxter regaled me – only slightly augmenting what Lena had said.

When I went down, Redhawk took charge. He called Baxter, told him that 'a government employee' had been shot in Ironstone's house. Baxter figured that the victim was some kind of FBI type, owing to Ironstone's questionable gestalt, and Redhawk let him think that. If he'd known it was me, there's no telling how he would have reacted. Ironstone's not a guy you'd want to mess with under ordinary circumstances.

Didn't matter. Philip brought me to Redhawk's car, stopped the bleeding, and got me to the hospital, like Lena'd told me. What Baxter filled in was the brouhaha at Ironstone's pad.

Baxter and a couple of his finest officers roared up the

mansion's front driveway, sirens blaring, moments after I had been whisked away. They found Ironstone, two of his 'employees,' some blood, a bullet hole, and a little furniture out of place.

Ironstone's story was that the person who had murdered his son had broken into his home, aided and abetted by one Foggy Moscowitz, in order that they both might kill him. When Ironstone began to describe the non-Jewish assailant, Baxter realized that it was the kid from the night before, and, apparently, laughed out loud.

'He actually wanted me to believe that you and that little girl broke into his house and tried to kill him,' Baxter concluded. 'I mean, Jesus, if you know what I mean.'

'I believe I do,' I assured him. 'And just for the record, he shot me. I'm the one who got shot. I'm wondering why you don't ask me about that.'

'So what were you doing there, Foggy,' he asked.

'Lena, the kid who shot David Waters at Mary's Shallow Grave, had information for Ironstone,' I said matter-of-factly. 'In fact, it was actually something Ironstone wanted to know.'

'Namely.'

'That David Waters had a daughter,' I said. 'Meaning Ironstone is a grandpa.'

'That's what you were there to tell him?' Baxter sounded very surprised. 'Why wouldn't he just tell me that, instead of telling me all that malarkey about you trying to kill him? What's the deal?'

'Search me,' I told him. 'He's a criminal. You know how they are: they're incapable of telling the truth.'

'This is a bit of a pot and kettle situation,' Baxter said, 'given that you were a car thief for so many years.'

'Yeah but that's different,' I assured him. 'I'm reformed. Ironstone's still in the life.'

'Uh huh, so tell me more about this alleged baby, Ironstone's granddaughter.'

'I don't know much more,' I began, 'And I can't find her, or the mother. I was actually going to come by your place tomorrow with a picture of the mother, see if you had any ideas where I might find her.'

'The baby's missing?'

'Ironstone did something to chase mother and child out of town a while back, or so I'm told,' I said to him. 'And the thing is, David Waters had a nice insurance policy. I've been thinking about finding the kid to make good on the policy.'

Baxter hummed into the phone. 'That ain't something the insurance company does?'

'Probably,' I agreed, 'but, see, it's associated with the whole thing that night at Mary's, with the kid and David – see, it's still my case, right?'

'Yeah, speaking of that,' Baxter said, 'where is the kid, the shooter? Because, *see*, it's still my case too.'

'I guess it is at that,' I told him. 'But *see*, I been in a coma. I wasn't even sure where my apartment was, let alone some gun-crazy juvenile.'

'So let's line this up,' he sighed. 'You can't find the shooter, you can't find David's wife or child, and you're still suffering the effects of your little coma.'

'Uh huh,' I yawned. 'That's about the size of it.'

'Foggy,' he began.

'I'll come in first thing, bright and early,' I promised. 'I want to show you this photo, see if you might know the aforementioned mother.'

'Good,' he concluded. 'And maybe then you can show me what you found in that safe deposit box you ransacked this morning.'

'Sybil Blessing is not supposed to give out the wherefores of a safe deposit box,' I told him.

'She didn't. Any more than Yudda told me whether or not you enjoyed the bouillabaisse.'

'You had me followed,' I said, hoping he heard my irritation.

'From the second you left the hospital.'

'Because?'

'See you in the morning, Foggy,' he answered. 'Bright and early. No kidding.'

He hung up before I could respond.

I loosened my tie. Why would he have me followed like that? Maybe Maggie Redhawk called him because she was concerned for my health and she was just watching out for me. After all, I had told her that Baxter would be asking for me. But it was really more likely that Ironstone had something to do with it. He'd sent a goon, Herbert, to ransack my office. And Herbert had related Ironstone's feelings about me, namely that he wouldn't mind much if I ended up dead.

Ironstone Waters was rich, mean, and unencumbered by morals – the kind of guy who would get what he wanted no matter what. The percentage I could play was to figure out exactly what he really did want and then try to give it to him.

Maybe that way he wouldn't want to kill me so much.

EIGHT

The next morning was very bright. After several years in Florida I still hadn't gotten used to the heat. And I insisted, against all good sense, on wearing the kind of suits I thought a gentleman ought to wear, to wit: the grey sharkskin with slick black Oxfords. The shirt was cotton but the tie was silk. In short, by the time I was in Baxter's un-air-conditioned office, I was sweating like a stool pigeon in Manny's back room.

The police station in Fry's Bay was modest. It was a stand-alone brick number about fifty square feet, windows on all sides. There was a front desk with a sergeant, there was a coffee pot on a table, there were two detectives, and there was Baxter. I didn't mind him because he knew about my questionable past in Brooklyn and he didn't care. He didn't mind me because I did my job at Child Protective Services better than anyone should have. I actually cared about the kids, which was a big surprise to me. And they often seemed to take to me, even more of a shock. So Baxter and I were on a more-or-less even keel. Still, he'd had me followed, and I suspected that he might be in bed with Ironstone. In a way that made me feel more at home. The cops in my neighborhood in Brooklyn were taking money from every third-rate crook on the block.

I sauntered in the door a little after eight in the morning. The guy at the desk was named Gilmore – bald, slow, and drunk.

'Officer,' I told him, 'Detective Baxter has expressed an interest in seeing me.'

'Hey, Foggy,' he said, waving the hand with the cigarette in it. 'Go on back.'

Baxter was the only one who had an actual enclosed office. It took up the back quarter of the big open room and was glassed in. The blinds were always up. Baxter was always in his shirt sleeves, drinking coffee.

I walked on back and knocked on the glass door. He looked up and motioned me in.

'How you feeling this morning?' he asked.

'Like I just got out of the hospital,' I said. 'Also like I got shot. Which reminds me, where do I file a complaint about that?'

Baxter nodded. 'You can get the form from Gilmore. I'll put it in this pile right here, on top of Ironstone's complaints about you: breaking and entering, attempted murder, harboring a fugitive – I forget what all else.'

'OK.' I sat down in the uncomfortable wooden chair in front of his desk. 'So you wanted me to come in. So here I am.'

'Where's the kid?' he asked. 'The one who killed David Waters?'

'Lena? You can't find her? I thought you'd have her here in jail. Last time I saw her was when we were both being shot at by Ironstone.'

'You saw her in the hospital after that.'

'I did?' I grinned. 'I was on a lot of pain medication.'

'Are you telling me you don't know where she is?'

'I swear to God, Baxter, I have absolutely no idea where Lena is.'

He leaned back in his chair. 'What about the stuff in the safe deposit box. She gave you the key.'

'She didn't. She put the key in my suit coat pocket when I was unconscious. I just discovered it there yesterday morning.'

'I don't care,' he sighed. 'What was in the box?'

'Got it right here,' I answered innocently.

I reached into the inside pocket of my sharp suit and produced the two photos, the birth certificates, and the insurance policy. The letters and the bullet were hidden in my apartment. I didn't even think to mention the cash I'd left in the box.

Baxter leaned forward and had a look.

I pointed to one of the photos. 'That's Lena, the alleged assailant in the David Waters murder. The other one is her older sister, Ellen Greenberg. That's who I'm looking for. The insurance policy is for her daughter, hers and David's, as you can see.'

He squinted. 'Yeah. Ironstone was asking about that little item.'

He made a move to grab it and I put my hand on it; slid it back my way a little.

'Look, Baxter,' I said, 'I don't know what you've got in mind, but I'm on an official case for the state of Florida that involves the welfare of several minors. I'm absolutely certain that you're not the type to interfere with a person such as myself, in the pursuit of his sworn duty, right?'

'Look, *Moscowitz*,' he snapped, 'I got a case too, and it don't make sense to me right now. I want to know what happened to David Waters. I want to know where his killer is. I want to know what went on at Ironstone Waters's big old house. And you seem to be in the middle of it all!'

I took a breath. 'So you don't know where Ellen Greenberg is?'

'Christ, Foggy!' he shouted. 'What the hell is going on here?'

My shoulders dropped a little.

'Tell you the truth,' I admitted, 'I don't know. Apparently Ironstone Waters didn't want his son David to be married to this Ellen Greenberg, who worked in some flower shop that, far as I can determine, doesn't exist. Still boys will be boys, and David married her anyway, I think. They had a baby, as married people will, and kept everything secret from Ironstone. But Ironstone found out anyway, and had Ellen shipped out of town, maybe permanently – or maybe Ellen just got scared and ran, I don't know. So David turns miserable, takes out this policy, but as is always the case, the policy won't pay off if it's suicide. So he arranged to have Lena kill him. That would accomplish several things. First, he'd be dead. Second, he'd be free. Third, his kid could collect a million bucks. And in addition, he could really upset his father, which seems to have happened a-go-go.'

'Yeah.' Baxter nodded. 'I think it's safe to say that Ironstone is pretty upset.'

'So what now? Can I get on with my work?'

He closed his eyes. 'They shut down your office, you understand that?'

'And somebody left it unlocked, so a lot of the junk is missing. But I'm going to straighten all that out – and get more furniture. I mailed a report to the state office the night David Waters got shot. Meaning they haven't finished processing the paperwork. Takes them this long to find a paper clip. Meaning the case is still open, so technically my office is still open. Get it?'

Baxter rubbed his forehead. 'OK. OK. *If* you get your office *officially* opened, and *if* you file the proper co-complaints with me, I'll see what I can do to stall Ironstone. But I got to keep on with the investigation into the David Waters murder until you give me some answers about all this mess, right?'

I smiled. 'Who could ask for anything more?'

'Yeah,' he sniffed. 'I give you a week.'

I blinked. 'A week? Baxter. Come on. I just got out of a *coma*.'

'Yeah, well, Ironstone Waters would be happy to put you back into a coma at this point, so you're lucky it's a week. You have no idea the kind of pressure I'm getting. It's not just the money. He's got muscle on the Tribal Council.'

I'd only been in Fry's Bay a couple of years, but it didn't take me long to understand the power of the Seminole Tribal Council. My favorite thing about them was their independence. A few Seminoles lived and worked in town, and a few came into town to work with some of the commercial fishermen. The census had it figured that there were seventy-three Seminoles in the whole place. What most people didn't know was that, out in the swamp, scattered over hundreds of miles, there were over fifty thousand Seminoles hidden from any sort of government scrutiny. That meant that the tribe was larger than Fry's Bay by about a million times. And *that* meant that no matter what anyone said, the Tribal Council ran most things in my part of Florida.

That's why I was happy to know Mister Redhawk.

'Yeah,' I told Baxter, 'Ironstone Waters has influence. But Mister Redhawk *is* the Council. And Redhawk likes me.'

Baxter nodded. 'So I've been told. But unless Redhawk has some kind of Seminole voodoo that can make you bulletproof, the fact that he likes you really don't cut no mustard.'

I nodded. 'So I got a week.'

'Yeah.' Baxter stood. 'So I guess you better get to work.'

'It's good, by the way,' I said, standing up.

'What? What's good?'

'You wondered last night if I liked Yudda's bouillabaisse. I did. You should try it.'

He smiled at me. 'Would you please get out of my office and go get shot somewhere else?'

'OK,' I told him, 'but I really wasn't planning on getting shot again anytime soon.'

He shrugged. 'You know what they say: if you want to hear God laugh, tell him your plan.'

NINE

I was back in my apartment twenty minutes later, packing. I figured I'd hustle on over to Lake Wales, see if anyone at the old Chalet Suzanne recognized the picture of Ellen Greenberg. Could be something.

Just as I folded the last tie, the phone rang.

'I'm busy,' I said into the phone.

'What are you doing at home?' the girl's voice demanded. 'I thought you'd be out finding my sister.'

'Lena?'

'Hey, Foggy.' Her voice softened considerably.

'Where the hell are you?'

'Um, you know. Around. Look, I called the hospital, they told me you got out. What are you doing?'

'Well,' I said, 'in short, I been looking for Ellen Greenberg. No one in town remembers her. And her flower shop took a Brigadoon. And P.S. my office is closed, at least temporarily. It's missing furniture and everything. Last but not least, Baxter gave me a week's grace period before he files charges against me for getting shot by Ironstone, and you for killing his son. I think those are the highlights.'

'In other words you've got nothing. What are you doing home?'

'Packing.'

'What? Where are you going?'

'Lake Wales.'

'Oh, the stationery. So you've been in the safe deposit box.'

'Right.' I closed my suitcase. 'I actually have a few questions about that.'

'Not now. I'll meet you at the Chalet Suzanne. You got the money?'

'What do you mean?'

'The money I left for you in the safe deposit box, Foggy,' she said wearily, like I was an idiot.

'That was for me?'

'What did you think it was for? Crimeny.'

'And did you just say you'd meet me in Lake Wales?'

'I'll try for room seven. They only have, like, sixteen rooms or something. And two plus five is my lucky number.'

'Seven is everybody's lucky number, I thought you were a little more original than that.'

'No, Igmo,' she complained, again with the attitude, 'my lucky number is two plus five.'

'Uh huh,' I said. 'I know better than to ask you a lot of questions now. But I just want to tell you—'

But I stopped talking because she hung up.

Ten minutes later I tossed my suitcase into the backseat of my car, a raven black 1957 Ford Thunderbird. It was the only one in town and something of a curiosity for the locals.

I thought I might head over to Abiaka Park before I split for Lake Wales. I'd only been a couple of times, but I'd never seen anyone there, which was odd to me. It was a beautiful park. You could sit there and watch the ocean, and there were always flowers.

As I drove over to it, I got to thinking about David Waters's reputation as a pervert. If the park was small and quiet and not many people ever went there, and if it was maintained by the tribe, then you had to wonder: who started the rumors about him?

In a small town like Fry's Bay there are all kinds of rumors. It had taken me a while to get used to that. I didn't gossip much in Brooklyn. I was too busy getting zonked and boosting cars. On the other hand, my mother and my aunt, who raised me as best they could, did nothing but gossip. They never once had a conversation about world events, politics, religion, philosophy, or even the weather. They talked about Mrs Grossinger in the apartment across the hall and how she always smelled of cabbage. Or her no-good son who used too much Brylcreem and never called her except to ask for money. Or the Veelander twins who lived upstairs and who were tramps.

I always assumed that all that gossip was the reason I couldn't stand to be at home with them, so for a long time I blamed my mom and Aunt Shayna for my nefarious lifestyle. Until I realized that I really, really liked the coke and I was really, really good at stealing. I had pride in my artistry. And when my friend Pan

Pan Washington started bragging that I could steal the shine off a policeman's badge, I thought I was really Mr Big Stuff.

The point is: I didn't get gossip. But even at that, the weirdness of David's rep was hard to understand just from a practical point of view. Who even saw him there at the park? If it was other Seminoles, why would they spread rumors about him in town, a very un-tribal-like phenomenon.

My conclusion, as I pulled up to the small, empty parking lot beside the park, was that people in general hated Ironstone Waters. And if there's one thing that poor people hate more than rich people, it's rich people's children. Most Seminoles were poor. And David was a drunk and a jerk even before he got pegged as a pervert.

As with all my other experiences at Abiaka Park, the joint was deserted. It was probably an acre or so of land. I didn't know anything about flowers, but there were plenty: shrubs and vines that had flowers, a half dozen small palms, cool looking green and yellow striped giant grass, a rock garden, and tons of shade. There were three benches, all handmade, all facing the ocean.

I sat down and watched the waves for a second, trying to reconcile the peace of the place with the unsavory small town talk associated with it.

I never saw the woman. She was just, all of a sudden, sitting on the bench beside me. It was spooky. She was wearing a pale blue sun dress, no shoes, shades, and a white straw fedora. Looked about twenty or so.

'Hi,' I said, because what else was there to say?

'You've been asking around town about Ellen Greenberg.' She didn't look at me; she stared out at the ocean.

'I have.'

'John Horse heard about that. He sent me.'

Good old John Horse was a kind of Seminole shaman, lived way in the swamp. I'd had enough significant interplay with him to consider him a friend. Sure, he'd once dosed me with some hallucinogenic tea and thrown me in a lake, but he'd done it as a favor, at least in his mind. And he was a guy who even Redhawk and Ironstone left alone. So he was a good friend to have.

'How is John Horse?' I asked.

She smiled. 'He's not dead.'

I took a second to think why she'd responded that way. John Horse was, according to plenty of other people, over a hundred years old. So 'not dead' was a pretty fair achievement. But he also had lots of enemies, mostly in the government, including several outstanding federal warrants. So he was also lucky not to be dead from some overzealous local authority. But I got the impression, from the way the woman said it, that she meant something else. She meant that John Horse wouldn't *ever* be dead.

That was the gossip about him.

'And he sent you to do what, exactly?' I asked her.

'Help you.'

'Yeah,' I said, turning her way, 'help me do what?'

'Find Ellen Greenberg, get her daughter the money from David's will, and keep you from getting killed.'

'Oh.' I sat back. 'Tall order.'

'Let's start this way.' She took off her hat, let her hair fall down over her shoulders, and stared at me. 'You couldn't find her yesterday for three main reasons. One is that she didn't go by the name of Ellen Greenberg here in Fry's Bay. Also she didn't look like the photograph you had – she'd dyed her hair and she wore glasses, fake glasses. Finally, she didn't work in a flower shop, exactly. She worked the flower counter in the gift shop at the hospital. Maggie Redhawk knew her; Maggie helped her when she was pregnant. See? I just saved you all kinds of time and trouble.'

I stared back at her. 'Yeah, you could have told me some of this before I ran all over town with the photo, but this is actually a pretty big boost. So you would understand if I told you I was in love with you all of a sudden.'

Her smile got bigger. 'It would never work out, Foggy. Religious differences.'

'You're anti-Semitic?'

That made her laugh. 'No. I mean religious *differences*, as in, I have a religion and you don't.'

'What makes you say that?' I asked, trying my best to sound offended.

'John Horse told me all about you.'

'Damn,' I said. 'Well, you're the road not taken, then.'

'One that got away,' she agreed solemnly.

'OK now that that's settled, maybe you can tell me how David Waters got such a terrible reputation in Fry's Bay.'

She nodded, a little contemplatively. 'Interesting question. I knew David most of his life. He wasn't a nice kid. You know: stuck-up rich dick with an Adonis complex. Nobody liked him. But then he met Ellen. Word is that she took him down a peg or two. That's what he needed. The Council was disposed to consider him a dick permanently. So when he ran into this trouble with his father – I mean his father not thinking Ellen was good enough for him, which, you understand, was the exact opposite of reality – he got worse. And with all the people saying that David was a child molester, it hurt Ironstone's heart and soiled his reputation. A couple of solid business deals went south on account of the rumors. What publicity-conscious white businessman wants to screw with a deal involving the father of a pervert?'

I folded my arms. 'This is quite a story. How much of it is real and how much of it is what John Horse told you to say to me?'

See, I was wise to John Horse. He fancied himself a trickster. He had sent this person to talk to me and to wind me up like a top; set me spinning around the countryside doing what I could only assume was *his* business.

She only smiled. 'I see that you really do know John Horse.'

'That's right,' I told her. 'I think you'd better tell me your name. If we can't get married, we can at least be friends.'

'Hachi,' she said.

'What does it mean? I know that's important.'

'It means *stream*. What does *Foggy* mean?'

'Um, it means, in my case, *vague, confused, bewildered*, right?'

She laughed. 'Who would give you such a name? Not your mother.'

'My so-called friends in Brooklyn,' I assured her.

'Why?'

'It's a long story,' I said, standing up, 'and I actually have to be going. Tell John Horse that your mission was only partly successful.'

'Oh?' She kept her seat and looked up at me.

'I believe that David Waters may have deliberately exacerbated his rep as a child molester in order to screw with his dad,' I allowed, 'but there's more to it than that, and I'll find out what it is. And I'll find out whatever it is that John Horse doesn't want me to know. Also tell him that Yudda's bouillabaisse is really good, if he's planning on coming into town anytime soon.'

No point wasting any more time in the park. John Horse had tossed an attractive young woman my way and a story that had just enough truth about it to be confusing. The real deal behind David Waters and his troublesome mythology was still as yet to be revealed.

Then, just as I was about to get into my car, Hachi called out.

'Hey?' Her voice was like a song.

I turned around. 'What?'

'David really loved to go fishing, John Horse says.'

And with that, she was gone, wandering back into the shadows of the park.

I cranked up my car and didn't look back.

Unfortunately, I spent half the trip to Lake Wales thinking about the way the ocean breeze had lifted the hem of Hachi's blue dress.

TEN

The roundabout in front of the Chalet Suzanne was empty when I got there. I had no idea what time it was, but it was late at night. The place was pink, lit up, with weird spires everywhere: an angular wedding cake of a building.

I parked, left my suitcase in the car, and ambled in.

The lobby was small, a perfect example of Florida haute décor: nice pictures and swell furniture – spotless, bright, welcoming. The guy at the desk, on the other hand, seemed very disappointed to see me.

'May I help you, sir?' he asked, but it was in a way that made me think he didn't really want to help me much at all.

'Yeah,' I told him, 'I have a room. My niece is already checked in, room seven I think.'

He stared. 'Your niece?'

'Fourteen going on fifty, about this tall, traveling light.'

He continued to stare. It made me uncomfortable.

'It would, of course, be illegal for a person of that age to register by herself.' He didn't blink. 'No one of that description has been here. May I have your name please?'

'I guess I beat her here.' I leaned forward, elbows on the counter. 'I'll take room seven.'

'Occupied.' He stood his ground.

'OK, give me rooms two and five.' I reached for my wallet. 'And while you're at it, you can tell me how long you've been working here.'

'How long I've been working here?' he repeated.

I zipped out my wallet, flashed my CPS badge, which looked very official, and I shoved it in his face.

'Let's start this again,' I said, 'only lose the attitude and answer my questions nicely, or I'll see what I can do about having you arrested.'

It was an idle boast. I was outside of my county, and as far as I could tell there weren't any children around who needed protecting, but it worked sometimes.

'What's this about?' he asked me, but his voice was a little less hard.

'It's about a woman named Ellen Greenberg,' I said right back.

I reached into my coat pocket and produced her picture.

'Now tell me how long you've been working here,' I said, smiling. 'Please.'

'I've been the night man for five years. And that woman's never been a guest, not since I've been here.'

'Could have been a year ago, or even two,' I said. 'You might not remember her. She would have had a kid with her, a little girl.'

He shook his head. 'Look, I've got a great memory for faces and an instinct for suspicious behavior. That badge of yours wasn't police. Are you a P.I.?'

'Child Protective Services,' I said. 'It's a very specific arm of law enforcement.'

He nodded. 'She steal the kid?'

'What? No. She's the mother. Look, why are you giving me such a hard time?'

'Am I?' He tried to sound innocent, but it didn't work.

I stared. 'When I came in, you seemed very startled.'

'We don't get many guests in the middle of the night, and we don't have any outstanding reservations.'

'And you're the suspicious type.'

'That's right. So why don't you tell me what you really want. And I should probably tell you that I have a pistol in my hand, underneath the counter here.'

'Here's how I work,' I told him. 'I latch onto something and I just keep at it until I get what I want. There are some stupid things about this job, but I love it. I help kids. It's what my Aunt Shayna would call "very rewarding." Also I have righteousness on my side: very few people want to be known as someone who doesn't help children in need. Your problem is: that's what I think of you, that you don't want to help the children. See?'

His face showed signs of a weakening will. 'If you'd just tell me your name, sir,' he began nervously, 'I think I might be able to help you.'

Suddenly I got it. Lena was already there. She'd told the guy that someone was after her and she probably gave him money to keep her secret. Only she'd also given him my name, a moniker that few would claim.

'Sorry,' I said, and even I could hear the sympathy in my voice. 'The name's Foggy Moscowitz.'

I held out my hand.

The guy's shoulders relaxed down about two inches, and he exhaled like he'd been holding his breath for an hour. He shook my hand.

'That's the name I was looking for.' He managed a smile. 'Sorry, but Lena, she—'

'I'm pretty sure I got the picture. She's in room seven?'

He nodded. 'Paid for two nights.'

'And gave you how much more?' I asked.

He looked down. 'It *was* a very generous tip.'

'You really got a gun under there?' I asked.

He nodded and very slowly pulled out a familiar looking 1951 Beretta.

'You can give it back to her now,' he said, his voice a little shaky in a post-adrenaline way. 'Guns make me nervous.'

'Me too,' I agreed, taking the thing from him. 'Room seven is—?'

He pointed. 'Just up those stairs, second on the right.'

I nodded, pocketed the Beretta, and headed up the stairs.

The door to room seven came into view, but I knew better than to just barge in on Lena. The Beretta in my pocket would not be her only gun. So I started whistling. Don't know why, it just seemed like the right thing to do. The tune was *Stardust* – none of that crap that they played on the radio. You couldn't get away from the Captain and Tennille and the idea that love would keep them together. If their only evidence was a clunky melody and a sentiment that had been soaking in warm milk for a week, I didn't hold out much hope for the couple.

So *Stardust* it was, from a time when people really knew how to write a song, and by *people* I meant Hoagy Carmichael. I knew Lena would get it.

I stopped short of the door, whistling the verse, and stood there.

After a second I said, 'Are you going to let me in? I'm hungry. I want another omelet'

The door flew open and Lena bounded into the hall.

'Foggy!'

She had a gun in one hand, and she threw the other arm around my neck, hugging me like I had a million dollars. She was wearing a tee shirt that said 'Disco Sucks' and what they used to call Capri pants.

'I don't have a kitchenette,' she went on, dragging me into the room. 'We'll have to go out for an omelet.'

'Forget it then,' I told her, allowing myself to be dragged. 'I only like the ones you make.'

'Yeah,' she agreed, 'because mine are fantastic.'

We were in, and she closed the door behind us.

'Now.' I exhaled. 'What the hell?'

'I see your point.' She nodded.

She tossed the gun onto the bed and flopped down into one of the two chairs in the room. It was a nice room, beige, a little too much frou frou for me, but clean and well appointed. The bed was one of those canopy jobs, and the off-white carpet on the floor was very lush. The bathroom was right by the door, and the only window in the room was rigged up with blackout curtains so there was no telling what was outside.

I took the other chair and stared at her.

'This is the last place my sister was seen,' she said without prelude.

'Yeah but that's just the thing: she wasn't seen. The guy downstairs has been here for five years, and he doesn't remember her.'

'Right,' she said, leaning forward. 'He doesn't remember. That doesn't mean she wasn't here.'

'Look, I know you think the stationery is a great clue,' I shot back, 'but it's very likely that she just got the stationery from this joint without ever actually staying here.'

'Why would she do that?' Lena glared. Then, before I could answer, she nodded. 'She'd do that to throw off anybody who came looking for her. Damn it. *Damn* it. I kept those letters all this time, and they're useless. Square one.'

'Not entirely,' I told her, slumping down in my chair. 'She got

the stationery somehow. Like, for instance, maybe she worked
here for a while. Never saw the night man, gave a false name,
never mentioned she had a kid; lived somewhere close by.'

She shook her head. 'That's kind of genius. How did you think
of that?'

'First, I thought of it because I'm a kind of genius, but more
to the point, I didn't actually think of it at all. Your sister did. If
she's half as smart as you are, she'd cook up something like that
pretty easily, right?'

Lena nodded. 'So – what? We, like, canvass the neighborhood?'

'I don't want to be too obvious. Your sister went to a lot of trouble
to hide. I don't want to go crashing around, drawing all kinds of
attention to her, showing her photo – it's got to be quieter than that.'

Lena sat up suddenly. 'You don't think she could still be around
here, do you? I mean in Lake Wales?'

'Possible.' I shrugged. 'But those letters aren't dated. There's
no telling how long ago they were written. When did you get
hold of them? And how?'

She hesitated; took a breath.

'David gave them to me about – maybe a month ago. He
said they'd tell me where to find her when the job was done,
get them their money. I just assumed that he meant she was
still here, at the Chalet.'

'Did you really read the letters?' I asked her.

She squirmed. 'A little. I don't go in much for the sugary snacks.'

'Yeah,' I agreed, 'and they *are* insulin resistant, but if you
take a deep breath and keep on reading until the third paragraph,
you get something pretty odd.'

'Odd?'

I sat up and leaned forward. 'Have a look.'

I fished in my suit coat pocket and pulled out the documents.

'You brought them with you?' She seemed to think I was an
idiot.

'Just have a look, wise guy. All three of them have some very
odd wording.'

'*What?*'

'Have a look, seriously.' I handed her the letters.

She studied them for a few minutes and then looked up.
'They're in code.'

'I think so.' I gave her a good strong look. 'How did you get this smart so young? And this tough?'

I was surprised to see that she avoided looking at me.

'When we have a little more time,' she answered me quietly, 'I'll tell you some stuff that happened to me, and you'll tell me how you got from Brooklyn to Florida, right? But for now, I really want to find my sister.'

'Got it. So. Let's really concentrate. Between the two of us, we'll figure it out in no time.'

Five hours later the sun was almost up and we hadn't figured it out. She was cross-legged on the bed and I was slouched down about as far as I could go in one of the over-stuffed chairs.

'Is there anything to the fact that the weird phrases are always in the third paragraph?' Lena mused out loud.

'Not as far as I can tell,' I mumbled, 'but I think I'm more confused now than I was when we started.'

'Me too,' she allowed. 'So maybe we should say out loud what we're thinking. You know, be spontaneous. What are you thinking right this second? Say it out loud.'

I sat up and rubbed my eyes. 'All right. I say, out loud, that what I'm thinking now is I need coffee and a big breakfast.'

She bounded out of bed like a golden retriever. 'See! I knew you'd think of something. Let's go.'

She didn't wait for a response, just headed for the door.

I hauled myself out of the chair and stumbled after her. She zipped down the stairs, through the lobby and the dining room, right into the kitchen. I did my best to keep up with her. When we flew through the lobby I checked to see if our friend at the front desk was going to object, but he pretended we were invisible.

Lena waded into the kitchen like she owned the place. Eggs in the fridge, bacon in the meat locker, day-old bread on the counter – she collected the ingredients without even looking at them.

Ten minutes later I was sitting in the dining room eating what she called 'toad in the hole.' She cut a circle out of the middle of a piece of bread, put it on a hot griddle, and cracked an egg into it; fried the bacon on the side. It was like French toast without the French. Plus, the kitchen had an espresso machine, a big one. I have no idea how she knew what to do with it – there were gears and knobs and cups, none of which made any sense to me. But there I was sipping first-class espresso and dining on a dish that was at once unfamiliar and very comforting.

She ate her food in ten seconds and then leaned forward, chin in elbow, watching me eat.

'Better?' she asked.

'And I'll tell you why,' I answered, downing the last of my espresso. 'Numbers.'

She hesitated. 'Sorry?'

'We've been going about the letters all wrong.'

'Explain,' she said.

'All right.' I finished my last corner of toast. 'The phrases are repeated in the third paragraph of each letter, right?'

'I'd forgotten about that. What about it?'

'That's to get your attention, so you'll know what phrase to look at. Now the idea of using the single words *telephones* and *pens* is also to isolate them. Then there's the odd phrase "in the same place." I think the number three and the single words are trying to tell us about a place. Some location, I mean, where your sister might actually be.'

'Maybe you need some sleep.'

'It was your idea to think out loud,' I told her.

She glared. 'And what, exactly, does your thinking get us, Einstein?'

'Numbers,' I repeated. 'One of the things I did in my callow youth in Brooklyn was I ran numbers for Red Levine, a relatively famous guy in my neighborhood. He took me under his wing, and I ran numbers until I graduated to boosting cars.'

She shook her head. 'Miscreant.'

'Yeah, but I'm telling you about numbers. It's a racket like a lottery where a schmo bets on numbers and if those numbers turn up in the paper the next day, the schmo wins a little money. Most people used the race track results, but Red liked the *bug*, the last digit of the day's New York bond sale.'

'OK, you're a hoodlum,' she conceded, 'but I still don't understand where this gets us.'

'Then I'll continue. We used to employ little codes if we ever had to write anything down, in case we got cracked. Simple stuff. We're looking for something – some place name with the number three in it. And the rest of the name is in the single words *telephones* and *pens*.'

She was doubtful. 'You're going a long way around to get home.'

'Yeah, but I got an ace in the hole. I was given a hint very recently that David Waters liked to fish. Liked it a lot.'

She squinted.

'Well,' I went on, 'maybe we need to find out what's a good fishing hole here abouts.'

'In Lake Wales? There's got to be, like, a hundred.'

'Yeah,' I agreed, 'but as luck would have it, I know where to start. Let's go.'

I got up from the table. Lena followed.

But in the Suzanne lobby, we got the stink eye from our boy on the front desk. He didn't say anything, but he didn't have to. Something was up.

'Doesn't that guy ever get off work?' I mumbled.

'Any chance someone followed you here?' Lena whispered, frozen in the lobby.

'Didn't see anybody,' I told her, 'but I know Ironstone's guys are after me.'

She moved very slowly toward the stairs. 'Well, I'm worried about whatever it is that's worrying Arnie.'

'Arnie's the desk guy?'

She nodded. 'And all my hardware is in the room.'

'So here's the plan,' I told her. 'You go to the room; I wait in the hall. You try to act a little more like a scared fourteen-year-old kid and a little less like a thirty-five-year-old mobster, and that will give us the element of surprise. Leave the door unlocked. Then, when the time is right, I bust in, and we get the jump.'

She turned her icy glare my way. 'Not really a plan, per se.'

'I like to improvise the details. Go on.'

She wasn't enthusiastic, but she went to the stairs. I stayed a little behind.

Up the steps to the second floor, she pulled ahead and, in a move that made me like her even more than I already did, she started whistling *Stardust.*

She only got louder at the door, shoved in the key, and pushed

into the room. I had my back to the wall just to the right of the
door. I watched her click the lock to make it stay open, and then
she looked into the room and stopped whistling.

'Hey,' she said, sounding very much like a whiney teenager,
'what're you doing in my room?'

'Shut up,' a deep voice said.

I didn't recognize it. She let the door close behind her. And
even though I had every confidence in her ability to take care of
herself, I was worried.

'Why don't you both just sit down,' I heard Lena say loudly.

Good. She was telling me how many guys there were.

There was mumbling that I couldn't hear, and then Lena
talked again.

'I'm on vacation,' she railed, 'what're *you* doing here is what
I'm asking?'

More mumbling and a little scuffling. Much as I hated guns,
I reached into my coat pocket and took out Lena's Beretta,
suddenly very happy that I hadn't given it back to her.

Then Lena gave out a little squeal, and that was enough for
me. I kicked in the door, plastered myself against the wall inside
her room, and pointed the Beretta everywhere at once.

The tableau that greeted me was, despite the situation, a little
comical. Two great big goons were flanking Lena. They were
both dressed in nice black pin-striped suits, also black shirts and
black ties, a long braid of hair trailing down their backs. They
had Lena by the arms and they were lifting her up. The three of
them looked like some sort of wrong-headed avant-garde dance
company.

'I'm pretty sure I can plug both you guys before you can set
down the girl and fish out your guns,' I said confidently. 'So let's
behave, OK?'

Without waiting for them to answer, Lena did some kind of
circus move: kicked her feet up over her head; somersaulted
backward in the air. In the next second she was free from the
goon-grip, landing pretty neatly on the bed. She rolled, reached
under her pillow, and came up on her feet with a gun in each
hand.

I had to laugh. 'Man,' I told the goons, 'did you guys ever
pick the wrong kid to screw with.'

They both looked around like they were audience dupes at a magic show.

'Now have a seat, gents,' Lena commanded, 'or I'll pop you both in the back. I'm a little girl and I got no morals.'

They hesitated.

Lena didn't.

She shot one of the guys through the back of his kneecap. He went down and passed out; didn't make much noise. Oddly, neither did her gun. Closer examination told me that she'd fired a Smith and Wesson 'hush puppy' – mostly used by Navy Seals in Vietnam, very quiet, nice and small, and impossible for a kid to get hold of.

I took a step farther into the room. The guy on the floor was bleeding all over the carpet. I looked at his pal.

'You should probably go into the bathroom and get a big towel,' I told him.

He looked at me with dead eyes. 'You should probably get away from me, Foggy. We're taking this girl to Mr Waters. I can't kill you because John Horse told me not to. But I can make it impossible for you to walk, or I can cut off your penis.'

He took a single step in my direction, but that's as far as he got.

Lena came up behind him, put her little pistol in the back of his calf, and fired. The bullet came through his leg and skidded across the carpet.

He went down.

Lena looked up at me. 'I don't know what's wrong with me. Six months ago I just would have iced these guys. I think I'm losing my nerve.'

'Could be stress,' I told her. 'I'm reading a very interesting new book by Dr Lewis Thomas, and he says stress is the cause of most of your modern maladies.'

'I do have a lot on my mind,' she agreed.

I walked over and knelt beside the guy who had threatened my ability to procreate.

'You do understand that this person here, this girl, just beat you, right?' I asked him. 'And she also killed David Waters in front of a crowd. *And* she would have killed Ironstone if I hadn't messed her up. So you're *really* on borrowed time, here.

I'm pretty sure she's going to get her mojo back any second now, and you'll be left rotting in some hotel room far away from home, with no burial, and no one to mourn your passing.'

'Why don't you kiss my ass?' he snapped.

'Well,' I said to Lena. 'I tried to tell him. Go on, then. Shoot him in the back of the head. That'll get you back in the old saddle.'

'Maybe you're right. I loosen up, do these two guys just for practice.'

She pressed the barrel of the hush puppy against the guy's skull.

'Wait a second,' the guy said.

I could tell that the shock of getting shot was wearing off and the pain in his wrecked leg was turning on.

'Wait for what?' I asked him.

'Wait for me to tell you *why* I came to get the kid,' he growled. 'Ironstone isn't interested in killing her anymore. He wants to help.'

'Bullshit,' Lena snapped. 'I killed his son and I tried to kill him. He's not the forgiving type.'

'Ordinarily I would agree with you,' he said. 'But the old guy is suddenly interested in family. He wants to see his granddaughter.'

'Me too,' Lena said. 'But I don't know where she is any more than he does.'

'It's true,' I chimed in. 'We came here looking for her, but she's gone.'

'God's honest truth,' she swore.

'So we can't help Ironstone at the moment,' I said. 'But if you would let us continue in our investigation without dogging us or shooting us or threatening to cut off important body parts, we'll probably find Ellen and her child within the week.'

'I'd say that's a good bet,' Lena added.

'And anyway,' I concluded, 'you both got shot. You can't really keep up with us. You need to go to the hospital. That's a great excuse to hand Ironstone.'

The guy sighed. 'OK.'

'There,' Lena said and took the gun away from the guy's head.

I pocketed her Beretta and offered the guy my hand. He took it and sat in one of the chairs, wincing.

'What's your name?' I asked him.

'Holata,' he said.

'Means *alligator*,' I told Lena.

'Impressive that you know,' she said.

'All right then,' I went on, 'I'll call an ambulance and Lena's going to pack her stuff. We're going to be gone when the ambulance gets here.'

He nodded.

Lena went to the bathroom and got a couple of towels. She tossed them at me and went to a small black suitcase that was lying on the floor underneath the only window in the room.

I tried to fix up Holata's wound and stop the other guy's bleeding – he was still out. I stared down at him and finally realized that I'd seen him before. He was Herbert, the one who'd ransacked my office.

'They'll fix Herbert's kneecap good as new,' I told the guy. 'And you're not in much trouble at all – the bullet went through clean.'

He nodded. 'Really hurts.'

'Yeah, I'm calling right now.'

I went to the phone, dialed the operator, and waited. After a moment a woman's voice answered.

'Yes,' I said cheerfully, 'we were on our way to the gun show in Miami, my friends and I, and we've had a little accident. One of our pistols fell off the bed and inadvertently fired. They're both shot in the leg, my friends.'

She asked me a question.

'No, ma'am,' I told her, 'it was just an accident. Nobody's mad. But we really could use an ambulance. They're both bleeding all over the nice carpet here at the Chalet Suzanne.'

That provoked more talk from her.

'Yes, ma'am. Chalet Suzanne. Room seven. And could you please hurry. One of my friends is unconscious. Thank you.'

I hung up.

'Let's go, Lena,' I said. 'I don't want to be here when the authorities get into this room.'

She clicked the suitcase closed. 'Done.'

'You heard what I told the nice lady dispatcher,' I said to Holata. 'Can you stick to that script?'

'Gun show in Miami,' he said, breathing heavily. 'Accident.'

'Tell John Horse I said *l'chaim.*'

'What?' he asked me, trying to focus his eyes.

I didn't bother explaining.

Outside it was getting hot. Somehow Lena had changed into a nice dress when nobody was looking. It was an elementary school look, pale blue, knee length, high collar. Still had the flip flops on.

As we climbed into my all-too-conspicuous car, I felt I had to ask, 'What's with the little kid look?'

'I know the advantage of a good costume,' she told me.

'Yeah.' I cranked the engine. 'Maybe now would be a good time for me to say something to you about shooting people with guns.'

'What did you have in mind to say?'

'I thought I would begin with, "Cut it out."'

She nodded. 'I know you think this is the part of our little story together where you ask me how a smart, good-looking person my age got involved in killing people. But I think I'm more like you than you realize. For example, I'm not the sharing type. Bad stuff happened to me when I was very young, and it was get tough or get dead. And I'm not dead.'

'I can see that,' I told her as we pulled out from the Chalet Suzanne.

'And my point is,' she interrupted, 'that you haven't told me how a Brooklyn crook got to Florida working this job you've got. I imagine you'd tell me that it's a complex issue.'

'It is.'

'And personal.'

'Yes.'

'Well.' She shrugged. 'Ditto.'

'There will come a time,' I warned her, 'when I'll have to make reports and tell tales, and I'm not any good at lying – not anymore. So when that time comes, I'll tell you all about my troubled youth, and you'll reciprocate.'

'It's a deal,' she said.

'But for now you'll have to explain to me again how you got those letters.'

The hot air was rushing all around us through the open

windows, and I was very much regretting wearing the old shark-skin suit.

'David gave me the letters when he hired me, like I said,' she told me, but she wouldn't look at me.

'Why'd he do it?' I asked, trying my best not to sound like I didn't believe her.

'Maybe Ellen told him about me,' she offered hesitantly, 'you know: about my work. Maybe David gave me the letters thinking I'd be able to figure them out, which, by the way, I never would have. You, on the other hand, are kind of a genius, have I mentioned that?'

'Not nearly enough,' I told her. 'But you're saying that David had the letters. Does that mean *he* figured them out? And came here?'

'Good questions.' She turned my way. 'Where are we going?'

'Remember I said I knew where to start,' I responded, 'about the question of fishing?'

'So we're going where?' she repeated

'To the Cherry Pocket,' I said, and stepped on the gas.

ELEVEN

The Cherry Pocket was a fish house restaurant that Yudda talked about. He said that if I ever wanted to watch a man wrestle an alligator and then eat that alligator cooked in lemon butter, the Cherry Pocket was my ticket.

The story was that some Floridian by the name of Cherry stumbled on a place between some canals, thought it looked like a pocket, hence the name. Once a place for cock-fighting, itinerant gambling, and exaggerated tales about how big a fish was, our current decade had tamed it somewhat. Now, Yudda said, it was a nice place to go for a decent piece of catfish or a dozen raw oysters. Not for me, obviously, since my mother and my aunt Shayna kept kosher and I still had the habit, but I thought the kid might get a kick out of the place. And it was the perfect spot for me to ask someone where a rich Seminole kid might go fishing.

I drove a little north and somewhat east from the Chalet Suzanne and ended up in a trailer park on the banks of Lake Pierce in front of a sign sporting a picture of an alligator standing up on his back legs. The sign read 'Cherry Pocket Fishing Resort Steak & Seafood Shak Tavern.' Yes, that's how they spelled *shack*.

I parked under a nearby tree and we ambled into the joint. While it was a lovely day outside, it was after midnight inside the place: low lights, fried fish, and tavern smell. Perfect. The hour being early, I was surprised to see so many people. They had the aspect of regulars, good old Florida beer-for-breakfast salt of the earth. They all made a point of ignoring us when we walked in. We took a table close to the door, backs to the wall – habit for both of us.

A guy wearing a dirty white apron came our way. He sported a pompadour hair style and a look of concern. He stood at the table and didn't speak.

'You wouldn't be Tony, would you?' I asked him.

'Don't no *Tony* work here, pal,' he said quickly.

I looked at Lena. 'Too bad. Here I am with twenty bucks from Yudda that he owes Tony, and don't no *Tony* work here.'

'Well,' she said, 'you tried. Let's go.'

She made as to get up.

'Hold on,' the guy in the apron said. 'I'm Tony.'

I shook my head. 'Not really. Tony's an older guy. Yudda told me.'

'Yudda owes me twenty from the last time he was in here,' the guy went on, 'because he lost a bet about eating raw oysters.'

I nodded. 'Go on.'

'You know what a big guy Yudda is,' he continued. 'He bet me he could eat twelve dozen raw oysters. He lost.'

'And?' I prompted him.

'And he got sick as a dog,' the guy laughed. 'That's why he didn't pay up. Said I give him bad oysters.'

I smiled, reaching into my pocket. 'That's the story he told me.'

I handed over a twenty. It wasn't actually from Yudda. He said he'd never pay the creep, or ever set foot in the place again, because the oysters *were* bad. My opinion was that even if they were supreme, it was disgusting to eat that much raw shellfish. But that's just me.

'What can I get for you?' Tony asked.

When he smiled he showed us that he was missing several teeth, and only one of them had been replaced with a gold substitute.

'I've never had gator,' Lena suggested.

'Well, you in for a treat, little lady,' Tony said. 'What about you, pal? You want to try the raw oyster bet?'

'Not for ten to one,' I told him, 'but I wouldn't mind a piece of grouper.'

He didn't move.

'You ain't come all this way to give me Yudda's twenty and fetch the little lady some gator,' he mused.

'Right.'

'What you want?' He lifted his chin.

'I'm trying to find the place where my friend David Waters goes fishing.'

I wanted to see what he'd have to say about that.

He stared back. 'You *what*?'

I shook my head. 'See, it does you no good to *act* stupid. You're so good at it naturally.'

'It's true,' Lena added. 'You have a real gift.'

'Ain't *David Waters* a Seminole name?' he sneered.

'You know it is.' I stared him right in the eye.

One of the codgers at the bar rumbled a little and said, 'He goes over to the campsite, over there by the old dock. Three Tee Pees. Like that: three separate words, for some reason.'

The codger was maybe a hundred and fifty years old, dressed in camo, and wheezing like a broken concertina in a vaguely Cuban accent.

'It's called *Three Tee Pees*?' Lena asked. 'Like that?'

The old guy nodded.

'David Waters goes fishing there?' I asked.

The old guy sighed, like talking was exhausting. 'Yes.'

'Could you point me in the right direction?' I asked him.

The codger hitched his thumb over his right shoulder. 'Down the dirt road, into the trees on your left. You'll see the sign.'

'What's it look like, the sign?' I asked him.

'It's got three triangles on it. Like teepees,' he answered me.

I looked at Lena. 'You see why we're idiots, right?'

She blinked.

'*T* for *telephones. P* for *pens.*'

'Three teepees.' Her jaw dropped.

'It used to be the campsite here,' Tony warned. 'But it ain't no more. Three Tee Pees campsite. All broke down now.'

'Can you get our food ready to go?' I asked Tony. 'We'll be back in a minute.'

'I got to get the money now,' he answered hesitantly.

I dug in my pants pocket and handed him a twenty. 'I'll be wanting the change.'

He mumbled something and headed for the kitchen. Lena and I made for the door.

'It's nothing over there,' the codger called out. 'Like he said.'

I turned to face him. 'No campers?'

The old guy shook his head and went back to his beer. Lena and I split.

We found the dirt road right away, but it was a bit of a hike into the woods. It didn't take long to figure why the place wasn't used much anymore. The lake had risen, apparently, and the dirt road vanished into a kind of boggy mess. We had to go away from the lake, higher ground, just to keep from getting my Florsheims messier than they already were.

Another five minutes tromping through the forest primeval, and we came across what was left of a couple of stone barbecue grills. We never found the sign that Tony mentioned.

'This can't be it,' she said, looking around at the rest of the area.

It was overgrown like an untended grave, and the air was a little hard to take, with the rotting vegetation and wafting fish smell.

'If I was to hide out,' I told her, 'I'd pick a place like this, because most people would come to it and say, "this can't be it."'

'Good point,' she admitted. 'So.'

'We look around.'

She nodded and headed off more or less toward the lake. I went around the other way. I knew we wouldn't find anything obvious, if we found anything at all. You wouldn't go to this much trouble to hide and then just set up a nice tent with a solid cook fire.

After a while I was pretty convinced that we'd hit a dead end. I was about to find Lena and tell her that when she called out.

'Foggy! I think I got something. Christ!'

I ran. It wasn't easy. The ground was littered and soggy and, every once in a while, I hit a sandy part. I fell twice. But I got up, and I dodged through the trees and the fallen limbs. Just when I got to the place where I thought Lena was, I heard something very wrong right behind me. It was the sound of a charging bull – a bull that was whispering curse words in the Seminole language.

Before I could turn around, a boulder fell on my head, and I rolled into a very dark cave, black as night and twice as cold.

When I woke up, it actually was dark. So I'd been out all day. The moon was bright enough, and I got a pretty good look around. No Lena. Nobody. No hint as to what it was she'd seen. I didn't know if she'd gotten away or been taken. I was worried no matter what, but after another half hour crashing around in the relative dark and finding not a single clue, I realized that I needed to regroup. I was dizzy, disoriented, and starving.

I did notice the cement picnic tables. All of them were in disarray, broken, mostly unusable. But on each bench there was a mold of three teepees.

We'd been in the right place.

I made it back to the Cherry Pocket restaurant and stumbled through the door. My head was killing me and I was wet all over.

Tony smiled. 'You ain't had a good day.'

'No,' I agreed. 'I have not.'

'Lost your little piece of jailbait, did you?'

Aside from how creepy that sentence was, it suddenly seemed to me that Tony might have had something to do with what happened, my getting bonked and Lena getting gone.

So just to make sure, and because I was wet, cold, and hurt, I motored up to him pretty fast and grabbed his ear. The ear is a remarkably sensitive place if you grab the whole thing just right. It gives you carte blanche with just about anybody's head. I moved his around like he was a sock puppet.

'First thing, she's my friend, so lay off with the *jailbait* talk,' I rasped. 'Second, where is she? And speaking of *where* – where's my food? *And* my change.'

'Christ!' he squealed. 'My ear!'

'Yeah,' I conceded, 'this probably hurts.'

'I kept your change, your food's cold, and I ain't got the first idea what happened to your little *friend*.'

I looked around. The codger in the camo was still at the bar, not looking our way.

'I found the campsite,' I told him.

'It's a mess,' the old guy said. 'There's nothing there.'

'Let go of my goddam ear!' Tony insisted.

I shoved his head backward. 'Would you mind heating my food up?' I asked politely.

'Christ!' he shouted.

'Now?' I asked politely.

He glared at me for a second, and then he went into the kitchen.

I sat next to the codger.

'Name's Foggy,' I said. 'If I take care of your bar tab, will you tell me how you know David Waters?'

'I drink for free.' That's all he said.

I looked around. The atmosphere was exactly the same at night as it was in the daytime: 3 AM in Purgatory. There was a drunken older couple in a booth, arguing quietly about poisonous snakes. She said the worst was the copperhead. He said the worst was her mother.

A guy in fishing gear, vest and hat festooned with lures, was eating shrimp with a kind of reckless abandon usually found in pornography.

Other than that, the joint was empty.

'How is it that you drink for free?' I asked.

'I own the place,' he answered, finishing his beer.

'That's how you knew about David Waters.'

'Probably.' He stood up.

'Where are you going?' I turned a little on the bar stool. 'Something I said?'

'Almost eight o'clock,' he mumbled, heading for the door. 'Time for *Columbo*.'

'OK but wait,' I said, sliding off the bar stool. 'I got a real life mystery on my hands: David Waters is dead and I'm investigating.'

He didn't even look back. 'I know.'

And with that he was gone.

I considered going after him, but Tony appeared with my food. It was hot and smelled like heaven. It reminded me how dizzy I was, so I sat back down. Grouper in capers and butter, crispy slaw, hush puppies, French fries, three sauces, and a whole lemon cut in half.

'Tony,' I admitted, 'this looks great.'

'My ear still hurts,' he said.

'Yeah, sorry,' I said, picking up the fork that was on the plate. 'I got knocked out over at the Three Tee Pees, and you shouldn't have said that about my friend. I'm worried about her and she's missing. Although, she can probably take care of herself.'

'All right.' He held his hand up to his ear. 'Go on. Try the grouper.'

I did. After a couple of chews, I looked up.

'This is fantastic,' I told him. 'You just warmed this up?'

'Naw,' he said, 'I cooked you a new one. Good, huh?'

'No,' I said, 'it's *fantastic*. You really got a certain way with a fish.'

He smiled, and I suddenly got why Yudda liked the guy, in spite of all the supficial anomosity. They both had pride in their work. Made me reevaluate my opinion of Tony. But as I reevaluated, I ate. Everything. I would have eaten the plate if he hadn't taken it away from me.

'You was hungry,' he observed, staring at that spotless plate.

'Tony,' I announced, 'I misjudged you, and I apologize. You and Yudda are cut from the same cloth.'

He nodded, not looking at me. 'I consider that high praise. Yudda, he's the best.'

'I agree. So keep my change, and the rest of the money I paid you for the kid's gator, and tell me who hit me over the head.'

He looked toward the door. I nodded.

'Your boss,' I began, 'the Cuban geezer who sits here all day drinking up the profits, he's not exactly what he seems to be.'

Tony was still staring at the door. 'I don't know what the hell he is.'

'But you're afraid of him, I can tell.'

He turned my way; his face was sour. 'What makes you to say that?'

'Your entire demeanor changed toward me once he left. He makes you tense.'

'Well, I don't know what that means' – he nodded – 'but he does make me nervous. He ain't been the boss but for six months. Don't do a thing in this world but drink beer all day and stay up all night watching TV. Don't sleep far as I can tell. And I ain't never seen him eat.'

'How long have you been working here?' I asked him.

'Near five years. Yudda got me this job, matter of fact. After I got out of Lake Correctional.'

'Ah.' That was all I said.

The Lake Correctional Institution had originally been a migrant labor camp. After that it was a bait farm, if my memory served me. A couple of years ago, maybe 1973, it was converted to a men's prison.

'You ain't ask me what I was in for?' he wanted to know.

'Not my business,' I said. 'You got a past. I do too.'

'I was Yudda's, like, apprentice after I got out,' he went on, a little relieved by my nonchalance. 'Which I always figured was just a fancy way to say busboy. But he was good to me.'

'Right. So what about the new boss?'

'Came in one day,' Tony said, 'and told me he'd bought the whole area. Said he liked to fish. Then he sat down and told me to order some beer ain't nobody heard of. I did. He's the only one that drinks it, and he drinks it all the time. And you're right about the profits. This place don't hardly break even.'

Something, some little spark, was trying to light up a darker corner of my brain.

'What's the beer with the odd name?'

'I can't pronounce it,' he complained.

He went behind the bar and got a bottle, plunked it down in front of me. It was a bottle of Cantillon Kriek, the same stuff that Yudda had given me at his place. I guess that was why I had the little spark pestering me.

'Look, Tony,' I began, 'I want you to know that I was a crook in a former life, in Brooklyn. So when I ask you something, I want you to be honest with me, and I promise I won't rat no matter what your answer is.'

'I got no idea what you're talking about,' he said warily.

'It's this: besides learning to cook a fish just right, what else did you do for Yudda?'

'I told you. I bussed tables, washed dishes, cleaned the joint – including the grease trap, which, let me tell you, is one disgusting way to spend Sunday morning.'

'No.' I stopped him. 'I mean what *else* did you do?'

I locked eyes with him.

He spent several seconds trying to figure out what to say to me, but in the end my winning ways got to him.

'You mean the stuff,' he said.

'A little more specific,' I encouraged.

'Yudda's from New Orleans,' he said.

'And won't go back there on account of his ex-wife. I know all that. Skip on down.'

'It's some of the finer weed ever grown down there in Louisiana. They say it's the climate.'

I was wise. 'And Yudda imports weed from his hometown.'

'And, you know, distributes it too. But it's just weed.'

'I always wondered how Yudda stayed in business when his place was empty except for me most of the time.'

'Oh, he's very well-to-do,' Tony assured me. 'Got a big old boat he bought from the Fort Lauderdale yacht brokerage.'

'Really.' I was beginning to add a few things up, and I really didn't like where my thinking was going.

It was a thin thread, but there was more to it than just a little harmless redistribution of cannabis. It was something that involved Ironstone Waters, I was sure of that. And he wasn't a small potatoes kind of person, worried about a dinky marijuana operation. His potatoes were, in fact, very much bigger than that.

TWELVE

My new friend Tony fixed me up with a discreet fishing cabin about halfway in between the bar and the so-called Three Tee Pees camp. I was sore, beat, and confused. I needed sleep, and I knew it wouldn't do any good romping around in the mud and moonlight looking for signs of what happened to Lena.

The cabin was a single room with a bed and a chair, a very small kitchen area in one corner, and a floor lamp that flickered. It smelled like mildew and bacon fat. I opened all the windows, but then I got a nice whiff of sulfur and fish guts, the natural ambience of the place. I didn't take my suit off, and I didn't get under the covers. I was absolutely certain that I would never fall asleep in this particular backroom of Purgatory.

So I was very surprised when the sun blasted in through the windows the next morning.

I sat up. Somehow the smell was better. Or maybe I'd just gotten used to it. I had no idea what time it was, and I thought again about getting a watch. But if I got a watch, then people would start thinking I was the sort of person who knew what time it was, so I rejected the idea, as I always did.

I felt the back of my head. There was quite a lump, but I've been told that's good. Maggie Redhawk had taught me that you had to have a lump after you got hit in the head or something was very wrong.

Then I checked my vision, and it seemed OK. I pronounced myself fit for work and launched myself off the bed and out the door.

The day was much nicer than the night had been: dry, warm, sunny.

I headed in the direction of the Three Tee Pees area.

It didn't look any better in the sunlight. There was Spanish moss hanging down to the ground. Roots had grown over some of the table bases. Fallen branches and dead leaves were everywhere.

I did my best to remember which way I'd been headed, toward Lena's voice, when I'd been conked, and wandered more or less in that direction.

After a minute I realized something odd about the whole area. There wasn't any garbage; no beer cans or paper plates or chip bags anywhere. Which made it, in my experience, an unusual picnic area.

The old guy had called it a campsite. I was only seeing the tables. Somewhere around there would be some kind of sectioned-off plots for campers' tents and the like. They just weren't immediately visible. Maybe that's what Lena had found.

I walked right up to a low growing hedge, stepped over it, muscled through a little more overgrowth, and there they were: half a dozen spacious campsites. Each one had a small stone grill and a knee-high water faucet on a pipe rising out of the ground.

And there was a very large tent pitched on the last site in the row closest to the lake.

It looked like it had been there for a while, but it was untended. There were black leaves on top, and there was a small rip in one side, near the base. Still, I approached it like there might be a bear inside.

'Hello?' I called out.

No answer.

I moved as quietly as I could to the front flap. I thought better of standing directly in front of it when I tossed it open. I was crouched way over to the side.

I threw the flap, half-expecting some kind of brouhaha, but there was nothing. I peeked inside. Two sleeping bags, a couple of Igloo coolers, and a duffle bag. There was also the smell of mildew and some evidence of critter droppings, along with more leaves and a little mold on the inside of the tent.

It was conceivable that Lena's sister Ellen had been hiding out in the tent, along with the daughter. But whoever'd pitched the tent, they hadn't been there for a while.

I looked around, making sure there weren't any other Seminole bulls snorting in my direction, and then I stood up.

I figured that Ironstone Waters had dispatched more goons than just the two Lena and I had found in the hotel room. We'd been followed to the Cherry Pocket. When we'd come to the campsite, these secondary goons had gotten the better of us. That meant Lena was in trouble, probably back in Fry's Bay with Ironstone. I didn't believe for a second that he was interested in helping out his grandchild. He was interested in revenge. And it wasn't for the murder of a son he didn't much like. Somehow Lena had messed up some larger picture.

What that larger picture was eluded me, but I knew I had to get back to Fry's Bay. The problem was, I also knew I had to stay at the Cherry Pocket and figure out who the new owner really was and what part he had to play in Ironstone's larger picture. I didn't want to believe that Yudda was involved, but he probably was. That was an odd trio to contemplate: Yudda, Ironstone, and the Cuban geezer. But I had a terrible intuition that they were somehow related.

What to do?

I backed away from the tent and was about to head for the bar when I noticed that there was something stuck in the tear I'd seen at the base of the tent. I took a few steps, got up close. I couldn't figure out what was stuck in the hole. It was like a flat half-circle of rubber. I pulled it out and wished I hadn't. It was a flip flop. Like the ones Lena had been wearing.

All the way back to the bar I worked hard not to picture how it had gotten there.

When I did make it back to the bar, it was empty. No Tony, no geezer, no general hoi polloi. I called out, I went into the kitchen – it was eerie, like no one had been in the place for years. The stove was cold, the place was clean – no dirty dishes, no pots left in the sink.

So I sat at the bar to gather what was left of my wits. Maybe I was making up the connection between Yudda and the Cherry Pocket, but the back of my neck felt prickly all the same.

I had to remind myself that Lena could take care of herself so that I could stop worrying about her and concentrate on the larger picture. The larger picture hung on David Waters.

Then all of a sudden out of nowhere, I thought about Hachi and her blue dress. She'd told me that Ellen Greenberg didn't look like the photograph I had, that she'd used a fake name in Fry's Bay. Also that she'd worked at the hospital with Maggie Redhawk, in the gift shop.

Maggie Redhawk knew the woman I was looking for.

Still, I just sat there all alone in the dark little bar. I knew that I had to get back to Fry's Bay almost immediately. Lena was at Ironstone's mansion. Maggie knew Ellen Greenberg, so she was my best hope of finding Ellen, not to mention the child who stood to inherit a lot of dough.

So why was it that I didn't get up off the bar stool and out to my car?

That question was answered about two seconds later. The door to the bar swung open and the geezer-owner, still in camo and wheezing like a squeeze box, stood in the doorway, back-lit by morning.

'You're still here?' he growled

'Where else would I be?' I smiled.

'Tony told me that your young friend has been abducted.' He didn't budge. 'I would have thought you'd be trying to find her.'

I faked nonchalance. 'She does a really good job of dealing with bad people. She'll be fine. I'm more worried about Ironstone's men. They're the ones in trouble.'

It was worth a gamble. If he didn't know who Ironstone was, no foul. But if he acknowledged their presence in his little fish camp, then that would be quite a nice bit of information.

'That little girl doesn't stand a chance against very large, very stoned Seminole men,' he snarled. 'God only knows what they're doing to her now.'

I slid off the bar stool. 'Yeah, you should probably check the hospital in Lake Wales to see what happened to the last Seminole gangsters that tried to mess with Lena.'

That shut him up, but only for a second.

He sighed. 'You have no idea what you've fallen into. It's a big, big ocean, and you're a little tiny fish.'

With that he drew a pistol out of some hidden pocket and leveled it right at me. The way he was lit made it impossible to see what kind of gun he had, but it didn't matter. There wasn't anything for me to hide behind or throw at him; I was too far away to lunge. So I tried psychology.

'I agree,' I told him, careful not to move. 'My thinking is that I ought to beat it out of here, go back home, and get some rest. You know I just got out of the hospital? I was in a coma on account of Ironstone Waters shot me. So I really don't need to do that again. You know the old saying: shoot me once, shame on you; shoot me twice . . .'

'Shut up!' he snapped. 'It's just your bad luck that you didn't leave this morning when you got up.'

I could read his body language. He was about to shoot me.

I sagged, like I was beaten, and leaned on the bar.

'Look,' I began, staring at the floor.

Then I dropped, took the stool by the leg, whirled around and tossed the stool right at him. He fired, but the shot went wild. The stool bashed right into him. I heaved myself over the bar and crouched down.

I could hear him stumbling over the stool and lumbering toward the bar.

I looked around for a *mediator*: most bars had one: a club or a gun, something to settle late-night disputes. After a second, there it was: a shotgun. Good choice for a bar of that ilk because it looked very intimidating, and it made a hell of a noise if you shot it.

I grabbed it and slid backward toward the far end of the bar.

He fired again and the bullet hit just to my left.

I moved another couple of inches, pointed the shotgun straight up, and pulled one of the triggers. Sounded like God's own thunder, and chunks of the ceiling rained down. Really scary.

I stood bolt up then with the gun pointed right at my nemesis.

'It's filled with buckshot,' I explained calmly. 'That's why it exploded the ceiling like that. It'll do the same thing to your gut.'

I was partially protected by the bar. He was out in the open.

And for the first time, really, I got a good look at the guy. His eyes were rimmed in red, his hair was like crazy white pipe cleaners sticking out of his head, and his hands were shaking, but not from nerves. He had the DTs. In short, he was a shambles.

'You really ought to put your gun on the floor,' I said.

'Are you going to shoot me?'

'Not if you put your gun on the floor,' I said louder.

And to make my point, I waved the shotgun around a little.

He thought about it for a minute, but eventually he threw his pistol down and backed away from me.

'I'm going to tell you again,' he said, and his Cuban accent was even more pronounced than it had been, 'you're wading into water way over your head.'

I lowered the shotgun. 'Since you seem to be anxious to tell me about it, just what have I stumbled into?'

He moved his hand slowly up to his neck and pulled out a medallion he was wearing. It was round, about the size of a silver dollar.

'Do you know what this is?' he whispered harshly.

'Can't see it.'

He moved toward me very slowly, the way Bela Lugosi used to come up on his victims. When he got close enough for me to actually see the necklace, I raised the shotgun again.

'Black Tuna,' I said.

He smiled, but it made his face look dead. 'That's right.'

The Black Tuna gang was, as far as I understood, the major marijuana smuggling ring in the United States. They got their name from the radio code for Raul Davila-Jimeno, supposedly a Colombian sugar grower. But he was the major supplier of the organization. And you knew a guy was in his gang if he wore a black tuna medallion like the old guy had around his neck. Raul had a small army at his beck and call, and he ruled Santa Marta, Colombia, like he was king.

They were very organized, and they had technology. They were good at eavesdropping on radio communications between U.S. Customs officials.

I'd heard that they operated out of the Fontainebleau Hotel in Miami and their deliveries came to some houseboat off the coast. I'd also heard that they had some association with the hoity-toity Fort Lauderdale yacht brokerage, so they could get a hold of special boats, the kind of thing that might carry a couple of tons of marijuana without sitting too low in the water. And that was the same place where Yudda had gotten his boat, at least according to Tony.

But I didn't buy it.

'If you were Black Tuna,' I told the old guy, 'you wouldn't be holed up in a joint like this, pickling your liver all day long.'

'Well,' he began, a little despondently, 'I'm Cuban.'

'I guessed the accent,' I agreed.

'And maybe you know that the whole Cuban operation has been taken over by the Columbians now. The whole thing. They keep me on because I know things that nobody else does, like safe houses and secret routes, so they need me. I'm here at the Cherry Pocket, like, in *storage*.'

'OK.' I wanted to see where he was going, so that's all I said. The silence encouraged him to go on.

'Can I sit down?' he asked.

I nodded, but I kept the gun on him. I knew better than to underestimate the guy just on account of his age. I'd seen what oldsters trained in *Juego de maní* could do. It was a combined martial art and dance thing that was developed in Cuba by African slaves, and I knew that a lot of these drug guys were wise to it. And a guy who knew it could kick my ass all over town before I could even pronounce it correctly – regardless of his age.

So, down he sat and leaned on the bar.

'Can I have a beer?' he asked.

'You like that Belgian number that Yudda turned you on to, right?' It was a little bit of a trick question.

'Yeah,' was all he said.

I kept my eye on him, but I fetched him a beer.

'So tell me about Columbia,' I said, plunking the bottle down onto the bar in front of him.

He took it, bit the top off with his teeth, drank half the bottle, and exhaled.

'It was just marijuana, you understand. I mean, it was a lot of marijuana, like maybe a billion dollars' worth. But, you know – it's harmless. That shit shouldn't even be illegal.'

'But the Columbians are a little more serious,' I guessed.

He nodded. 'Cocaine. By the ton. And it's good business. I mean, it's so much money that they *weigh* it instead of counting it. Can you imagine?'

'I don't really care,' I said, 'I just want to find Ellen Greenberg and her child – and my friend Lena.'

'Ellen's little sister.' He nodded and took another long pull on the beer.

How could he know that? Lena hadn't told anybody but me that Ellen was her sister. Plus, of course, how did he know Ellen?

'Ellen stayed here for a while,' I guessed, 'over there in that crappy campground.'

'She was hiding out from Ironstone Waters,' he said, 'but you already knew that.'

'Yes.' The less I said, the more he'd think I knew.

'You came here to get her,' he went on.

'I did.'

He flashed that corpse-like smile again. 'But you had bad information. She hasn't been here in six months.'

'Where is she now?' I asked before I thought better of it.

'How should I know? Another beer.'

I stared at him for a minute, and then reached over to get him another bottle.

That was my mistake. My eyes only looked away for a second, but in that second he grabbed the barrel of the shotgun and pulled it out of my hands. He jumped backward off the barstool, flipped the gun around, and blasted it in my direction.

I barely had time to duck behind the bar, and even at that, some of the shot did damage to my suit at the shoulder.

I heard him throw away the empty shotgun and scurry for his pistol. I knew I had to move fast. I grabbed two of his favorite beer bottles, nearly frozen in their ice bath. I threw myself a couple of feet to the right behind the bar. Then I stood and heaved one of the bottles as hard as I could at his head.

It hit, and he staggered. He hadn't retrieved his pistol yet.

I fell back behind the bar, moved all the way to the left, and stood again. He was trying to see straight, but I tossed the second bottle. I was a little amped up, so I threw it really hard. It smashed against his skull and he went down.

I took that moment to roll over the top of the bar and land on the floor right beside him. I kicked his head as hard as I could, but he refused to become unconscious.

He turned over onto his back, lying there on the floor, with his pistol in both hands.

I jumped sideways. The gun went off. I turned and kicked his arms. The gun went flying against the wall and went off again. Hair trigger.

He was scrambling to get up. I got a hold of him from behind, my arm around his neck. I squeezed. He elbowed. We were the worst dancing partners in history, turning, rolling onto the floor, biting, scratching.

Before I knew it, we were nearly to the front door, and neither one of us could find the pistol.

He let out an animal-like scream and belted me right in the stomach with both hands. I doubled over, lost my breath for a couple of seconds, and when I opened my eyes, he was gone.

I sat down on the floor. I felt like a train had run over me. Twice.

On the other hand, a whole lot of things were beginning to make more sense to me. For instance, the old guy was right. I was in way over my head.

I had stumbled right into the middle of the Florida Cocaine Wars.

THIRTEEN

That's what the papers called it, 'The Florida Cocaine Wars.' And in all fairness, 'The Black Tuna Gang' was something of a media appellation as well. I was familiar with the way that worked. My own dear Pops had been a card-carrying member of a group he called the *Combination*, an organization insultingly dubbed 'Murder, Inc.' by an overly-dramatic press.

But it didn't matter what you called these Columbians, they were seriously wrong guys. They weighed the money instead of counting it; they also measured their progress in blood. I had no idea how things were in Columbia, but in certain parts of Florida, it was a war zone like Poland after Hitler.

I sat there on the floor of the Cherry Pocket bar and tried to think my way through all the landmines. If Ironstone Waters, and, by association, David, had anything to do with Black Tuna, I wasn't remotely equipped to soldier on with my little escapade. My best bet was to find Lena, try to get her into a good school and out of the killing game, then go back to my little office and pretend that the previous several weeks had never happened.

Except that I'd promised Lena I'd find her sister. And since I'd turned over a new leaf a few years back, I wouldn't allow myself to break a promise. Ever.

So, step one: I stood up. Step two: I counted my blessings (such as the fact that the old guy hadn't kill me, *and* I finally knew what I was really up against.) Step three: call home. Home in Brooklyn.

I wasn't going to call my mother or my Aunt Shayna. I was calling Pan Pan Washington. For one thing, he was an artist with a blowtorch. He could make a VW bug look like a Jaguar XKE if he wanted to. But that wasn't why I needed to call him.

In my raucous youth, only a few years previous, I had been, shall we say, an aficionado of the coca plant. I was pretty sure that one week I single-handedly cleared out the entire coke reserves of my hometown borough. I could never be sure, because it was all kind of blurry, but I was told that I boosted thirty-five high-end cars that week, also won a mountain of cash on the ponies, and wrecked two perfectly good friendships. Regardless, I was familiar with the milieu.

And Pan Pan had been my supplier. If I wanted information about the coke business in general, he would be the guy to call, because he was very thorough, very knowledgeable, and one of the guys I *hadn't* pissed off before I left Brooklyn.

Finding Lena wouldn't be that hard either, really. Ironstone's men had taken her, so all I had to do was go to Ironstone – the guy who shot me.

As for Ellen Greenberg, or whatever her name was, that would have to wait. Clearly she was clever and good at hiding. She'd keep, at least for a while. I'd eventually ask Maggie Redhawk about her, and get somewhere, but for now: homeward bound.

So despite my aches and pains, I moved carefully out the front door of the dingy bar. I had to be certain that the Cuban codger wasn't out there waiting for me, even though I was pretty sure that he would be trying to get as far away from me as he possibly could. I thought about getting the shotgun, reloading, and sticking it out in front of me, just to see what would happen. But after considering how it had gone the last time I'd pointed a gun at the guy, I decided that I would employ stealth instead.

I crouched low when I nudged the door open with the tip of my Florsheim.

Nothing.

I poked my head out, very low to the ground.

Nothing.

Then I felt a little stupid, so I stood up. I gave the outside a good look. The sun was slanting through the trees, made a lot of shadows, places to hide. My car was pretty visible, but he could have been hiding behind it.

I stepped through the doorway, trying to remember that stupid poem I had to memorize in elementary school: 'Into the valley of death rode the something-or-other.' A clear rip-off of Mizmor Kaf Gimmel in the book of Tehillim, the Twenty-third Psalm. I actually *did* know that one by heart: 'Yea though I walk through the valley of the shadow of death.'

Neither quote was very comforting to me. I moved very stiffly toward my T-Bird.

As luck or God or poetry would have it: the guy was gone. I slid into the driver's seat, cranked the car, and backed it out fast, like I was stealing it. Once I was on the main road, the accelerator went to the floor. After a while I glanced down at the speedometer. It said I was going 102 miles an hour, but it was an old car and I was sure that was wrong.

I felt like I was crawling and might not ever make it back to Fry's Bay.

The sun was high by the time I parked in front of my apartment. Given recent events, I was wary of just walking in, so I slipped around back, beachside, and managed a peek through the sliding glass doors.

My place seemed empty.

I fished in my pocket for the back door key, clicked the lock, and oozed in as quietly as I could. I was relieved to discover that I was alone in the apartment. I was still sore from my tussle, and sitting in the car for a while, tense and speeding, had only made it worse.

I took off my coat, worried that it was permanently ruined, and made it to the bathroom for aspirin. I thought six or eight might do the trick – as long as I chased it with single malt Scotch and heroin, neither of which I had, alas.

Still, down went the aspirin, and then I sat on the bed going over all the plans I'd made on the drive back to Fry's Bay. I would, in order, shower, put on a new suit, drive to the big old Ironstone Waters mansion, stroll in, and probably get shot dead. The end.

But in the unlikely event that I wasn't dead, I would lay down a little mixture of truth and invention for Ironstone to consider. I would tell him that I knew all about his involvement in Black Tuna, the cocaine wars, and the real reason his son David had been killed.

That was a little something I'd been pondering the entire drive. Why had Ironstone been so against his son's involvement with Ellen Greenberg? Sure, some of it was racism – he didn't want David marrying an inferior Caucasian. But why remove the girl from town altogether? It seemed like an emotional overreaction from a very calculating man. I had no idea what was really going on with David and Ellen. Maybe it was love, maybe it was something even more treacherous. But my play was to tell Ironstone that I knew the real reason his son had been killed and then watch to see what he'd do or say. And *then* he'd shoot me dead.

But if *that* didn't happen, I would use whatever *did* happen to leverage Lena's liberation. If Lena wasn't dead already.

As I pondered, sitting there on my bed, it occurred to me that a lot of my predictions about the future ended with people getting dead.

Lost in such thoughts, I almost didn't hear the gentle tapping at my front door. It was so timid, in fact, that I considered for a second that no one was really there at all. Still, caution was my friend. I slipped out the back sliding doors and inched around the side of the building to get a gander at my visitor. And what I saw popped my eyes.

My new girlfriend Hachi was there, holding some kind of package in her hand. And there beside her: none other than John Horse.

I stepped out into the open, headed toward them.

'Nobody home,' I called.

Hachi turned my way. John Horse didn't bother looking, but he smiled.

'There you are,' Hachi said. 'We brought you something for the aches and pains.'

I stopped.

'What makes you think I got aches and pains?' I asked.

John Horse laughed. 'You got shot. You were in a coma. Then you got hit on the head. Then you wrestled with an alligator and a black tuna. I saw it all.'

He looked exactly like he did the first time I saw him. There were wrinkles in his wrinkles. He was dressed in a red flannel shirt, clean jeans, and ornate cowboy boots. His hair was white smoke all around his head. Everything about him was the oldest thing I'd ever seen, and then he turned my way. He had the eyes of a very young child, and they were smiling even though the rest of his face wasn't.

In short, I was glad to see him.

'Hello, John Horse,' I said. 'You saw me wrestle two animals?'

He nodded.

'Let's go inside,' Hachi urged.

She looked around. She was nervous.

'OK,' I agreed.

I went to the front door, unlocked it, and let them go in first.

John Horse went immediately to the sofa. Hachi went into the kitchen and unwrapped her package, set three bottles on the counter. One was small, filled with some kind of powder. One had pills in it. The third was a bottle of Bowmore 25-year-old single malt Scotch. For my money it was the best in the world, even though I didn't actually have the money, because it was also one of the most expensive spirits around.

'I suggest a combination of all three,' John Horse said, nodding toward the bottles.

'Where did you get the dough for the scotch?' I had to know.

John Horse smiled. 'I didn't buy it. I took it from Ironstone Waters. He had a lot of bottles. I don't think he'll miss one.'

'This particular one,' I explained, 'he might. It's very expensive.'

John Horse just stared.

'And besides,' I went on, 'the last time I drank something you gave me, I was in an altered state for a couple of days, if I remember correctly.'

The first time I met John Horse, on tribal land in the middle of the swamp, he'd dosed me with some sort of hallucinogenic tea and I'd visited a couple of other realities, none of which had a street address.

'That was so that I could know who you were,' he said calmly. 'I know that now, even if you don't.'

'Yeah,' I countered, 'I know who I am just fine. It's you I'm worried about. Sending Hachi to fill my head with all kinds of distractions, that's about your speed. But showing up here knowing that I had an encounter with Holata, one of Ironstone's men, and some guy from the Black Tuna gang? That smacks of *involvement*.'

'I don't know what you mean when you say *involvement*.' He had no expression in his voice or on his face.

'Well we could go on like this all day,' I snapped, 'but I'm really not in great shape, so excuse me if I'm rude: what do you want?'

'I want to help.' He stared.

I looked at Hachi and she smiled.

'What do you want, then?' I asked her.

'I want to help John Horse,' she answered.

'Hachi is kind of a protégé of mine,' John Horse said. 'I'm teaching her a few things, and she's teaching me a few things.'

That was the kind of thing John Horse said that was more than the sum of its words. I don't know how he managed it, but he could say things a certain way that implied a larger picture.

I gave up trying to figure him out, for the moment, and sat down in my big comfortable chair.

'I think I'll skip the beverage for the time being,' I told him, 'and just listen to what you came to say. You say you want to help me.'

'Yes.'

'So help me.'

Hachi came into the room and sat on the sofa beside John Horse.

'There are a few things you need to know.' He leaned forward. 'First, Ellen Greenberg doesn't exist. She's a figment of someone's imagination.'

It was such a strange thing to say that it didn't have any effect on me for a second. I wasn't sure I'd heard him right.

'What do you mean?' I finally managed to ask.

'She's made up,' John Horse said.

'No.' I jutted my chin in his direction. 'First, I trust Lena. She wouldn't make up a sister. Second, Hachi said that Maggie Redhawk knew her. Third, I found a tent near Lake Wales where she used to stay and confirmation of her visit there from the Black Tuna guy. So, no – she's not *made up*.'

'Lena probably has a sister,' he answered. 'And there was a woman who was working at the hospital with Maggie; she probably did spend some time at the Cherry Pocket. But those are two different people. I have no idea about Lena's sister, but the woman we're talking about was an agent of Nixon's new

Drug Enforcement Agency. She was here in Fry's Bay to arrest David Waters and to try to get the goods on Ironstone.'

That made me feel a little dizzy.

'Are you trying to tell me that a federal agent had a *child* with David Waters?'

'Oh, no,' he answered, 'I think that the child might be made up too. Or, actually, Hachi thinks that David made her up and started rumors about her so that he could go on molesting little children in the park. But I'm not sure about that.'

I sat back and rubbed my eyes. 'No. David Waters asked Lena to kill him so that he could get insurance money to his child.'

'Does that sound at all plausible,' John Horse asked softly, 'when you say it out loud like that?'

I had to admit that it didn't, but any other explanation of David's murder was just as impossible to swallow.

Still, I had to ask, 'Then why did Lena kill him?'

John Horse looked at Hachi and then back at me. 'We'd like to know that too.'

'So, in essence,' I said slowly, 'everything I know is wrong.'

'Not everything,' Hachi said.

'Look,' I explained, 'I like Lena. I don't think she'd make all this up.'

'No,' John Horse agreed, 'as I was saying, she probably does have a sister. And that sister may somehow be involved in all this. But the woman known to her as Ellen Greenberg was a federal agent.'

'No,' I protested, 'what about the love letters and the photographs I found in the safe deposit box?'

'When you showed that picture all over town,' John Horse answered, 'did anyone recognize it?'

'No.'

'Then maybe that photograph is of Lena's real sister and not the agent.'

'Doesn't resolve the love letters,' I insisted.

'How did Lena get them?'

'She said that David Waters gave them to her,' I told him, 'but I guess you're going to tell me that they were all a part of some grand plan on David's part, or Ironstone's drug cartel.'

'I haven't seen the letters.' He shrugged.

I heaved a sigh the size of New Jersey, hoisted myself out of my chair, and went to my ruined suit coat to retrieve the letters in question.

Twenty minutes later John Horse made his pronouncement. 'Fake.'

He tossed them onto the coffee table between us.

'There's more to it than that,' I said, knowing that he had something else to say.

'The child-like code encouraging you to go to the Three Tee Pees campground.'

'What about it?' I asked, not even bothering to marvel at how quickly he'd solved that particular riddle.

He ignored me. 'And the handwriting. Hachi?'

She nodded. 'A man wrote those letters.'

'Probably David Waters,' John Horse agreed.

I shook my head. 'Why in the world would he make up these letters?'

'To confuse Lena.'

'And why would he want to do that?' I went on.

'So she wouldn't kill him.' John Horse closed his eyes. 'Lena is a strange child.'

'Agreed,' I told him, 'but if David Waters didn't hire her to kill him, what's her motive?'

'Her sister, maybe? This supposed Ellen Greenberg?' He shrugged.

I slumped down even farther into my chair. 'Look, I know it's your way to dazzle people with confusion in the guise of the artful lie, but I don't understand why you're doing this to me.'

Hachi folded her hands in her lap. 'Ironstone Waters has got to be stopped. He's going to cause a lot of trouble for the Seminole people in Florida if his *business* continues unchecked. And if he's killed a federal agent, then more people from the white government will come here. That won't be good for us.'

I knew what she meant. The United States Government had no idea how many Seminoles lived in the swampland around Fry's Bay, and the Seminoles wanted to keep it that way. I couldn't blame them. In the 1850s the government tried to relocate all the Seminoles to Oklahoma. Over 40 million dollars was spent, and the soldiers didn't even find half the tribe. They did take away some three thousand never to return again. The Seminole Wars were never completely settled, and no peace treaty had ever been signed. Technically, they're still at war with America. So who could blame John Horse for wanting the federal government to stay far away from his home?

'Did you know that one of the American soldiers involved in the Seminole Wars,' John Horse said, as if he'd read my mind, 'wrote a letter home that said, "If the Devil owned both Hell and Florida, he would rent out Florida and live in Hell!"'

Then he smiled.

I nodded. 'OK. This is a lot to take in. And my primary concern, actually, is getting Lena out of trouble. She's at Ironstone's house, I'm pretty sure.'

'She is,' Hachi confirmed.

I ignored my impulse to ask her why she was so sure of that.

'So you say you want to help me?' I continued. 'Go with me to Ironstone's house.'

John Horse stood up immediately. 'Let's go.'

I blinked. 'Now? I can't go now. I don't think I could walk to the door, let alone into another version of the valley of the shadow of death.'

He rolled his eyes. 'That's why I brought you the three bottles. Take them now. All three.'

I glanced in their direction. 'I might drink a little Scotch, and I already took some aspirin, but there's no chance in hell that I'm going anywhere near that white powder, whatever it is.'

'It's an herbal remedy,' Hachi said, bounding from the sofa and going to fetch the bottles. 'If you're nervous about it, I'll take some too.'

'Me too,' John Horse chimed in. 'Let's all have some.'

'I need to rest,' I whined.

'You need to move,' John Horse said.

And he said it in a certain tone of voice I'd heard before. It was the voice of the absolute. I really didn't have any choice. I got to my feet. Hachi opened the Scotch and put the bottle in my hand.

'You said you already took aspirin?' she asked.

'Eight,' I told her.

'OK, then you don't need what's in the other bottle, just this.'
She opened one of the mystery containers and measured about
a tablespoon of the white powder into her hand.

I stared at it. 'Do I snort it?'

She laughed. 'Just let me put it into your mouth, and then
wash it back with the Scotch.'

Before I could answer, her palm was touching my lips. The
powder had a pleasant peppery sensation and a kind of anise
taste. But the skin of her hand against my face was a lot more
intoxicating.

I tried to swallow the powder, had trouble, swigged the Scotch,
and coughed.

While I was recovering, Hachi and John Horse both took
some of the powder too. Hachi took the bottle from me, gave
it to John Horse; he took a single swallow. Then she drank too
and we all stood there for a second. I was waiting for some kind
of kick. It didn't come.

'What is this stuff?' I asked, still tasting it in my mouth.

'It will restore your soul,' John Horse said, smiling. 'Goodness
and mercy will follow you now.'

'Are you quoting Torah to me?' I asked.

'Seems appropriate,' he said calmly.

'Interesting,' I countered. 'I was just thinking of another one
of – oh for God's sake.'

'What?' he asked.

'I was thinking, just earlier this morning, about another one
of King David's poems,' I explained, 'and I just now realized
why: the name David is in my head. And, P.S., you seem to be
in my head too, John Horse. In my head.'

I realized then that my voice had an odd sound to it, and
there were a lot of missing steps in my pronouncement. I was
feeling more than a little dazed, uncertain of what I was saying.

'What *is* this stuff?' I asked again. 'All of a sudden I feel
great.'

'Me too,' John Horse said.

'Come on,' Hachi said, grinning, 'let's go over to Ironstone's
house and watch Foggy get shot again.'

'OK,' I said cheerfully.

I stumbled toward the front door.

'Wait,' Hachi commanded. 'You can't go like that. Man of your style. Where's your suit coat?'

'Oh.' I nodded. 'Right. Gotta look my best.'

I ambled unsteadily into my bedroom, shuffled through the old closet, and found a little Harris Tweed number – not my usual daywear, but for some reason I felt it gave me an air of sophistication otherwise missing from our insanely foolhardy endeavor. Plus, it went with the pants.

Moments later we were out in the parking lot in front of my apartment, arguing about who was going to drive. It was a short debate. Hachi snatched the keys out of my hand and went to the driver's side.

'You're too beat up, Foggy,' she said decisively, 'and John Horse is too old. This is a job for a young woman.'

John Horse and I looked at each other and started laughing, although I couldn't have told you why, exactly. I got in the passenger seat, and John Horse squeezed in between Hachi and me, cross-legged on the seat to avoid the gearshift. It had to be a very uncomfortable posture. He didn't seem to mind.

FOURTEEN

It was actually kind of great to ride in my car instead of drive it. I could watch the scenery and feel the air on my face. It was very invigorating. By the time we got to Ironstone's house – and I had no idea how long we'd been in the car at that point – I was feeling like I could do anything.

'What would you think if I just lifted up the whole house,' I announced when the car came to a stop, 'and shook it until Lena fell out?'

'I'd like to see that,' John Horse said very seriously.

'Both of you behave,' Hachi said. 'Here.'

She handed me the Scotch. I hadn't seen her bring it, but I was glad it was there. I swigged back a couple of healthy pulls and handed the bottle to John Horse. He drank for a while, it seemed, then he handed it back to me.

'We should save some for Ironstone,' he said, still in earnest. 'It *is* his liquor, after all.'

'Good point,' I agreed. 'Let's go.'

The three of us loped toward the front door like a troop of puppies. I was struck, once again, by the appearance of the monstrous house, its resemblance to Citizen Kane's pad. And there was a kind of informal garden around the front walk, very inviting, although I realized that my sense of well-being had less to do with the garden than the mysterious powder John Horse had concocted.

Still, I made bold to *blam* on the front door. I hit it harder than I meant to, and it was really loud. John Horse laughed.

A second later who should appear in the doorway but Holata, the guy whose name meant *alligator*.

'Hey!' I grinned. 'Do you know who this is?'

John Horse held out his hand to the guy. 'Hello, Holata. Shouldn't you be in the hospital?'

'Probably,' he agreed, stone-faced. 'Maybe I'll go when I get off work.'

He stepped aside gingerly, and I saw that he had a massive bandage wrapped around his calf. He was still in the same pin-striped suit he'd worn in the hotel room in Lake Wales.

'Bet that leg hurts,' I whispered to no one in particular.

'Did I already tell you to kiss my ass?' Holata asked.

'Yes,' I confirmed. 'Yes, you did.'

'Good,' he said. 'Still goes.'

He ushered us into the room where I'd been shot, the one that was a ringer for the one in the movie, huge fireplace and all.

Ironstone was seated in a great big old chair, cross-legged, in a dressing gown.

'Man,' I said, 'you are *really* going for the Orson Welles prize here. How many times did your architect have to watch the movie before—'

'Shut up,' Holata said calmly.

'OK,' I said, 'but here's what's left of your Scotch. We brought it back.'

Ironstone barely glanced at the bottle.

'Please have a seat,' he said. His voice was gravelly, like maybe he had a cold.

In a bizarre kind of unison, Hachi, John Horse, and I sat down on a very large sofa, side by side, smiling.

'I was rather expecting Mr Moscowitz,' Ironstone went on, 'but I'm honored to entertain John Horse.'

'And this is my protégé, Hachi,' John Horse said instantly, nodding in her direction.

Ironstone licked his lips. He looked like a Gila monster. 'You're the one who spied on my son,' he said to Hachi.

'No.' She locked eyes with Ironstone. 'I'm the one who reported your son to the police after he molested Teresa Jumper, Betty Mae Jumper's relative.'

'Betty Mae Jumper,' Ironstone growled, like he was saying a group of dirty words.

John Horse looked at me. 'Betty Mae is a remarkable woman. She's the first Seminole to graduate high school, and the first woman head of our tribal council. A couple of years ago, Nixon appointed her to the National Congress on Indian Opportunity – a great honor, even if the Congress is a sham, and Nixon, you know—'

'She's a *woman*!' Ironstone interrupted, spitting.

Hachi just smiled bigger. 'Our tribe was just about bankrupt in 1967 when she took over. When she left office in 1971, we had half a million dollars in the bank.'

'Any chance you could get her to look at my bank book?' I asked.

'The point is,' Hachi insisted, 'David Waters molested Teresa Jumper, and I reported it.'

'Completely false accusation!' Ironstone roared, leaning forward.

'I'm so confused,' I moaned. 'Was David a child molester or not?'

'Where's Lena?' John Horse said, crashing through all the extraneous conversation.

A moment of silence ensued.

'Who?' Ironstone asked.

I burst out laughing. '*Who?* The girl who killed your son, tried to kill you when you tried to kill her and I caught your bullet. And then you kidnapped her in Lake Wales and brought her here! You're asking *who*?'

'She's here,' John Horse whispered.

I stood up and hollered, 'Lena!'

Holata was at my side instantly, with an automatic in my ribs.

'Sit.' He pushed the muzzle into my side.

I turned to look him in the eye.

'I've just about had it with you guys,' I said.

And without further ado, I turned, grabbed the gun, broke at least one of Holata's fingers in the process, then kicked him in his wounded leg as hard as I could.

He howled. The gun went off. He went down. I kept turning and, when I stopped, I was standing right in front of Ironstone with Holata's pistol in my hand. The gun almost touched his nose.

The whole ballet took three seconds.

'What *is* this stuff you gave me?' I asked John Horse, staring down Ironstone. 'I feel like Superman.'

A couple of other Seminole gorillas barged into the room, but they paused when they saw that I had a gun in Ironstone's face.

'I have a lot of questions,' I said to Ironstone, oblivious to my own peril, 'about drugs and federal agents, and the reality of your son's wife and child, but at the moment I'll settle for Lena. Let me take her into my own very professional custody or I swear to God all kinds of hell will break loose. Beginning with a bullet in your forehead.'

I leveled the gun and twitched my trigger finger, though that was mostly for show.

'Foggy,' John Horse said cautiously, 'don't let the medicine encourage you to do something you don't really want to do.'

And, for the first time, Ironstone looked worried.

'What medicine?' he asked softly.

'Oh, you know,' John Horse said, 'Snakeroot, cedar leaf, some secret bark and, of course, belladonna.'

Ironstone froze. 'You gave this white man the nightshade powder?'

'I did.' John Horse laughed. 'I have no idea how it will affect him.'

I got it then: John Horse had dosed me at least in part so that he could scare Ironstone. I had to admit, loopy as I was, it was a good plan. Especially since it was working.

'I'm not even sure what's real and what's not,' I lied.

'Foggy,' Hachi chimed in, 'you might actually kill that man. Do you understand?'

'I might?' I asked her, deliberately sounding confused.

'Listen to me, Mr Moscowitz,' Ironstone said quickly. 'Lena's here, in this house, and nothing whatsoever has happened to her. She's absolutely unharmed.'

'Except for the trauma of being kidnapped by brutes in suits.' I turned to Hachi. 'That's funny: *brutes in suits*.'

'It's a scream,' she responded.

'Lena!' I shouted again.

'Go get her!' Ironstone snapped at one of his men. 'Now!'

The guy flew away. Holata moaned.

'Everything happens to me,' he said. 'Now I got broken fingers!'

John Horse leaned down and said very softly into his ear, 'That's because you're engaged in the wrong employment. You need to leave Ironstone's house and never come back.'

I recognized the tone in the old man's voice; he'd used it

on me before. It was charged with such absolute authority and conviction that it was impossible to ignore.

'You're right,' Holata responded, as if he'd just discovered something. 'Everything bad that ever happened to me started when I went to work for Ironstone Waters.'

He stood.

'What are you doing?' Ironstone snapped at him.

Holata didn't say a word. He drifted out of the room like he was hypnotized.

'Where do you think you're going, Holata?' Ironstone yelled.

His only answer was the slam of the front door closing.

'One down,' John Horse said, grinning.

Hachi stood then. 'I think I'll go see if Lena needs any help.' And she was gone.

Ironstone started to get up. I flinched. The pistol in my hand went off. The bullet whizzed past Ironstone's head and planted a nice hole in the chair he was sitting in.

'I told you to be careful,' John Horse warned half-heartedly.

I couldn't tell if he was talking to me or to Ironstone. I was still trying to figure out how the gun had gone off. It was only luck that made the bullet go into the chair instead of Ironstone's head. He sat back down, a whole lot less certain of himself.

'Listen, Moscowitz,' he whispered harshly, 'you're not in your right mind. That crazy old man gave you a drug that's impairing your judgment.'

'You know,' I began philosophically, 'that's what people always say about drugs, that they impair something or other. But that's not strictly true. More often than not, the drug just offers you another explanation of reality. And on some occasions, your vision is actually clarified, not impaired.'

Ironstone glared at John Horse. 'Tell him! Tell him that he's not in his right mind.'

'You're not in your right mind, Foggy,' John Horse said at once.

'You think I don't know that?' I answered. 'I would *never* hold a gun to a rich man's head in his own house. Too many complications. But the thing is, see, Mr Waters, you've just said, in front of witnesses, that my judgment was impaired. So from now on, legally speaking, I'm "not criminally responsible" for anything I do. Isn't that a great law? My people invented it.'

'Your people?' Ironstone was confused. 'The Jews?'

'Well,' I admitted, 'we had a little help from Aristotle. But the law holds up in America today: impaired judgment. Perfect defense.'

'It's true, I'm afraid,' John Horse chimed in. 'He'd get off even if he'd killed you just now. I might be in a little trouble, since I gave him the drug. But what experience do I have with white people? I had no idea how it might alter him. So it's not really my fault either.'

'And in any case,' I observed, 'how many times has the law tried to find you way back in that swamp?'

'Hundreds,' he said. 'But never once successfully.'

'There you are,' I said to Ironstone.

I saw, out of the corner of my eye, the only other guy in the room, another one of Ironstone's henchmen, trying to slink my way. Without a thought I turned the pistol on him and shot his shoe.

The guy yelped like a dog.

'See,' John Horse said, 'you can really hit what you're aiming at if you just concentrate.'

'Right,' I acknowledged, swinging the gun back to Ironstone's forehead.

John Horse got up off the sofa and went to the wounded man, who was having a hard time standing up.

John Horse put his arm around the man and whispered into his ear. I couldn't hear what he was saying, but the man calmed down and started nodding. Then John Horse took something out of his pocket and handed it to the guy. He looked down at it and, in seconds, he was crying like a child.

I glanced over to see what had caused such a display, and there in the wounded guy's hand was a very small turtle shell, bleached white.

John Horse said to me, 'Long life, good health, perseverance, and protection. That's what's in a turtle shell. Do you remember that turtle stew you had at my house a while back?'

'With the little potatoes in it?' I nodded. 'It was fantastic.'

John Horse patted the wounded guy on the arm. 'His mother made it for us.'

I blinked. 'Wait. Taft?'

I turned to get a good look at the guy. I'd met him before at John Horse's place in the swamp. Nice guy.

He avoided eye contact.

'Taft,' I said. 'Man, I'm sorry I shot you. What the hell are you doing working for this schmeckel?'

'I need the money,' he lamented, still not looking at me. 'My mother is real sick.'

'I'm sorry to hear that,' I began.

'Get that gun out of my face!' Ironstone demanded.

I turned his way, flicked my hand a little to the left, and fired the pistol a third time. The bullet just barely missed his ear. It probably damaged his hearing, and it absolutely dampened his motivation. He sat more still than the chair – that poor old, shot-up chair.

Before any further mayhem could ensue, Lena appeared in the room, Hachi at her side, followed by Ironstone's last visible play pal.

Lena smiled at me. She was still wearing the ridiculous outfit, and she was barefoot.

'Go ahead, Foggy,' she encouraged, 'that chair's only suffering now; you need to put it out of its misery. One more shot ought to do it.'

I lowered the pistol.

'There you are,' I said to Lena. 'Look, I wouldn't have bothered you while you're working, but you owe me three-ninety-five for the gator basket back at the Cherry Pocket.'

'It's good to see you too,' she said softly.

'She was in a back room, just sitting there,' Hachi assured me.

'OK,' I said to Ironstone, 'would you mind telling me what the hell you thought you were doing kidnapping a minor from my official state custody? Do you have any idea how much trouble you could get for that?'

'I want to find my grandchild,' Ironstone told me through clenched teeth, 'and that girl is the only one who knows where my grandchild is.'

'She *doesn't* know,' I insisted.

'I tried to tell him that,' Lena assured me.

'On the other hand,' I went on, 'I did find out about your son's involvement in Black Tuna and a whole lot of cocaine.'

Ironstone didn't say anything, which was, of course, saying a lot. The fact that he didn't deny my allegation and didn't defend his son spoke volumes.

'Come on, Foggy,' John Horse said, patting Taft on the shoulder and standing up. 'We got what we came for. Let's go.'

I locked eyes with Ironstone.

'You understand that I have to file charges against Holata and the other guy we shot in Lake Wales,' I told him. 'I assume he's in the hospital there, the other guy. And I don't think Holata's going to be much help to you from now on; I think I can get him to admit your part in Lena's abduction. Makes you a party to kidnapping of a minor. It's a felony that judges especially hate.'

Ironstone just smiled, his eyes dead. 'Do you really think there's a judge in this state that I can't buy? Or a cop? You know that Baxter's on my payroll.'

And even though I'd suspected that, I lost just a little bit of my swagger. Ironstone could see that on my face.

'Here's the thing about money, Mr Moscowitz,' he said. 'It gives me the kind of feeling you're getting right now from John Horse's medicine. The difference is, your feeling isn't even real, and it'll wear off in a couple of hours. My feeling *makes* things real, and it lasts forever.'

John Horse roared laughing.

'Money isn't real,' he said when he could catch his breath. 'Ironstone, your life doesn't have any reality. You don't even live in a real house, it's a set from a movie.'

'You live in a cinder block house!' Ironstone countered very loudly.

'No I don't,' John Horse corrected, shaking his head, still smiling. 'Sometimes I sleep or eat in a place like that, but I live in the air, and on the ground, and sometimes in the water. Come on, my friends, let's leave this sad place. And this walking corpse that thinks he's a living man.'

Ironstone sat very still on his wrecked chair.

'Get up, Taft,' he said, 'and show our guests out.'

Taft glanced down at the little turtle shell in his hand.

'Yes, sir,' he said and stumbled to his feet.

He was bleeding, and his foot had to be killing him. John

Horse put his arm out and Taft leaned on the old man. They headed for the door, so I followed. Hachi and Lena caught up with us.

'Man,' Lena whispered, 'you came in like the cavalry.'

'I was worried about you,' I acknowledged. 'I told you: if anything happens to you while you are in my alleged care, I have a ton of paperwork to fill out. I hate that.'

'You're in over your head,' Ironstone called out. 'All of you.'

I nudged Lena. 'That's just what the guy in the Cherry Pocket restaurant told me.'

'Tony?'

'No, the old geezer at the bar,' I said. 'Wait 'til you hear all the things I found out.'

'Is one of those things the notion that my sister was never actually in Fry's Bay?' she asked as we neared the front door. 'That some other woman masqueraded as the fabled Ellen Greenberg? I figured that out from some of the questions Ironstone was asking me. So now I have no idea what the hell is going on.'

I stopped walking because it was hard for me to think and move at the same time.

I glared at Lena. 'I just realized that Ellen Greenberg is a false name. Your last name's not Greenberg. I don't know what your last name is.'

But she kept walking toward the door.

'That's right,' she said without looking back. 'You don't.'

FIFTEEN

By the time we got back to my place, the 'medicine' was beginning to wear off. John Horse was very quiet. Worst of all, Lena had to ride in the trunk. There wasn't any other way to fit all four of us in my car. We left the trunk lid open, which made it impossible for Hachi to see out the back window, so not only were we breaking about ten traffic laws, we were also pressed up against the boundaries of highway safety.

Hachi parked. I jumped out in a hurry and went around to check on Lena. She was curled up and sleeping.

I looked down at her.

'Wouldn't you rather do this inside on the sofa?' I asked her.

She didn't open her eyes, but she smiled.

'It is a nice sofa, if memory serves.' She yawned and unpacked herself.

The four of us stood in the parking lot for a second not knowing what to say, exactly.

'Well,' John Horse announced at length, 'I'm going home. Foggy, you should get some sleep. You look terrible.'

I nodded.

John Horse headed off toward town. Hachi handed over my keys. Lena headed for the front door. I was surprised to see Hachi do the same.

'Where do you think you're going?' I asked her.

'You and Lena need to sleep,' she answered me. 'I don't. I'll stay awake.'

I started to argue, but then I realized that it would probably be useless, and also that John Horse had most likely told her to stay. If that was the case, there wouldn't be anything I could do to get her to walk away.

So I nodded. 'OK. But I have to say that you are the most singularly attractive watchdog in the United States and Canada.'

'Agreed,' Lena called out over her shoulder, standing at the door.

'Flattery from both of you,' she observed. 'You must be exhausted.'

And she was right. Lena and I were done for the nonce. I don't remember anything after that.

I woke up with a start, very disoriented. I was still in my tweed, face down on the bed, shoes still attached.

'Hey?' I called out.

'Kitchen!' Hachi sang.

I smeared myself across the bed and managed to get vertical. Something smelled fantastic.

I stumbled out of the bedroom, when what to my wondering eyes should appear but Yudda, larger than ever, carousing in my kitchen.

'This is a surprise,' I mumbled.

Lena was sitting up on the sofa, nearly as groggy as I was, and Hachi was standing next to Yudda in front of my stove.

'What's going on?' Lena wanted to know.

'That's Yudda,' I answered.

'Tony's Yudda?' she asked.

'None other,' I confirmed. 'I just can't figure out why he's here.'

Yudda glanced up from his labors. 'Yes you can.'

And then he went right back to work.

'No I can't,' I assured him. 'What are you doing in there?'

'Okra pancakes, caramelized onions, blanched celery root with a goat cheese froth, and Duck Eggs Anna.' He smiled, not looking up.

Hachi was watching him work, fascinated.

'Eggs Anna?' I called out.

'Met a guy at Columbia University a couple of years ago,' Yudda said distractedly, 'name of Jacques. He was getting his master's degree in French literature, but he was a hell of a chef. His mother used to do this thing with eggs, hard-boiled, then mustard added to the yolk, then pan seared face down – gonna kill you.'

I stared. 'I don't understand about half of that, but Columbia University is in *my* town. What were you doing there?'

'Hiding.' He shrugged.

He'd always made a big deal about being on the lam from his nefarious mischief in New Orleans. I never asked because I lived in a glass house. I just accepted him as a fellow traveler and left it at that – despite how curious I was about Yudda at a university.

'OK and you met a French guy there?'

He nodded. 'Ready!'

He looked up at last.

Hachi announced, 'This is going to be wonderful.'

Lena stood. I motivated. We all gathered at my classy little kitchen table, Formica top and all.

And while the repast was indeed wonderful, my thoughts turned quickly to the collection of questions I had in my brain.

'Yudda,' I began unceremoniously, 'these eggs are perfect, what's the deal with Tony?'

He looked up from his plate.

'Who?'

'Tony,' I repeated, 'at the Cherry Pocket near Lake Wales.'

'Oh, that bastard.' Yudda returned to his food. 'He tried to poison me with oysters.'

'And he used to be involved in your weed business.'

Yudda's fork froze halfway between plate and mouth.

'Says who?' he wanted to know.

'I don't care about that,' I went on, 'I care about what's happened to the business. I'm putting in a call to my pal Pan Pan Washington in Brooklyn just as soon as I finish this delectable breakfast, and he'll know all about the subject, to wit: the Columbian/Cuban ruckus here in our sunny little state.'

'That's a mouthful.' Lena grinned.

'I don't know what Tony's been telling you,' Yudda said, setting down his fork, 'but all I ever done was collect a little weed for a rainy day.'

'And sell it.'

He held up an index finger. 'Only to friends.'

'You made enough profit to buy a big boat from the Fort Lauderdale yacht brokerage.'

'Well,' he hedged. 'Yeah. I like to go fishing.'

'Uh huh,' I said. 'Don't really care about that either, but when the Columbians came in and took over the general apparatus, they also introduced coke into the mix, am I right?'

He nodded, unsure what to say.

'And David Waters was involved.' I said it like I knew what was what, which I did not. But I wanted to see what Yudda would say about it.

'That kid.' Yudda shook his head. 'Jesus what a mess he was.'

I took that as a *yes*.

'And when I showed you the photo of the so-called Ellen Greenberg, you didn't bat an eye.'

'Because I never seen the woman in that pitcher,' he protested.

'Yeah, but my guess is that you knew more than you were telling me.'

'Such as?' he snapped.

'Such as there *was* a woman going around town calling herself Ellen Greenberg, and you knew *that* woman.'

He shifted in his chair uncomfortably. 'Jesus, if I knew you was such a pain in the ass, I never would have come here with Hachi.'

'Yes, you would,' I said, 'because Hachi is John Horse's pal, and you're afraid of John Horse.'

That was another guess, but it was a good one. Lots of people were afraid of John Horse. If I'd had any sense, I would have been one of them.

Hachi put her hand on Yudda's big forearm. 'You might as well tell him everything. That's why you're here. And, as you can see, he's figured out most of it anyway.'

'Which, may I say, is impressive,' Yudda sighed. 'It ain't a single cop that's ever figured all this out. You go to Lake Wales for ten minutes and all of a sudden you're an expert.'

'So give,' I told Yudda.

He did. His story was odd. He had friends in the bayou who grew great stuff, and they would send it to him when they sent crawfish. It was a great gimmick, the fish smell covered the pot smell. It was an enterprise that had gone on for a while. Nobody got hurt, everybody got high.

Enter the Columbians. They followed all the pot trails, found Yudda, and convinced him to take them on as his new partners. The convincing involved snipping off one of his toes and insulting his food. He didn't say which one had been the final straw, but shortly after their visit, two of his cousins in Louisiana were found face down and bloody in the swamp near the pot farm. They'd apparently been less cooperative than Yudda.

After that it was just a matter of bringing some of their powdery product into the swamp, hiding it in the crawfish boxes instead of pot, and sending it to Yudda. Yudda got Tony the job in Lake Wales so they could use it as a kind of changing station. The old Cuban guy at the Cherry Pocket was not just on ice there, more or less like he'd told me. He was an *administrative assistant*.

'All of this is very interesting,' I interrupted, 'but I have two questions. Why bring in the stuff through Louisiana? And what about David Waters?'

'I'm getting to that,' Yudda protested. 'The answer to your first question is diversity. Bring in all your stuff through one port, you have a greater risk of getting nabbed than if you spread it out. These guys, this Black Tuna outfit, they really know what they're doing. And they're more organized than any legit business I ever heard of.'

'And David Waters?' I prompted.

'Christ you're impatient,' he complained. 'David insinuated himself. He was, by any measure, a wreck waiting to happen. The guy did more coke in a day than most people do in a year. Honestly, he knew all about the back and forth between the Cubans and the Columbians, and he went into business with them both. *Both*. I'm surprised the guy didn't get killed sooner.'

All eyes turned to Lena. She had stopped eating.

'That whole line about David Waters asking you to kill him,' I said softly, 'was garbage.'

She nodded. 'It was.'

Finally: the truth.

'But it's not what you think,' Lena went on quickly

'What do I think?' I asked, leaning back in my chair.

'You think I might be connected with one of the drug gangs. That's what I'd think. But the truth is a whole lot more personal, Foggy. You have to believe me.'

'Let's hear a little more of the truth, for a change, and I'll see what I believe.'

'I have an older sister,' she began. 'She went by the name of Ellen Greenberg; it was a last name she picked out of the obituaries. We were born in Rio, Florida – population around four hundred. She left when she was twelve and I was nine. I left a year later.'

'You left home at the age of ten?' I blurted.

'We didn't have parents. Same mother, one of Rio's three hookers and a real fan of the needle. Two different fathers – identities unknown. I'm pretty sure our mother thinks we're still around the house somewhere. Anyway, Ellen fell in with a Seminole crowd, far as I've been able to determine, and met David Waters. He encouraged her to do coke and play around in bed, both of which she apparently did with aplomb. When she came up pregnant, she tripped on a moment of clarity and fell out of love with the sporting life right away. Something about not wanting to be just like our mother. She took off, hid out in Lake Wales, and somehow sent for me. I came running, but she was gone by the time I got there. Vanished. I went looking; came across her connection with David Waters. Did some research and called him. Arranged a meeting.'

'Don't tell me,' I began.

She nodded. 'That night at Mary's Shallow Grave. That was our first meeting.'

'And he really didn't want to be dead,' I observed.

'Probably not,' she agreed.

I leaned forward, eyes narrow. 'So tell me. Why did you kill him?'

She locked eyes with me. 'I'll tell you. He didn't know I was the person he was meeting there that night. He just saw an under-aged girl. He slithered over to me, obviously coked up. When he leaned over to whisper in my ear, he had a syringe in his hand. He jabbed my arm and was about to push the plunger when I shot him. My guess is that's how he got Ellen involved in drugs. Given our family history, it wouldn't have been that difficult, we probably have a genetic disposition.'

I was momentarily stunned, but I managed to say, 'Nobody found a syringe.'

'No,' she said tersely. 'Someone at the bar, or with the police, found it, got it, and took it away.'

I sat back. 'Baxter.'

'Could be.' She stared down at her plate.

'All we need now,' Hachi intervened, 'is for Foggy to tell us about his life of crime, and me to explain why I'm John Horse's apprentice, and we've got ourselves a real Encounter Group going on here.'

It was just the right thing to say. It wasn't exactly funny, but we all laughed, and a whole lot of tension left the room.

'So what now?' Yudda said after a moment.

'Now I'd like to ask Lena, here, what the hell she was talking about at Ironstone's,' I said, 'the first time we met him. What was all that about David wanting you to kill him?'

'I was scared!' she said. 'I lied! Sue me.'

No. There was more to it than that.

'Well,' I began, 'I'd like to spend another couple of hours on the subject of how you got guns and got so good at using them, but the more pressing issue may be finding Ellen and her baby, and sorting out this insurance policy business. That's actually real. I got it here in the apartment. Why would David have arranged such a thing?'

Silence ensued, so I kept going.

'Ellen is three years older than you,' I said to Lena, 'meaning, if you didn't lie about your age, she'd be seventeen now, right?'

Lena shrugged. 'Far as I know.'

'That photo that's supposed to be a picture of her,' I mused. 'Where did you really get it?'

'Safe deposit box. I didn't put the stuff in there, she did. She sent me the key. Told me if I couldn't find her, check the box. I don't know how she got that photo of me.'

I was about to continue in the same vein when Hachi interrupted my train of thought.

'I wonder why you haven't asked Lena what happened to her at Ironstone's house,' Hachi said softly.

'I was getting to that,' I told her.

'It was *weird*,' Lena said right away.

'Start from when they nabbed you,' I instructed her.

She nodded. 'I saw a tent,' she began.

'Yeah, I found the tent too, the next day,' I interrupted. 'Skip ahead.'

'It was the guy with the wounded leg, Holata, and the other guy, whose name was Taft. They grabbed me and smacked a strip of duct tape over my mouth. I saw you lying on the ground and panicked, so they shot me up with something, don't know what, and I was out. Woke up in a wood-paneled den that was so perfect I thought I was tripping.'

'That house is very strange,' Hachi said.

'Next thing I know,' Lena went on, 'there's Ironstone, sipping tea and talking with me like I'm company. He was asking me all kinds of questions about Ellen. Nothing about David.'

'What kind of questions?' I interjected.

'Like, first, did I have a photo, which I did not. Then what did she look like. Then where she might be. And what about the campsite. And what about the Chalet Suzanne, and why did I go there. It was very confusing, but I think I was still trying to recover from whatever was in the shot they gave me.'

'And Ironstone was just – calm? The whole time?' I shook my head. 'I don't understand.'

'Neither did I. But now that I know some of the stuff you figured out about the Florida drug battles, I have to guess that it all has something to do with that mess.'

'Yeah,' I said, 'it does. Let's add up. David's a cokehead and an embarrassment to his father. David takes advantage of underage girls. David was involved in the cocaine wars and brought business troubles to Ironstone's empire. Maybe the old man isn't quite as unhappy about David's demise as he seemed to be when we first met him.'

'You mean when he tried to kill me,' Lena said, 'and you saved my life.'

'What?' Hachi asked.

'A story for another time,' I assured her. 'I come off very noble, but at the moment I'm trying to understand – hold on.'

Lena looked at Hachi. 'You can almost hear his brain heating up.'

'I've seen this before,' Yudda agreed. 'He's making some kind of calculation, like when he ran numbers.'

'When we first encountered Ironstone at his big old mansion,' I began, 'he figured you'd killed David as a part of the cocaine wars; that you were in the employ of the Cubans or the Columbians, right? But then he did some research. Maybe you've killed other people and maybe you haven't, but he soon found out that you had nothing to do with his business. You were just looking for your sister. Now, first he assumed that your sister was the woman in town who was *calling* herself Ellen Greenberg. But that woman was a federal agent on Nixon's new – what do you call it – Drug Enforcement Agency. But when he found out that your sister was, in fact, just one more kid that David jumped, he had to spend some time sorting out what you knew and what you didn't. And to do that, he was only asking you questions about your sister, deliberately steering away from what he actually wanted to know, to see if you'd confront him about any of his business matters. He's not afraid of you now, he's afraid of the DEA.'

'How much of that is guesswork,' Hachi asked, 'and how much is factual?'

'No idea,' I admitted, 'but it sounded pretty convincing to me, so that's my starter premise.'

'You also have to consider what happened to the DEA agent,' Lena added. 'Where is she?'

Yudda stood up and started clearing the table.

'I just want to cook crawfish and smoke a little weed,' he said distractedly. 'The rest of this is too much for me to think about.'

'Look,' I said to Lena, 'your sister is on the run with a small child. We need to find her. We need to actualize David's insurance policy as soon as we can, no matter why he took it out. I'm convinced it's legit. And in the process, we have to find out what happened to a federal agent, why she was using your sister's chosen name – all the while dodging bullets and Columbians.'

'Have you heard from Mister Redhawk about the disposition of the policy?' Hachi asked. 'He's looking into it. That's why you're sure it's a legitimate document.'

'You know about that,' I said.

'John Horse knows everything. He tells me some of it.'

'In fact I've been a little busy lately,' I said to her, 'so, no, I haven't spoken to Mister Redhawk for a while.'

She tilted her head. 'No one has.'

It was very spooky the way she said it, and everyone in the room could probably feel the chill.

'What does that mean?' I asked.

She shrugged, but it wasn't a casual gesture.

'Look,' Yudda inserted, 'if there's nothing more, I really got to get back to my establishment.'

'Yeah, how did you get here?' I asked.

Yudda inclined his head in Hachi's direction. 'She drove. In your car.'

'Why did you come?'

'She's very convincing,' he complained. 'Plus, you know, pretty.'

I turned her way. 'And why did you bring him here?'

'So that you could discover some of the things you've just told us,' Hachi answered calmly, 'and so you could trust him again, see his face; know that he's not really mixed up in anything beyond his life here in Fry's Bay.'

'So I could eliminate him from my palate of concerns.' I nodded.

'And get on with your work,' she agreed, standing. 'Let's go, Yudda.'

He nodded and headed for the door.

Lena stood. 'I'll do the dishes.'

Hachi leaned over the table. 'I'll bring your car right back. Take a shower. Get dressed. We have things to do.'

And with that, she was gone.

I stared at Lena's back. She was standing at the sink, still dressed in that stupid school uniform look.

'Now are you going to tell me?' I asked her.

'Tell you what?' She didn't turn around.

'You know what.'

She stopped washing. 'OK.'

She turned around but didn't say anything.

'Just say it,' I told her.

'David Waters is the only person I ever killed.'

She held together for about three seconds and then burst into tears.

SIXTEEN

A little while later I was showered and shorn and on the phone with Pan Pan Washington. Lena was curled up on the sofa under a blanket, just staring into space.

'I don't hear from you for three years,' he yelled into the phone, 'and your first call is that you want to score?'

'No,' I interrupted, 'if you'd just listen, I don't want dope, I want information. What I told you the last time I talked to you still goes: I'm sober and I actually have a government job. So stop shouting and listen, could you do that for just ten seconds?'

'Foggy,' he began.

'I'm in the middle of the great big mess in Florida.'

That shut him up for a split second, but he recovered.

'You're in the cocaine wars?'

'You tell me,' I answered. 'I almost got killed by a Cuban who was afraid of a bunch of Columbians who are taking over an apparatus that used to just offer weed.'

'What branch of the government do you work for?' he demanded. 'The Bureau of *Stupid*?'

'I told you, I'm Child Protective Services,' I snapped. 'The whole coke thing is tangential.'

'Tangential?' he was compelled to repeat. 'These Columbians will tangential up your ass and back down your spine, man. They are not nice men.'

'Yeah, I already know that, but could you please just settle down and tell me what I want to know.'

'What do you want to know?' he growled, attempting to display his ire.

'Names.' That's all I said.

Again, he was stunned. This time he didn't respond at all.

'So how's your grandmother?' I asked him.

'I got her a new wheelchair,' he answered softly. 'You know what she did? She embroidered a little, like, banner that she put on the back of it that says "Hell On Wheels."'

'Sounds like her.' His grandmother was the nicest mean woman I ever met. She made the best fried pies in Brooklyn every Thursday just because she knew that Pan Pan and I liked them. She also shot and killed her husband because he was seeing another woman. That was years ago. She and the other woman lived together ever since then. Pan Pan's grandmother lost a leg to diabetes when I was still in New York. Probably all those fried pies.

'Raul Davila-Jimeno,' he said after a minute. 'Starts with him.'

'The Black Tuna guy, I know. Everybody knows him. I was hoping for a more local name, meaning somebody here in Florida.'

'Ramon Fidestra,' he said more seriously. 'He's a Cuban guy that the Columbians kept on because he knows everything. He's like a go-between for both sides. Plus, did you know there was a weed highway from New Orleans to Florida? They're using that now for the more diversified distribution of product from South America. They boat right up between Cuba and that pointy part of Mexico into the Gulf and take a slight left to Louisiana. From there it's the same route as the older weed rode: pack the coke in seafood and ice, ship it to Florida restaurants connected with the organization. And Fidestra is in charge of it all, even though he likes to tell people he's only on the sidelines.'

I smiled. 'And that's why I called you. To get that name. I'm pretty sure I met the guy.'

'No you didn't,' he assured me. 'If you'd met him, you'd be dead, and I wouldn't have this aggravation.'

'He kicked my ass, if that's any compensation for you,' I offered.

'I'm serious, Foggy,' he said. 'He's old. You don't get to be old in his line of work without being one big badass. He's, like, one of the Ancient Kamikaze Drug Lords of the Sunbelt.'

'I'll keep that in mind. Nice turn of phrase, P.S.'

'You want me to tell your Ma and Shayna that you called?'

I thought about it.

'I guess you'd better not,' I said after a minute. 'Why stir it up? So, OK, anything else?'

'Such as?'

'Such as any other names or any news you would like to relate.'

'Little Phil got iced,' he offered casually.

I nodded. 'Probably had it coming.'

'Oh, wait. What's that new guy's name? Hang on.'

'There's a new guy in Brooklyn?'

'No,' he said, 'a new guy in Florida, some rich kid. Thinks he knows what's on, but don't.'

'Rich kid?' I asked, pretty certain who it was.

'David Waters!' Pan Pan shouted. 'I knew I could remember it if I – did I tell you I started using your memory system, that stuff you used to teach me when you was in numbers? It really works! David Waters. Jesus is this guy an idiot – somebody'll shoot him dead before long. But at the moment, he controls the entire supply from New Orleans to Florida. Thinks the money makes him immune. Lords it over Fidestra. *Man* has he pissed everybody off – like, I hear it's even his own father that might have him hit.'

I tried to think of what to say to that, but too many ideas were in my brain. It was very crowded in there.

'Foggy?' Pan Pan said after too long a silence.

'Hey, Pan Pan,' I said softly, 'could you forget all about this call? I mean permanently.'

'Um, OK,' he ventured slowly. 'What's up?'

'Not sure.'

'I thought you left Brooklyn to get *out* of trouble,' he admonished.

'Yeah,' I agreed, 'that's what I thought too. I'll call later just to chat.'

'That's what you said three years ago.'

I hung up. I stared at Lena, trying to decide how much she knew, or how much I should tell her.

'*Pan Pan* is a funny name for a person,' she said, still staring. 'Does everybody in Brooklyn have a nickname like that: Foggy, Pan Pan?'

I sat in my chair.

'The first time I ever boosted a car – an amazing Corvette Stingray, 1953, first year they rolled them out to the public. It was sky blue with a snow white interior and silver wheels. I popped it right away, but I drove it around for a while just because it was so fine. Anyway, I had been instructed to take it to a certain garage, and when I did, there was Albertus T. Washington waiting for me.'

'Albertus?'

'I know,' I agreed. 'He was new to the nefarious enterprises, new as me, impatient, probably nervous, and ready to get everything over with. I pulled the car in, he slammed down the garage door and slid under the car. He was mad right away because he said I hit something when I was driving it around. And I said, "Hit what?" And he said, "Oil pan." But I didn't hear him so I said, "What?" and he started yelling, "Pan, pan, pan!"'

'Ah,' she acknowledged.

'I thought it was funny and spread the story around. Within a week everybody was calling him "Pan Pan." It stuck.'

She focused, sat up, and eyed me. 'So what about "Foggy?"'

'What about it?'

'How'd that happen? What's your real name?'

I stared right back. 'Since you asked a two-part question, I will offer these two answers, in order: a) doesn't matter, and b) none of your business.'

She smiled. 'That's not very nice.'

'David Waters wasn't a dabbler,' I said to change the subject. 'He was trying to be the boss – the new boss of the new business. There's a good shot that everybody wanted him dead. Even his dear old dad.'

She shook her head. 'You think Ironstone put out a hit on his own son? Then why would he be so mad that I killed him?'

'You know, a lot of this would have added up easier,' I began, 'if you'd just told me the truth from the beginning. Why in God's name would you make up such a weird story? I was going to ask you before, but you were crying, so.'

Her eyes narrowed. 'I think I related my upbringing, right? Not the kind of environment that encourages trust.'

'You didn't trust me?'

'I didn't trust *anybody*, Foggy,' she snapped. 'How was I supposed to know that you were some kind of Jewish Ninja Monk?'

I blinked. 'What makes you think I'm a monk?'

She sat back. 'I'm straight as an arrow, but even *I* am attracted to Hachi. And you don't give her the time of day.'

'Nice change of subject,' I accused.

'You did it to me first when I asked about your name,' she

answered. 'Plus, I think of you as a monk because you never tried anything with me.'

'With *you*?' I laughed. 'Look, one of the reasons I'm so good at my job is that I got a very clear sense of who's a child and who's not. As far as I'm concerned, anything goes between adults as long as they agree. But a kid does not have the wherewithal to make such decisions.'

'Oh, yes they do,' she protested.

'No!' I insisted. 'That's just the problem: you think you're equipped, but you're not. You're an apprentice adult. Nothing more dangerous than a novice who doesn't know what a novice is.'

'An apprentice adult,' she sneered.

'We're getting off the topic,' I complained.

'What's the topic?' she steamed. 'How to insult me?'

'No the topic is – just a minute.' I stared at her like I was a cop. 'If you were raised in the environment you described, how come you're so smart?'

'Maybe my father was a brain surgeon,' she snapped.

'Maybe, but you're educated,' I countered.

Her shoulders sagged a little. 'I didn't ever want to go home at the end of the day. I stayed at school as long as I could. Extra projects, library time, talking with the teachers. Miss May said I had a real aptitude – she was my sixth grade teacher. I skipped grades, and she had me take the SAT when I was ten.'

'I thought that was the year you left home'

'It was. I got into FSU. I just didn't have the money. So I left home. Got a job at that new Disneyland, the one near Kissimmee. I was Dopey.'

'Sorry, you were *what* now?'

'Not what,' she said, 'who. I was Dopey the dwarf; followed Snow White around the park. Hot as hell. $2.10 an hour.'

'No.' I folded my arms. 'No Dead End Kid ever worked for Disney.'

'Again with the Dead End Kids. Will you shut up about that?'

'No!' I snapped. 'How did you get from working in fairyland to shooting people? Jesus!'

'Again,' she railed. 'Background! I had a gun in my hand for the first time when I was around seven. My mother had dozens of guns lying around the house. You don't even want to *think* about the kind of men my mother entertained. I was scared. I had guns.'

'But you never used them.'

'The guns.' She sighed. 'No. Not until that night at the place.'

'So why make up a story about being a hit man?'

'Seemed like a great way to get invisible protection. If it gets around that I kill people for a living, then people are less likely to mess with me.'

I shook my head. 'This is just how little you know of actual human nature. Maybe you scared one or two citizens with that line, but a guy like Ironstone, that kind of thing just makes him curious – like it made me.'

She looked away. 'Yeah, OK, maybe I said it a little to impress you, too. I thought you were cool, and I wanted you to like me. And you seemed to like me when you thought I was a bad ass, so.'

I stood up. 'I like you just fine. And I'm going to make certain you're taken care of. For example, I promised you that I'd find your sister, and I'm going to do that. Partly just *because* I promised, but mostly because I'm in the middle of something I don't understand.'

'You mean the drug war.'

'I mean you and your sister. I don't care what the criminal class does with their time. I care about you. I care about what's happening with your sister, who is still legally a child, and her baby, who is by any definition a child. And, because of those concerns, I also have to figure out about this alleged DEA agent, what happened to her, what she was doing, and why she was posing as your sister, or at least using your sister's name. See, for me, it all comes down to that night in Mary's when David Waters tried to collect you and you pronounced him dead.'

'You care about me?' She had a funny kind of expression on her face. 'Why?'

I stood up. 'That falls under the heading of *my* background. The short version is that I messed up in Brooklyn, and because of me there's a kid who's got no parents. My fault. So I started caring about you because it was a part of my atonement for that. And now I care about you because I know you, and I like you

– whether or not you're a bad ass – and I want you to be all right. Now enough with the psychology from both of us. Let's get to work.'

'Work?' She blinked.

'Yeah,' I said, motioning for her to get off the sofa. 'However you got to this point, you don't seem to mind shooting guys in the leg now. That being the case, I assume you're not shy about doing the work we need to do to find your sister. Whatever it is.'

She tossed off the blanket and stood up. 'You want me to shoot people?'

'No,' I said quickly. 'But I do want you to maintain the attitude that you've had so far, the whole take-no-prisoners gestalt.'

'I'm confused,' she admitted.

'Good.' I headed for the door. 'Me too.'

SEVENTEEN

Now that I knew Baxter was on Ironstone's payroll, it would be a lot easier to deal with him. He had an agenda. He was interested in protecting Ironstone and his little fiefdom. That would color all of his behavior, and I could manipulate him.

But he wasn't the first stop I intended to make. Lena and I packed ourselves into my car and zipped right over to the hospital for a chat with Maggie Redhawk.

Maggie and I knew each other pretty well. She was my primary contact at the hospital when I need something for the kids I was helping. And she'd taken care of me more than once when I had run afoul of the more unsavory element.

Fry's Bay Hospital was a little ratty around the edges, but it was efficient and small enough to be personal.

Maggie was the head nurse, in her fifties, and Mister Redhawk's older sister. When we'd first met she'd made a big deal out of her opinion that I looked more like a Seminole than she did. I didn't argue because it bonded us.

I parked the car and we headed in.

Maggie smiled when she saw me coming. As usual, her hospital uniform was so ill-fitting that she looked like a bag of laundry in a nurse's hat.

'Foggy!' she sang. 'You're not dead!'

'Not yet,' I agreed, 'but I'm working on it.'

'And this must be the little girl who killed David Waters for us,' Maggie went on, beaming. 'Come here.'

Before Lena could protest, Maggie had rounded the nurse's desk and was squeezing the life out of the kid.

'Her name's Lena,' I said. 'What have you heard about her?'

'Lena,' Maggie repeated, holding the kid at arm's length. 'Everybody's talking about you. Let me get a good look.'

'She's actually the reason we're here,' I went on. 'We're looking for her sister. Ellen Greenberg.'

'Ellen's your sister?' Maggie asked. 'The woman who worked in the gift shop? Gee. You don't look anything alike.'

I produced the picture I had in my pocket. 'This is Ellen Greenberg.'

Maggie stared. 'No, it's not.'

'This woman,' I said, 'in this picture – is not the person you know as Ellen Greenberg?'

'No.' Maggie studied the picture. 'But I see that Lena, here, *does* look like this person. I'm confused.'

'The woman you know,' I continued, 'worked here for how long?'

'I don't know, maybe a year – less. She was real nice.'

'How long has it been since you've seen her?'

'Four or five months, I guess.' She cocked her head. 'What's it about, Foggy?'

'That's what I'm trying to figure out.' I put the picture away. 'Look, is there any chance that there would be a picture of the woman you know around here? Like in her employment record or maybe she had an ID badge with her mug on it?'

'Well,' Maggie said, 'we don't have photo IDs, and I don't know about her personnel file. Let me just go get it.'

And away she went, down the hall to some office.

Lena poked me in the arm.

'We're not looking for the person who worked here,' she said under her breath. 'We're looking for my sister.'

'Yeah, but you see they're connected, right? If we find this person who borrowed your sister's made-up name – if she's still alive – then don't you think she might shed some light on this whole business?'

'I guess.'

'Let me get this timeline clear in my head,' I said, leaning against the countertop of the nurse's station. 'Your sister left home five years ago. In that time, she fell in with a Seminole crowd, as you said, and got mixed up with David Waters. The unsavory manner of their first encounter led to your sister's baby and probably a drug habit. But at some point she got wise enough to get in touch with you. Was that at home in Rio?'

'No,' she answered, 'I'd already gone to Disney.'

'Which, P.S., you were ten; how did they hire you?'

'I lied about my age,' she told me like I was stupid. 'You've met me. I *seem* older than my age. I told them that I had a form of dwarfism. They believed me. And then they hired me to *be* a dwarf. I mean, you have to see the humor in that.'

'Yeah, but back to our story,' I said. 'How did your sister know you were at Disneyland or whatever it's called?'

'We kept in touch. She wrote me letters all the time. I wrote back.'

I suddenly smacked the top of the counter. 'Wait a minute. If you'd never met David before the night you zotzed him, where did you get the letters that you put in the safe deposit box?'

'Oh, yeah – about those.' She pursed her lips. 'Maybe I should have mentioned before that my sister is crazy.'

I stared.

When I refused to say anything, she went on.

'She wasn't all that stable before she left home,' Lena said quietly. 'But after what happened with David, she lost it completely. I guess. She sent those letters to me. To my address in Kissimmee. They were written to her fantasy of David. It didn't take me long to figure that out. So I realized she'd really gone round the bend. When I met you, I thought you might help me, so I left them in the safe deposit box. And then, you know, you *did* help me. So say something.'

'You just went right to the Chalet Suzanne when you left my hospital room.'

She nodded. 'Good guess.'

'Because you thought that was the last place she'd been, on account of the stationery.'

'Yes.'

'You came to Fry's Bay to look for David, thinking he might help you,' I surmised. 'But then you found out all the dirt on the guy and realized that your sister might have been a little off. And *then* you had your encounter, and *then* David was dead and you didn't know what to do.'

'And that brings us back to Doe a Deer,' she said impatiently. 'I think we found the place where my sister and her baby were hiding out, in that crummy camp-slum in the Cherry Pocket. I don't know why we're not back there, following the trail!'

'Because it's not a trail,' I said. 'If that *was* her place, she hadn't been there in months. Your sister came here to Fry's Bay. That's where everything went wrong for her, and for you too. We may have to go back to the Cherry Pocket eventually, but would you let me handle this my way?'

Before she could answer, Maggie returned with a manila folder.

'This is very odd,' she said, setting the folder down in front of me.

'What's odd?' I asked.

'Ellen – the Ellen I knew? She was hired directly by Dr Glendale.'

'And he is?' I wanted to know.

'The chief hospital administrator. He hires head surgeons, not gift shop girls.'

'That is odd,' I agreed. 'Is there a picture?'

'No,' Maggie said. 'There's really not anything. No application, no references, no time sheet. Nothing. Just a letter of approval confirming her hiring and a note that says everything else is in Dr Glendale's office.'

I didn't even bother to look in the folder. 'Then I guess I'd better go speak with Dr Glendale.'

'No, Foggy,' Maggie insisted. 'You can't just go careening into the boss's office!'

'I wasn't planning on careening,' I told her. 'Just talking. Which way is it?'

'No!' Maggie insisted.

'Look,' I said reasonably, 'if you don't tell me, I'll just go ask someone else, very politely, and I'll get there one way or the other. I won't mention your name.'

'I don't care if you mention my name,' she snapped. 'I've been the head nurse here for three administrators. They can all kiss my ass. I just don't want you messing with something that you don't know anything about.'

That stopped me.

'What?' I stared at Maggie.

She avoided eye contact. 'You don't know what you're getting into.'

'And you do?'

Lena looked back and forth between us for a minute and then said, 'David Waters got my sister pregnant, hooked on drugs, and then abandoned her. She was only fourteen or fifteen when it happened. We're trying to save her life. You have to help us.'

Coming from me, that wouldn't have meant much, but coming from an urchin in a school girl outfit, it packed a wallop. I didn't know how much of Lena's little speech was genuine and how much was theatre, but it didn't matter. Because it worked.

'The Ellen Greenberg that I knew,' Maggie said to Lena, 'that worked here, was undercover for the Drug Enforcement Agency. Why she took your sister's name I don't know. If I had to guess, I'd say that it gave her some sort of edge with David Waters and his growing cocaine enterprise.'

I wasn't surprised that Maggie knew such a secret – she was Mister Redhawk's sister, and Redhawk knew everything. I just moved on.

'If David really did accost lots of people the way he did with you,' I said to Lena, 'and he's sampling the product that he sells, it's possible that he might not know the difference between your sister and this woman.'

'Or that the ancillary thugs who worked for David would know the name and the general look of the girl,' Lena added, 'and just assume they were the same person.'

'Then it's possible that this DEA agent approached your sister with the idea of taking over her identity,' I went on, 'to get closer to the inner workings of David's operation.'

'My sister looked older than she was,' Lena told me. 'You said that. If this DEA agent was in her twenties . . .'

'Yeah.' I didn't move.

'What is it?' Lena asked me.

I squinted. 'You know how you said your upbringing didn't exactly encourage you to be trusting?'

She nodded.

'Me too. I don't have any idea who to trust at the moment. I mean, I trust Maggie, but maybe this Dr Gladstone—'

'Glendale,' Maggie corrected.

'Maybe he's involved in the wrong end of all this. Baxter probably is. And it's possible that Yudda's not telling us everything.'

'Foggy,' Lena began.

'Also you have not exactly helped matters,' I interrupted,

irritated. 'Every five seconds you tell me a new story. I have no idea what's what with you.'

As it turned out, that hurt her feelings. She looked down and mumbled, 'Yeah, well most of the time I don't know what's what with me either.'

Maggie didn't quite understand what was going on.

'So,' she began, 'what are you going to do now?'

I just shrugged.

'You can't give up on this, Foggy,' Lena said, sounding especially like a little kid.

Then, like a smack in the head, I remembered the other item that had been in the safe deposit box.

'Where did that bullet come from?' I asked Lena. 'The one that was in there with the letters and the photos?'

'Came in that last letter,' she said. 'It scared me. It's what made me leave Kissimmee and come to Fry's Bay to find my sister.'

'Why in God's name would your sister send you a spent bullet?' I asked.

'That's what scared me, I said,' she insisted.

'Unless she didn't,' I said slowly. 'Here's a weird idea. Your sister wrote those letters and actually sent them to David. But the mystery girl, the DEA agent, found them, got them, maybe intercepted them, and sent them to you instead. That would make the bullet really important. Like: evidence in something big.'

'This is either the most far-fetched invention of the decade,' Lena said, 'or the best guess of the century.'

'Not really a guess, entirely,' I said. 'Given the facts at this point, and the cast of characters, who would be the most likely person to send a spent bullet from a Colt M1911A1?'

'A what?' Maggie asked.

'That's the gun that fired a bullet that Ellen, one of the Ellens, sent to the kid, here, in a letter.'

'This is too much for me.' Maggie shook her head. 'Probably why my brother told me to stay out of all this mess. He told me you'd come looking for this woman, and he told me not to tell you anything.'

'Mister Redhawk told you to hide things from me?'

'No,' she said quickly, 'he just didn't want me getting involved.

But now that you've talked with me and gotten me involved – you'd better go see him.'

I nodded. 'OK.'

Without further ado I headed for the exit.

'Wait,' Lena protested, 'you don't trust the cops and you don't trust me but you do trust the Indian who busted your door down and scared me out of my wits?'

'First, what did I tell you about the word *Indian*?' I began. 'And second, you didn't seem remotely scared out of your wits.'

'I was hyper!' she snapped.

'We're going to see Mister Redhawk!' I countered as we exited the hospital.

EIGHTEEN

Mister Redhawk stayed in a big condo when he was in Fry's Bay. His was the only building in town designed for the very wealthy. It was a swanky edifice right downtown that was lousy with phony art deco details and a big marble lobby, all show-off and no comfort. If Redhawk was in town, that was as good a place as any to start looking for him.

I insisted that Lena change out of her ridiculous costume before we went to see him. Rolled up in her torn backpack was a pair of jeans and a flapper fringe top she'd found in a thrift store, also platform sandals with cork soles. I'd changed my tie: a thin burgundy number that was so far out of fashion it was cool again. Wardrobe refreshed, we sallied forth to the rich man's condo.

As we navigated through the odd revolving door, all glass and copper, I prepared myself for the security guard. We'd had several encounters. Once we were in the lobby, I was momentarily distracted by the paintings on the walls: women in blue dresses playing musical instruments. The floor sported an angular sunburst design, and the ceiling was a huge chandelier. I'd forgotten about all that.

Lena was impressed. 'Jesus,' she whispered.

The security guard stood up.

'You again?' he whined.

I reached in my hip pocket and showed my badge. 'Florida Child Protective Services,' I reminded him. 'And this is a child.'

Lena waved.

'Part of protecting her involves seeing Mister Redhawk.' I stopped right there. I thought it best to let silence convince him that I was serious.

He was staring at Lena, trying to decide what to do. It was obvious that thinking hurt his brain. So he gave up.

'Yeah, all right,' he mumbled, reaching for the phone at his station.

'Thank you, sir,' Lena said in a very small voice.

I tried to keep from smiling.

'Yes, sir, Mister Redhawk, sorry to bother you,' the guard said tentatively, 'there's someone here in the lobby that wants to see you. It's Moscowitz, that guy from . . .'

He trailed off, listening to whatever it was that Redhawk was saying. He nodded and hung up.

'Third floor,' he said.

'The top floor suite?' I asked. 'The whole floor, right?'

The guy nodded, 'Just renovated it.'

'You've been there before,' Lena surmised.

'I have.' That was all. No need burdening the child with past exploits when there was so much to be done in the present. 'Let's go.'

In no time we were standing in the elevator as the door opened onto a foyer that would lead to the rest of the suite.

And when that door opened, who should be standing there but my old friend Philip. His normal Hawaiian shirt and jeans had been replaced by a tux – he was dressed to the nines.

'Hey,' Lena said when she saw him, 'it's Hawaiian shirt guy, all dressed up!'

'Hey,' Philip fired right back 'it's pint-sized hit girl.'

'We should really get better nicknames,' Lena said, stepping out of the elevator.

'Agreed,' Philip told her. 'Hello, Foggy.'

'Philip,' I said, putting my hand on his giant bicep, 'I didn't get a chance to thank you for everything you did for me when I got shot at Ironstone's. Every time I think you can't get any better, you do.'

He smiled. 'You'd do the same for me.'

'In a heartbeat,' I vowed.

'Philip!' Redhawk called from an inner room. 'Bring them in. We're in a hurry.'

Philip indicated the way in with his hand. 'After you. He's kind of impatient.'

The suite was a lot different than the last time I'd seen it. It was ultra-simple, clean like an operating room, spare, cool, and with pale walls like a sunrise. The fireplace in the center of the living room area was see-through, and it operated from both sides. The living room had one huge Stickley sofa flanked by two similar armchairs, a craftsman table with a Currier and Ives book opened to some *Winter* pages – all sitting on a twenty by twenty antique carpet. With the fire going in the show-stopping fireplace, the room looked more like a millionaire's hunting lodge from the 1920s than a swank penthouse condo in No-Place, Florida.

'I like the new look,' I began.

'Sit down, both of you,' Redhawk interrupted, no-nonsense. 'On the sofa.'

We sat. His voice was very commanding.

He took one of the armchairs and stared a hole into Lena.

After a minute he said, very softly, 'You do look like your sister.'

I couldn't say how that hit Lena, but the sound of his voice was so warm and, at the same time, in pain that I had no idea what to say.

Lena saved the day. 'You know my sister?'

Redhawk closed his eyes for a second. 'I rarely admit this, but David Waters was my nephew.'

So that was another hand grenade. This time I took the lead. 'You're Ironstone's brother?'

'No,' he said, and his voice grated at the mere suggestion of such an association. 'He married my sister. Not Maggie, obviously; my younger sister, May. He hasn't always been the man you know today. Once he was a wild young man with more ambition than most, which was a very attractive trait in a crowd of young men lost to alcohol and ennui. He was going someplace.'

'It's just that where he was going turned out to be wrong,' Lena said before she could stop herself.

Redhawk nodded once.

'So you knew about David's . . . what's the word? *Association* with Lena's sister?' I asked.

'Ellen was a lovely child,' he said sadly. 'I don't know where you were ten years ago, Mr Moscowitz, but in certain parts of Florida there were beautiful, winsome young people whom the press ridiculously called flower children. Ellen reminded me of them: open, loving, tied to nature. You may have heard what David did to her. What you probably don't know is that it didn't change her basic nature. Having sex with a relative stranger, taking drugs for days at a time – these were normal pastimes for her, and I mean that in the most positive sense. Her notion of moral behavior was entirely liberated. She was not ruined by her encounter with my nephew. For her, it was only another experience that she collected, like collecting sunlight in brown layers on her skin.'

'Whether or not that's a fantasy on your part is a matter for another time,' I butted in. 'My concern is that you keep using the past tense when you talk about her.'

'Only because I haven't seen her in six months,' he said quickly. 'She's gone.'

'Gone where?' I asked point blank.

'Yes.' He crossed his legs and stared into the fire. 'That's why you're here.'

'You say that like you summoned us,' I railed. 'We came to get answers from you.'

He smiled, not looking at me.

'Mr Moscowitz,' he intoned indulgently, 'I have a great respect for your powers of deduction and investigation. After you spoke to my sister at the hospital, I knew you'd come to see me.'

I shook my head, hoping to convey my skepticism. 'All right, we came to see you. Where is Ellen Greenberg?'

He sighed, still unwilling to look at us.

'When I saw what David was doing, I went to Ellen and spoke with her. She needed help. I gave it to her.'

'Hold on,' Lena interrupted. 'What kind of *help*.'

'I got her into the hospital with Maggie,' he said tonelessly. 'Got her straight, helped her with the birth of her daughter. And I was going to send her back home, until she told me what her home was like. At that point, something happened.'

I leaned forward. 'Let me guess. David's insane pretensions in the drug world drew the attention of the Drug Enforcement Agency. Enter Madame X, some agent that looked enough like Ellen to pass for her in town. And the DEA put Ellen into some kind of Witness Protection Program.'

Lena blinked. 'What's that?'

I turned to her. 'About, like, five years ago, Nixon passed the Organized Crime Control Act, and a part of it is that certain people can be relocated and hidden by the federal government if they help catch the bad guys.'

Lena turned to Redhawk. 'You got my sister to rat on David?'

'This is all conjecture on the part of Mr Moscowitz,' Redhawk objected.

'And you can't tell me that I'm right because it would be breaking some kind of rule.'

At last he turned to face us.

'Ellen is safe.' That's all he said.

Lena stood up. 'Not good enough! I need to know where she is, how to find her! I have to see my sister!'

'I understand,' he said patiently, 'but there is, in fact, a more pressing matter.'

'The woman who took Ellen's place is missing,' I said plainly. 'And the whole deal with the DEA is falling apart.'

He sighed and focused on Lena. 'Unfortunately, the case was being built on David's activities. However unwittingly, you damaged that work very significantly when you killed him. You didn't mean to, but you've put your sister at risk.'

'Hold it,' I broke in. 'The woman who was impersonating Ellen has been missing for months. That's now Lena's fault? Six months ago she was a dwarf in Kissimmee.'

Redhawk turned my way and stared. 'I have absolutely no idea what that means.'

'If there was a whole operation around David,' Lena snapped, 'and the government was making some big case, why the hell didn't someone step in when I killed him?'

'Nobody knew who you were at first,' Redhawk said. 'And by the time anyone figured it out, you were gone.'

'Ironstone's guys didn't seem to have much trouble finding her,' I said.

And then, for the first time in my association with Mister Redhawk, he raised his voice in anger.

'Not the point!' He glared. 'We have to find the agent!'

It took me a second, but then I understood.

'Sit down, kid,' I told Lena. 'This woman, the DEA agent? She's the only one who knows where your sister is.'

'Oh, Christ,' she said and collapsed back onto the sofa. 'Great.'

'If she told anyone where Ellen is,' Redhawk went on, his

composure restored, 'then Ellen's in a lot of trouble. It's not just David's people now. The Black Tuna group is involved, and they don't seem to mind killing anyone.'

Lena swallowed. 'What are we going to do, Foggy?'

I put my hand on her shoulder. 'Nothing to it. We find the agent, she tells us where your sister is; then we all put the Columbians out of business so you can go back to Disneyland with your sister and your little niece. Shouldn't take more than a couple of days.'

Lena glanced over at Philip. 'You've known him longer than I have. Is he nuts or is he just a cockeyed optometrist?'

Philip grinned. *'Optometrist.* That's funny.'

'It's a scream,' she dead-panned. 'Can he really do it? Can he find my sister?'

'What?' I interjected. 'You don't trust me anymore?'

'I just think there might be something wrong with you,' she answered.

'Oh.' I nodded. 'Well, there probably is something wrong with me. Let's go.'

'Hang on,' she demurred. 'I have several questions for Mister Redhawk.'

Redhawk gave her his most serene look. 'Ask.'

'How do you know all about this DEA agent and my sister?' she blurted. 'Are you working with the government?'

And then something else happened that I'd never seen before. Mister Redhawk laughed. Out loud. It was actually a very musical sound.

'The government of the United States is an entity I will never trust.' That was his answer.

'With good reason,' I added.

'I know about this entire affair because I try to know everything that affects my tribe.' He looked away, back into the fire again.

'But,' I suggested, 'you were more than an observer in the matter.'

'What makes you say that?' he asked, still watching the flames play.

'How did the DEA know about Ellen?'

'I don't know,' he said.

'But you set the agent up at the hospital,' I went on. 'You got

her the job there because you wanted to make sure Maggie kept
an eye on her.'

He lifted his eyebrows.

'And we haven't even touched on the idea that this DEA agent
looked enough like Ellen to convince David that she *was* Ellen,
but when I showed Ellen's picture all over town, no one recognized it.'

That got his attention.

'You have a picture of Ellen?' he asked, turning my way.

'Right here.' I reached into my suit coat and produced it.

Philip came and got it, took it to Redhawk. He studied it.

'Interesting,' he said at last.

'In what way?' I pressed.

All of a sudden Redhawk looked me right in the eye.

'This doesn't look anything like the Ellen Greenberg I knew,'
he assured me.

Lena leaned forward, eyes wide. 'That's my sister. That
picture.'

Redhawk shook his head.

'I see a resemblance,' he began.

'In what way does this picture look different from the real live
girl?' I asked.

'Ellen – the girl I knew – had red hair and green eyes. She
was twenty pounds heavier than the person in the picture, and
at least ten years older. Also the nose was different. Ellen's nose
– the Ellen I knew – her nose was crooked. You'd have to look
really hard at the photo to see any similarity at all.'

'A dye job, some contact lenses, a couple of hard years and
Yudda's food,' I said slowly. 'And maybe her nose got broken?'

'All possible.' Redhawk handed the picture back to Philip.

Philip took a moment to look at it.

'It's also the look on her face,' he mused.

'How's that?' I asked.

'This girl in the picture looks a little lost. The Ellen that was
around here knew what was what.'

Lena shook her head. 'I don't understand any of this.'

I agreed. 'It's a tangled web.'

'Foggy,' Redhawk began.

I stood up. 'We're going now, and thanks for your time. Come on, Lena.'

'But . . .' she protested.

'I've got some ideas.' That's as far as I was willing to go in front of Redhawk, but I really did have a pretty fair plan.

Philip handed me the photo. Then he leaned over a little to speak with Lena.

'It's been my experience,' he told the kid, 'that when Foggy says he's got ideas, that means it's all going to work out.'

His words sounded so sincere that even I was convinced I knew what I was doing. Almost.

NINETEEN

We were in my car and driving through the center of town before either of us said anything. Lena broke the silence.

'Where are we going?' she wanted to know. 'You're driving too fast.'

'Well,' I suggested, 'when you know what you want to do, you also want to get started on it as soon as possible.'

'And what do I want to do?'

'You want to find your sister and the niece you never met.' I eased the accelerator forward and the T-Bird lunged. 'So that's just what we're going to do.'

'OK,' she protested, 'but where are we going?'

'To Ironstone's place.'

'What?' I thought she was going to jump out of the car.

'I don't want to plan this out *too* much,' I began, 'because if I do it'll trip me up. I like to improvise. And also I want you to react just the way you'd react if you didn't know what was going on.'

'That's going to be easy since I don't know what's going on.'

'Then we're set,' I said.

We didn't talk again until Ironstone's house came into view.

'Are you going to tell me what we're doing?' she asked under her breath.

'Just be exactly who you are,' I said.

'I don't know this John Horse guy,' she told me in what seemed at first a non-sequitur, 'but that sounds like something he'd say.'

I thought about it. 'Maybe it does. The old guy might be rubbing off on me. Which is lucky for you and me. He's the real item.'

'A genuine rabbi,' she added.

'Don't get all Jewish with me, pal,' I warned her.

I slowed the car and eased up to the front of the estate. We were greeted by a fresh face; someone I'd never seen before. That meant to me that Holata and Taft were gone. Good for them. Bad for me.

The new guy was dressed in a tan suit. He had his hair in a crew cut, unusual for a Seminole in my experience. He was very happy to show us his gun, a Heckler & Koch HK11, a relatively new machine gun that some of the Special Forces used in Vietnam.

I opened my door slowly and kept my hands in sight.

'Nice gun,' I said. 'We really need to see Ironstone. It's about his son.'

The guy didn't budge. It was like he didn't understand English, which maybe he didn't.

Lena got out of the car then but stayed on her side, with the car in between her and Mr Crew Cut.

'I'm the one who killed David Waters,' she said calmly.

That was all. We let that sink in.

Then, of all things, the guy smiled.

'I heard about that,' he said softly. 'You got him with a Heckler and Koch VP70.'

She nodded. 'We like the same brand name.'

He glanced down at his gun. 'They're good.'

'The thing is,' I interrupted, 'I can tell Ironstone what's happening with a certain government investigation, and all about how he really needs to help us find Ellen Greenberg, the real Ellen Greenberg – which he wants to do anyway. What we have here is a win/win kind of situation.'

'What government investigation?' he wanted to know.

'See, that's just what I want to talk to Ironstone about.' I glanced at the house. 'And you have to believe me: he really does want to hear about it.'

'Don't you have trouble with the sight on that thing?' Lena asked the guy out of nowhere.

'I *do*,' he told her. 'I thought it was me. I need glasses. But then I read that it's maybe a design flaw.'

'It is,' she assured him. 'You're really better off just pulling and spraying a general havoc than sighting for single shots.'

'Yeah,' he smiled. 'That makes a hell of a *havoc*.'

'Let's not test it out right at the moment,' I suggested. 'And time is actually of the essence. So can we go talk with Ironstone or not?'

He nodded and lowered his gun. 'Sure.'

With that he turned his back on us and headed toward the front door.

I glanced at Lena and shook my head, she batted her eyes, and we both followed Crew Cut.

'Mr Waters,' Crew Cut called out. 'It's that guy Moscowitz and the kid who shot David.'

'What?' his voice echoed from the ridiculously giant living room.

'It's true,' I sang out. 'And you're going to want to speak with us. It's about the federal investigation into your business.'

There was a moment of silence before he responded.

'Which one?'

I kept on walking, and there he was in his robe and slippers, sipping tea and staring up at me as I came into the room.

'Do you mean which business or which investigation?' I asked grimly.

'What do you want? I'm really just about at the end of my patience—'

'This new Drug Enforcement Agency they got?' I interrupted him. 'Do you know about them? Because they know about you. And they're about to tear your playhouse down. The cocaine wars are no joke. The DEA had a bead on David, and now that he's gone, they're all over you.'

He was momentarily silenced, so I pulled out my photo of Ellen.

'Who is this?' I snapped.

He stared, squinted, shook his head.

'No idea,' he said, returning to his tea.

'This, Ironstone, is Ellen Greenberg.'

He swallowed and looked my way again.

'No,' he assured me. 'Ellen Greenberg had red hair—'

'This,' I interrupted, 'is the real Ellen Greenberg. Lena's sister. The person you killed was a DEA agent. That's why the government is looking to burn it all down: you killed a Fed.'

I stared right into his eyes like I hadn't made most of that up.

'You thought you killed my sister,' Lena growled, standing right beside me, 'but you killed a cop!'

Good for her, following my lead.

Ironstone hesitated, then set down his cup. Before he could speak, I went on.

'The thing is,' I said, 'that David pissed everybody off. And I mean *everybody*. The Seminoles hated him because he's a child molester; the Cubans hated him because he sold them out to the Columbians; and the Columbians hated him on general principle. It's a wonder he didn't end up dead before Lena plugged him. Which, by the way, was lucky for you, because it threw a monkey wrench into the investigation. The woman you had killed took over Ellen's identity and was peripherally involved in David's life. Just enough to get into the operation, to know what he was doing. You killed her because, excuse me for saying so, you're an idiot. The real Ellen wasn't in love with David. And he wasn't in love with her. She would never have asked you for a thing. Not for herself and not for David's baby. But now you're in a mess, and it's one you made for yourself. I wouldn't be here at all except that I want to find Ellen, the real Ellen. I don't care about the rest of it. That's for someone else.'

I stopped. I wanted to see what effect my little tirade might have had.

Ironstone sighed and closed his eyes.

'First,' he said wearily, 'I didn't kill anyone or have anyone killed. David did. For the last two years he's been loaded. Cocaine hydrochloride mixed with morphine sulfate.'

'Speedball,' Lena said softly to me. 'One of Mom's favorite cocktails.'

'I'm not surprised he couldn't tell the difference between the woman in this picture and the woman who worked at the hospital,' Ironstone concluded. 'Sometimes he couldn't tell the difference between me and the sofa.'

I shook my head. 'In the first place, it's probably the case that Lena's sister dyed her hair and maybe gained a few pounds since this picture was taken. In the second place I just realized why the DEA agent went to work at the hospital.'

'Pharmaceuticals!' Lena concluded. 'She was supplying David!'

'Not exactly,' I told her. 'She was giving him, like, a control group. He could test the coke and the morphine from the hospital against the stuff he got from the Columbians to see how much the South American stuff had been stepped on.'

'Stepped on?' Ironstone interrupted.

I gazed at him for a moment and got socked with another realization.

'You're not involved in the drug part of your business,' I said to him. 'That was all David.'

'Otherwise you'd know that the term refers to how much the drugs have been diluted,' Lena explained with the condescension of youth, 'to make a little bit into a lot.'

'You can dilute cocaine?' he asked before he could stop himself.

'My mother used to cut it with baby laxative when she sold it,' Lena told him.

'The point is,' I insisted, 'David did think that the agent was the real Ellen, helping him out with his enterprise. He didn't kill her.'

'But if Ironstone didn't kill her,' Lena protested, 'and David didn't – then who the hell did? Did anyone? Maybe she *isn't* dead.'

'Yeah,' I said, 'I guess we'd better find that out. All the more reason for us all to work together.'

'We have to find out what happened to the DEA agent,' Ironstone agreed. 'Unfortunately, that might mean dealing with the Columbians. Black Tuna. They're the most likely culprits, wouldn't you say?'

I nodded. 'And I agree that it's unfortunate that we have to mess with them. But I know someone on the inside of their little club who might be willing to help.'

The drive back to the Cherry Pocket was tense. Lena and I were in the lead in my black T-Bird, Ironstone followed in a sleek blue Cadillac Fleetwood. We were more obvious than a parade, and we had no idea what was waiting for us at the other end.

Lena was staring out the window, thinking, and I didn't want to interrupt her. But I was relieved when she finally spoke.

'You think that Tony is a part of the gang that killed the agent?' she said softly.

'Tony? No. I didn't tell you about – do you remember the geezer at the bar who told us about the Three Tee Pees campground?'

She nodded silently.

'Him. He's Cuban, one of the original drug guys in the region – one of the few that made the transition once the Columbians took over. He has valuable information.

'And you got to know him?'

'In the sense that he kicked my ass, yes,' I admitted. 'And he would have killed me if I'd let him.'

She turned herself my way. 'Then what makes you think he'll help us?'

'I got the impression that he hated the Columbians.' I shrugged. 'It's worth a try to get him to help us. If I'd really thought it through, I probably would have asked you to wait in Fry's Bay, because this might not be so pleasant.'

'I guess you could have tried to make me stay in your little apartment,' she sneered. 'But how has that sort of thing worked out for you so far?'

'Yeah,' I agreed. 'It's just that since I found out that your badass quotient is a little less – realistic than I thought, I worry about you.'

She dismissed that with a wave of her hand. 'Aw, you worried about me before that. You're a worrier by nature. And, P.S., who shot those guys in the Chalet Suzanne?'

'OK.' That was all I said. I decided not to bring up the fact that she'd been crying in my living room. She might not have been tough as nails, but she certainly wasn't a typical fourteen-year-old kid either.

'Besides,' she said.

And with that she drew a neat Lilliput pistol out of one pocket in her jeans. Right around four inches long, it was one of the smallest semiautomatic handguns ever made, a German 4.25mm number.

'Where the hell do you get all these guns?' I asked her.

'I told you,' she answered, examining the thing, 'my mother was a collector.'

'Well that thing's an antique,' I warned her.

'Yeah,' she said, 'so are you, but you both seem to work all right.'

'I'm not a – how old do you think I am?' I railed.

'Slow down, Speed Racer,' she said, glancing in the rear view, 'you're losing our new friend.'

I glanced back at the Fleetwood and eased off the accelerator.

'Speed Racer?' I asked.

'You never saw that television show? I watched it all the time when I was a kid. It's a Japanese animation thing.'

'You watched it when you were a kid,' I said, attempting to demonstrate that I still considered her an apprentice adult. 'I see.'

'Television, school, and hiding with a gun in my hand,' she snapped. 'That was my so-called childhood. I'm a Dead End Kid, remember? How old was Leo Gorcey? He was your hero.'

'Right' I acquiesced, 'and Speed Racer was yours?'

'No,' she said. 'My hero when I was little? I'd have to think about that.'

'Yeah, well I grew out of the Leo Gorcey phase. After a while, unfortunately, my heroes were low-level criminals. But then I came to Florida, and now I got no hero, unless it's maybe John Horse. And that's some tough shoes to follow.'

'I outgrew cartoons,' she mused. 'But I guess I still have a – I feel the need for, you know, heroes.'

'Like who?'

'I don't know.' She turned back straight in her seat, staring out the window again. 'Bobby Fischer's pretty cool. And, I guess, you.'

They say there are things you won't know until you have a kid of your own, but I'm pretty sure I came close at that moment.

TWENTY

We pulled into the gravel parking lot of the restaurant at the Cherry Pocket just as the sun was beginning to sink low. The Fleetwood pulled up beside my car, and we all just sat there for a minute.

After a couple of minutes, I glanced over at Lena.

'Any way I could get you to wait in the car?'

She smiled. 'Hit me on the head, wrap me in duct tape, and weld the doors shut?'

I sighed. 'Well, I don't have any duct tape.'

She nodded and opened her door.

I got out, followed almost immediately by Crew Cut and Ironstone. Crew Cut had his machine gun in his hands.

'I don't know what's in there,' I said to him softly, 'but no good can come from sauntering through the door with that in your hands.'

Lena glanced at him, reached into her pocket, and showed him her Lilliput.

He nodded, tossed the machine gun back into the car, and opened his tan suit jacket. He had a remarkable holster system that held three different pistols and something that looked like a small hand grenade.

Lena nodded approvingly.

'Could we all just settle down,' I suggested, 'and let me see what I can accomplish with my gab before we start shooting up the joint?'

Everyone agreed, but the reluctance was thicker than the humidity.

I took the lead and headed for the door; the others flanked me, following. We didn't remotely resemble ordinary customers or fishing enthusiasts.

As I forged through the door I caught sight of Tony behind the bar and the old Cuban guy sitting in front of him. They turned my way. There were a couple of guys in a booth eating crab legs and some woman at a table looking over the menu.

I lifted my chin in Tony's direction. He wasn't happy to see me. When he saw my entourage, he actually took a step back. The Cuban guy got off his stool lightning fast.

'Mr Fidestra,' I said quickly, 'we just want to talk. Look. We have Ellen Greenberg's sister with us.'

I made sure he could see Lena, and then I put myself in between the two of them.

It was a risk, just calling out the name like that. But if he was Fidestra, it would cut right to the punch line. And if he wasn't, the name might at least give this guy pause.

I took advantage of his silence to say, 'Is there some place we can talk?'

He stared, ice-eyed and frozen.

Ironstone spoke up before I could stop him. 'I'm Ironstone Waters. David Waters was my son. This little girl killed him.'

It was short and to the point. I had to admire that.

The old Cuban guy took a deep breath.

'Mr Moscowitz,' he said in his gravelly voice, 'I understand that you enjoyed our grouper the last time you were here. Would you care to see how it was prepared?'

I smiled. 'Tony is really something of a chef,' I responded. 'I'd love to see how he does it. The kitchen?'

The old guy nodded. 'Right this way.'

And just like that, we all repaired to the kitchen. It was a very small affair: an eight-eye stove, a wood grill, a prep table, and a deep sink, all stainless steel. The floor was spotless and everything was gleaming.

'The fact that you know my name,' the Cuban said, 'means something.'

He stared. He wasn't going to say anything else until I told him how I'd found him out. So I explained about Pan Pan Washington and my former life in Brooklyn – only a little, but enough that he believed me.

'There is more to you than meets the eye,' he said. 'And in my life, I am not very often surprised like this.'

'The point is,' I pressed, 'I'm not here – we're not here – to mess with you. We're here to find Ellen Greenberg, and that's all.'

He looked us over. 'Not entirely true. You want to find out what happened to the DEA agent who was protecting her.'

I held my breath. I wanted to choose my words very carefully. Unfortunately, Lena didn't have the same constraint.

'Did you kill my sister?' It was a blistering sound in the small, cramped space.

It was so searing, in fact, that Fidestra grimaced.

'No,' he answered. 'Nobody killed your sister. That I know of.'

'But you killed the Fed,' she went on.

'Not me.'

'Your guys,' she pressed.

'My *guys*,' he barked, 'are all dead. The men from Columbia killed them all.'

'Which is why,' I interrupted before he could go any further, 'you'll help us. You work for those men, but you hate them.'

His eyes narrowed.

'Do you know who I am?' Ironstone butted in.

Fidestra looked at him. 'Ironstone Waters is a name I have heard, even before I met your idiot son. No offense.'

'None taken,' Ironstone said evenly. 'Being an idiot was only one of my son's foibles. I ask you because if you know who I am, you also know that I can offer you a way out of your current situation.'

'How's that?' Fidestra asked.

'You'll come work for me.'

'It's not a bad gig,' Crew Cut chimed in. 'You should see his place. I stay in a guest house all to myself. With a pool.'

Steel in his voice, Fidestra dead-panned, 'Yeah, but how's the food?'

I smiled. 'Tony learned from Yudda, as maybe he's mentioned. And Yudda lives in our little town.'

'Yudda,' he mused. 'He got screwed over by these damned Columbians too.'

'He did,' I agreed.

Fidestra looked around the kitchen for a minute. 'This place is the nicest prison I ever stayed in. But it's a prison to me.'

'Because you're not your own man,' I said.

'Not for a long time,' he acknowledged. 'I'm an old man. But I'm not dead. I just feel like I am.'

'So let's fix that,' I told him.

He hesitated.

'Some people get comfortable in prison,' I suggested. 'They like the routine; they don't like change. So I guess you have to decide if you're a prisoner or not.'

He reached into an inner pocket of his camo jacket. Before his hand got there, Crew Cut had a pistol out and Lena was pointing her Lilliput.

Fidestra noticed the guns, but he didn't care. He pulled out his own.

Just as I was about to shove Lena out of the way and prepare myself to get shot again, Fidestra turned and headed toward the back door of the kitchen.

'Let's go,' he told us; he didn't look back.

We all followed him.

We were out into the growing shadows of the late afternoon, walking a mulch path that smelled like pine and mildew. I was trying to figure out how you could get the whole woods to smell that way when we rounded a bend in the path and came across a circle of cars.

There were maybe twenty guys standing around, all armed to the teeth – those few who had teeth at all. Fidestra kept walking. I couldn't figure his play.

He called out, 'Hola!'

A couple of the guys turned his way. Then they saw the rest of us, and the guns all moved. We didn't have time to think, let alone duck or move.

Fidestra turned toward us and backed away, into the circle of heavy arms, grinning.

'What the hell made you think I'd just switch over like that?' he asked me.

It was very clear that we were about to have a serious problem. Guns were aimed, eyes were narrowed.

Then with absolutely no warning, Lena threw herself against my side, knocking me to the ground, and hit the deck herself. She rolled and, when she was on her stomach, she had the pistol in her hand aimed at the gang of Columbians. Two seconds later I had Holata's pistol in my hand, the one I'd used to shoot up Ironstone's chair. I'd almost forgotten it was there. We were both partly hidden by the general flora surrounding the path.

I was surprised that no one had fired off a shot.

Ironstone and Crew Cut were just standing there, unblinking. They were about fifteen feet away from the circle of men and cars. There was plenty of undergrowth around the path, places to hide. But that wasn't Ironstone's style.

'You understand what will happen to you if you do anything to me,' Ironstone said.

His words sounded like flint on rocks.

'We know about your deal with Raul,' Fidestra answered calmly. 'Why do you think you're not dead already?'

Ironstone laughed. 'I'm not the one who's already dead.'

'Um, boys,' Lena interrupted from the ground, 'I'm getting my vintage top all dirty.'

It wasn't clear who she was talking to.

'You want to find your sister?' Fidestra called out. 'I know where she is. Come here.'

'Oh,' Lena answered, 'OK, I'll just stand up now so your guys will have a perfect target.'

I was certain we were dead, me and Lena. No doubt in my mind. Otherwise I would never have done what I did next.

In a single move I was up off the ground, right behind Ironstone, my arm around his neck in a sleeper hold – the gun pointed at his head.

'Here's my thinking,' I began.

Crew Cut moved, but Lena was faster. She rolled and shot him in the foot with her little gun. I kicked the back of his other leg, and he went down like a water buffalo. Lena was on top of him with her gun jabbed into the poor guy's eye. Looked like it hurt.

'Here's my thinking, as I was saying,' I continued. 'I'm going to shoot Ironstone, then his bodyguard, and I'm going to make sure everyone knows that you guys did it. You have connections? So do I. I've already spoken to Brooklyn. Carmine Galante.'

That put a lot of ice on everybody. Galante was the de facto boss of the Bonanno family. He supposedly organized the murders of a whole bunch of Gambino family members. If he did it, it was so that he could take over their drug business. Currently no one involved in the drug trade would mess with Galante. Because if you did, you were dead.

Of course, I hadn't actually said I'd spoken to the guy, but I *had* called Brooklyn, so the angel of truth was on my side at least a little. And I'd also swung a guess at the whole notion that Galante was somehow invested in the Columbians. But it wasn't a bad guess. The drugs went to Miami, and Miami is where Pan Pan always used to go for his stash.

Plus, Ironstone was standing between me and the guys with guns.

'Moscowitz,' Ironstone snarled underneath his breath.

'Relax,' I whispered. 'Nobody's going to shoot. Not even me. Although the fact that you have a deal with the Columbians gives me pause.'

'I don't have a deal with the Columbians!' he whispered. 'David used my name!'

'That's probably right,' I agreed. 'It's also what's keeping us alive for a minute. Tell your guy not to hurt Lena.'

Without looking, Ironstone mumbled, '*Hattisits cheh.*'

It was one of the Seminole languages; I thought it meant *stop.*

Crew Cut relaxed and Lena rolled away.

'Good,' I whispered. 'Now will you go along with what I say? I can get us out of this.'

'Let's just see how it goes,' Ironstone answered.

'Look, Fidestra,' I called out, 'you can start a war if you want to. But you should probably think about what it would mean to have Italian families from the north and Seminole tribes from the south both coming at you with all kinds of malice.'

Nobody moved.

'We could kill you all right now,' he answered at length, 'and bury you in the swamp. No one would ever know.'

'You can't be serious.' I mustered a laugh. 'I'm an agent of the state. If I don't fill out paperwork, everybody and his brother comes looking for me. And if Ironstone disappears, every Seminole within a hundred miles would slog through the swamp until they'd found him. And they would find him. To you this is a wild place. To them, it's a back yard. Don't you get that?'

Lena stood up then, against every good instinct, and leveled an evil eye right at Fidestra.

'And I can top all of that!' she barked. 'I work for Walt Disney!'

Nobody laughed. She somehow managed to make it sound like she had J. Edgar Hoover on her side.

Crew Cut got to his feet and murmured, '*Tuchanocakin.*'

Ironstone nodded.

'Don't know that word,' I admitted.

'Thirteen,' Ironstone said. 'That's how many men there are in that parking lot.'

I didn't bother counting.

'I'm not in the mood to start shooting and hope for the best,' I began. 'And I kind of have to keep the kid out of harm's way, you understand.'

'I wasn't thinking of shooting,' Crew Cut whispered.

'He was thinking of crows,' Ironstone said.

It was such a weird thing to say that I didn't know how to respond. So Crew Cut went on.

'John Horse told me once,' he said, 'that if you have one or two crows, you can shoot and probably get one for dinner, if you want it. But if you have thirteen, they scramble. There's chaos. All you can do with thirteen is scare them away – before they start thinking they can peck your eyes out.'

I nodded. 'Creepy, but I think I get it. If we can stir up a little chaos, we might be able to slip back to our cars and get away.'

'No!' Lena protested. 'We came here to get my sister. And that stupid DEA agent. We can't just run away.'

'Yeah,' I admitted, 'she's got a point.'

'Right,' Crew Cut said, 'so we do this: we all try to shoot up those cars over there, then Ironstone and I head back to the Fleetwood. We'll see if we can get some of the bad guys to chase us while you and the kid look around here.'

'That's insane,' I said.

'I'm in,' Lena told him.

Without another word she aimed her little pistol at a Buick and popped off a shot. There was nothing for it after that but to duck and fire. Crew Cut had a gun in each hand, Ironstone wielded a big Smith and Wesson something-or-other, and I managed to shoot the tires out of three cars before Holata's gun was empty.

There was a lot of complaint about what we were doing, mostly in the form of returned gunfire, and also in plenty of Spanish cursing.

The four of us had cover, trees and palmetto plants and wiry shrubs. The Columbians were out in the open. They tried diving behind cars or dropping to the ground. After a minute they understood that nobody'd been hit, not a single bullet wound.

Ironstone and Crew Cut sensed that moment, and ran, back toward the restaurant and their Cadillac. Lena managed to slink away into some fairly dense undergrowth. I got myself behind a tree. Seconds later, maybe ten guys flew past us on the path, chasing after Ironstone.

Fidestra and a couple of stragglers were still by the cars. I was trying to decide the best course of action when Fidestra turned and shot the two guys standing next to him. Shot them dead.

'OK,' he called out. 'I know you're still here. Come on out.'

Lena knew better than to move, and I stayed mute.

'I'm an old man,' Fidestra went on. 'You made some good points in your little speech: what do I want with Italians and Indians on my ass? I should be in the Cuban part of Miami right now, drinking rum and Coca-Cola and trying to score with a girl half my age. You know. So I can die happy in bed.'

I sighed. 'Not five minutes ago,' I called out, 'you were going to kill us.'

'I wasn't going to kill you.' He paused. 'They were.'

'Where's my sister?' Lena shouted.

'I don't know,' Fidestra answered, 'and that's the truth. But I can take you to the DEA agent you're talking about.'

I didn't believe him. Lena didn't believe him. That's why it was so surprising when we both walked out onto the path.

He didn't have a gun in his hands. He made sure to show us that. We kept ours pointed at him. Mine was useless, of course; I didn't know about Lena's.

'I'm with Dr Moscowitz on this,' Lena snarled, pointing her gun very carefully at his face. 'Your third change of heart in under ten minutes – doesn't seem especially reliable.'

'Look,' he said, staring down the gun, 'sometimes I don't know when I'm telling the truth and when I'm saying whatever it is I have to say so that I won't get killed. I've been at this a long time. And I'm also pretty drunk, so that counts for something.'

That had a certain ring of truth. He probably was a little dazed and confused. It was fairly common knowledge that lots of

Cubans had been killed. This guy was wily, but he was also tired. Anybody could see that.

'Take us to the agent,' Lena said, cold as January.

He nodded. 'Come on, then.'

He turned his back on us and headed away.

I leaned close to Lena. 'My gun's empty.'

'So's mine,' she whispered.

'Any chance I could get you to kind of hang back?' I suggested.

She laughed and followed Fidestra.

We weaved our way through the cars in the gravel parking lot and past some sort of out building, maybe a restroom. After that the path got narrow again, surrounded by live oaks and Spanish moss, the pervasive palmettos, and sandier ground. The light was dappled and the shadows moved quickly in a dank breeze. We caught up with Fidestra fairly quickly, Lena behind him on his right, me on his left, my gun still foolishly leveled at his back.

After a couple of silent minutes, we came to a gaggle of concrete picnic tables, all in better shape than the place where we'd found the sad little tent.

Without warning, Fidestra stopped. I bumped into him.

'There,' he said, and he pointed to one of the tables – an empty table.

Lena put the short barrel of her pistol against the back of his neck. 'There's no one there.'

He didn't move. 'She's buried underneath the table.'

'Damn it,' I said, glancing down at my shoes.

I dropped like I was going to tie one of my Florsheims, but when my knee hit the deck I took hold of Fidestra's ankle, locked on, and stood up. It had worked before, and it worked again. He went tumbling down. I had his foot and I twisted it hard enough to break his ankle. I put my foot right between his legs, ready to kick.

'Just lie there,' I warned him, 'or I'll crack your eggs.'

Lena took a few steps back.

Fidestra did his best not to move, but he was in a very uncomfortable position. He rolled a little to the left and I twisted his foot harder. He grunted. His jacket fell open. He had two pistols tucked into his pants.

Lena saw and moved so fast he didn't see her coming. She

pocketed her Lilliput and dropped down, retrieving the two guns like she was picking wildflowers. She kept one and handed me the other. They were the same: police issue Smith & Wesson Model 10, commonly called the .38 Special, an old-timer's gun, to my mind.

'The idea was that we would—what was your idea?' I asked.

He was wincing from the popped ankle. 'Let me up and I'll just kill you right now. Otherwise you'll be alive for a long time watching what I do to *esta plaga*!'

He'd used the word that meant vermin or insect. I didn't know if Lena understood the exact translation, but she correctly interpreted the intention. She responded by kicking the guy in the head.

'You're a worthless piece of crap,' she told him. 'And we're going to kill you now.'

'No you're not,' he said calmly. 'I know things. I made a deal with the DEA so they could stop all the drug traffic in Florida. They know that. Why do you think they kept me alive?'

I didn't think he meant to say that, but it really brought down the house as far as I was concerned. This guy had convinced the Feds that he was working with them. He'd convinced the Columbians that he was on their side. And he had tried, a couple of times, to convince me and Lena that he wanted to help us. He was a trickster.

'My Aunt Shayna used to tell me, when I was little, stories about old rabbis who would work miracles. One of these guys was bragging about his abilities one day. He says, "When I climb up on my chair, I can see with my luminous eyes to the very ends of the earth!" And one of his students says, "What? You need a chair?" The idea in this case is that you can brag about your miracles all day long. But in the end, I can see farther than you can, and I don't need a chair.'

Fidestra just stared.

Lena leaned in, keeping her gun pointed at Fidestra.

'You're going to have to unpack that a little more, Foggy,' she said.

'He's boasting about stuff that he really can't do, and I'm going to take him down a notch,' I said simply. 'I'm going to finish breaking his ankle for messing with us. We're going to take his guns and get back to my car, if it's still there. And then I'm going to tell Detective Baxter how great it was that Fidestra helped us by ratting out his Columbian cohorts.'

That got a rise out of Fidestra. He started kicking and rolling.

I twisted his foot past the halfway mark, and the ankle popped like a hatchet falling. He howled. Then, just for good measure, I shot him in his right hand.

'Let's go,' I told Lena.

She didn't hesitate. She took off running back toward the restaurant and my T-Bird.

'So that means Baxter is working with the Columbians?' she asked me as we raced.

'Something like that,' I mused. 'Ironstone. The Columbians. The police. That's who we're up against. We're really going to need some reinforcements, here.'

We ran. Moments later we slowed down to make sure there was no one waiting for us near the restaurant. The parking lot there seemed empty. The Fleetwood was gone, and there were only two other cars evident, mine and a beat-up Ford pickup I'd never seen before. I hoped it belonged to a customer of the establishment, took a deep breath, and headed for my car. Lena was stuck to my side.

We made it to the car. I started it. I backed out. No trouble.

I had a very eerie sensation that we were being watched, but nothing happened. We got out of the Cherry Pocket and onto the main road. Neither one of us had put our guns away.

After a minute or two, Lena put her gun in her lap and leaned back.

'My sister's dead, isn't she, Foggy?' she asked me softly.

I kept my eyes on the road. 'You have to at least consider that as a possibility, yeah.'

She looked down. 'So you're going to stop looking for her.'

'No,' I said instantly. 'When I woke up in the hospital and you were there, I promised you I'd find her. That still goes. Even if she's buried under a picnic table.'

It was such a cruel, macabre image, we both started laughing, for some reason. Probably just the tension.

'Could we, like, *never* go back to the Cherry Pocket?' she demanded. 'I mean, like, *ever* again? It's the opposite of Disneyland. It's the *least* fun place in the world.'

'I don't know,' I told her, 'what's so fun about Disneyland?'

She looked out the window. 'Nothing there is real.'

TWENTY-ONE

Back in Fry's Bay, Lena conked out on the sofa and I sat in the kitchen pondering a couple of the toughest problems I'd had in a while.

The first was about the insurance policy that David had taken out for Ellen and the baby. If he really didn't know Ellen well enough not to confuse her with a look-alike; if he really had juiced her, boinked her, and cut her loose – why would he have taken out a million dollars' worth of insurance on himself with them as the beneficiaries?

Second, it was really hard to believe that a spoiled rich kid, which was his modus, could intimidate people like Fidestra and take over an operation that guys much tougher had put together.

Third, if David was a child molester and the whole tribe hated him, why hadn't John Horse stopped the guy? That was the sort of thing John Horse would do: run a punk off the rails. And yet David had lived to molest another day – that day being the one when he messed with the wrong kid, in the person of the one sleeping on my couch.

The rest of it was standard to me. Baxter was on Ironstone's payroll? My experience in Brooklyn was that a cop who didn't take at least a little pocket change was not to be trusted, didn't know the game. Ironstone was involved in the drug mess in and around Miami? What else was new? Rich people get rich by seeing that everybody else gets dosed. Get poor people hooked on drugs or fast food or Coca-Cola – whatever makes them zombies, whatever kills them off, whatever keeps them in line.

So if I eliminated the standard, what I was left with was David Waters. Who was he, exactly?

And that question made me realize that Hachi had been trying to get me to think about David from the very first time I met her. Which meant that John Horse wanted me to find out about David. Find out about *what* I had no clue at that point. It was all a muddle.

I stood up.

'Hey,' I called out gently.

Lena shifted on the sofa. 'What?'

'I'm going out for a minute. Got to check my office – what's left of it.'

'What time is it?' she mumbled.

'Early. You slept for a while. It's dawn. You want me to bring anything back?'

'Donuts.'

'Right. I'm locking up. Don't let anyone in.'

'Yes.'

'*Anyone*, Lena.'

She rolled over and looked at me. 'OK.'

I nodded, and I was gone.

I actually did go to my office. Someone had replaced the S so that the signage read 'Child Protective Services' again, like it was supposed to. But most of the furniture was still gone. My desk was a mess. There was no chair for it.

I picked up the phone and was very surprised to hear a dial tone. I made a few calls. The big office in Miami was very sympathetic to my plight. They'd already reinstated the office. I told them about the whole mess with David Waters. They gave it an official case number. They were also giving me a hundred dollars to 'refurbish.' So that was nice.

My second call was to Escalante Insurance Agency, the group that administered David's questionable insurance policy. I laid the policy on my desk and waited for someone to answer the phone.

'Escalante,' a woman's voice said, 'how may I help you?'

'I'd like to speak to Mr Lopez,' I said.

It was the other signature on the policy beside David's.

'What is it regarding?' she asked tonelessly.

'Insurance policy for David Waters. He's dead. I'm with Child Protective Services and we're looking to collect on behalf of the beneficiary, a juvenile: Ester Greenberg Waters. Mr Lopez issued the policy.'

'Oh.' Her tone changed considerably. 'David Waters. Yes. That's quite a – Mr Lopez? Someone from the Child Projected Service is calling regarding David Waters!'

There was a click on the other end and a sudden voice.

'Hello? This is Charlie Lopez.'

'Yes, Moscowitz with Child *Protective* Services,' I said, trying to sound as official and impatient as I could. 'We represent Ester Greenberg Waters in the collection of the insurance policy you wrote for David Waters, now deceased.'

'Yes.' He shifted the phone to his other ear. 'Of course.'

'What steps need to be taken?'

He paused. 'Oh. Well, we would need the death certificate, of course, and Letters Testamentary demonstrating your power of attorney in the matter.'

'Of course. And then?'

'Well, then – I mean, we would issue – there are several options. We prefer to set up a convenience account for the beneficiary. We would administer it for a nominal fee and said beneficiary could withdraw from it whenever needed. Like a bank account.'

'Is one of the options that you just write out a check for the insured amount and hand it over to *said beneficiary*?'

Again with the hesitation.

'Well. Yes, that is possible. But we prefer—'

'I'll bring the papers to you on Tuesday,' I said like a Frigidaire. 'You'll hand over a cashier's check then. Shall we say eleven AM?'

'Now, you're with who, exactly?'

'Child Protective Services. We protect children. From people like you. If you like you can call the main office there in Miami. Just got off the phone with them. Ask about Case Number 2247J. Anything else?'

'And your name was?' he asked very deferentially.

'Moscowitz. With a Z. Tuesday at eleven.'

I hung up before he could get in another word. The advantage of a call like that was simple: it got the guy nervous. I wanted him nervous.

Getting a copy of the death certificate wouldn't be hard. Maggie Redhawk could handle that. The Letters Testamentary were more difficult. They could take weeks. I'd just have to get them forged. It was important to get the check as soon as possible. Once I had the money, I had leverage. Someone had gone to the trouble of making sure there was a million-dollar policy. If it had been David, then I'd be serving his interest. If it had been someone else, that someone would come looking for me and the money, and I'd figure out why there was a policy in the first place.

My third call was to Baxter. Time to figure out just how deep he was into the stew.

He answered right away, but he wasn't happy about it.

'What?' he barked.

'It's Foggy,' I said. 'Ramon Fidestra just tried to kill me.'

Silence.

So he did know at least a little something about what was going on.

By the time he realized that his silence had told me things, it was too late. He stammered and tried to recover, but I was wise.

'W–who?' he hiccupped.

'Yeah, nice try, but you know Fidestra.'

'I–I really don't. He tried to kill you? Where?'

'Baxter,' I moaned. 'I don't care if you take a little folding money. I just want to put David Waters behind me. And right now I got about ten different theories about the guy and about his business. So quit play-acting and let's get a donut.'

More silence.

Then: 'Right. Let's get a donut.'

The aptly named Donuts was a prominent business in the center of Fry's Bay. Always smelled like heaven and wasn't too brightly lit.

At the helm was one Cass, sixty years old, barely five feet tall, cheeks artificially red, eyes the same color naturally. Henna hair sprouted out of her hairnet every which way, and her face was clearer than any book about what her life had been like.

'Cass,' I said when I sauntered through the door.

'Foggy,' she grated, 'ain't you supposed to be at the hospital?'

I sat down in front of her at the bar. 'Naw. I'm fine. Meeting Baxter. Got a case.'

She nodded. 'I heard. Some half-breed spawn of David Waters.'

Cass was a nice enough person, but her perspectives were of the more conservative bent. If by *conservative,* you meant *racist.*

'You heard,' I said.

'I got ears,' she growled. 'I hear things.'

'What exactly did you hear?'

'It was two Indians in here last night,' she began, 'says David Waters got shot, and then his father shot you. Did you kill David?'

'No,' I began, about to explain what had happened.

But Cass went on.

'Says David had a kid. That's why you was in here the other day showing me the photograph. That was the half-breed's mother.'

'And you came to that conclusion how?' I asked.

'I got a brain connected to my ears,' she snapped. 'I can add things up.'

Cass was especially crotchety; I wondered why.

'You seem a little on edge,' I told her, 'if you don't mind my saying.'

'Everybody thinks I'm stupid!' she exploded.

Baxter chose that moment to walk into the shop.

'Cass,' he said, 'you all right?'

'Kiss my ass,' she muttered and went into the back.

'I'll want some coffee,' Baxter called out after her, 'and a cruller.'

She took off to the kitchen and Baxter sat down at the bar, leaving one stool in between us.

'What's got her riled up?' he asked me. 'You been pestering her?'

I shook my head. Something had happened to Cass to put her on edge. It could have been anything, but her ire was unusual. I wanted to ask her about it, but not with Baxter around. So I just got on with the business at hand.

'I went to the Cherry Pocket,' I began.

'Why?' he interrupted.

'Ellen Greenberg wrote letters to David Waters on stationery from the Chalet Suzanne in Lake Wales. One thing led to another.'

'And that's where you met Fidestra,' he sighed. 'At that seafood joint at the Cherry Pocket.'

I nodded. 'He kicked my ass. I was lucky to get away alive.'

'You were. He's a really mean guy. And, yes, I met him. How much of this whole mess do you know?'

'Just enough to scare me,' I admitted. 'Looks like David tried to take over some drug rights and got in between Columbians and Cubans.'

'Here's the thing,' he interrupted, 'Ironstone gives me, like, a retainer. I was supposed to keep David out of the mess.'

'How'd that work out?'

'It was fine,' he insisted, 'until Goldilocks killed him.'

'You know what was about to happen to her.' I leaned closer to him. 'You collected his syringe before you called me. And you only called me because Mary was there to look out for the kid. Otherwise she would have ended up in a cell or worse.'

He didn't look at me.

'You tampered with significant evidence, man,' I went on. 'It wasn't just Lena who saw the syringe. Other people are asking where it went to.'

That was a lie, of course, but it was in the service of the truth, so to me it was legit.

'Things have gotten out of hand,' he said at length.

Before I could respond, Cass banged through the kitchen door with a percolator and two cups.

'Here.' She set the cups on the counter. 'Made a special batch just for you two. This is the good stuff – what I drink. Maxwell House.'

She poured.

'Thanks,' I said.

'Ain't got no crullers – not fresh.' She set the coffee pot down. 'You want the lemon-filled. They just come out.'

'OK,' Baxter said.

'I think I'd like,' I began.

'I know what you want!' she interrupted. 'Why a man would come in a donut shop and eat a English muffin don't make no sense to me. But I got one toasting now.'

I sensed that Cass was somehow trying to make amends for losing her temper, but I didn't understand it.

'I also need an assortment,' I said, 'for the kid.'

She nodded. 'Now,' she announced, 'I'm going to tell you both something.'

That was all. She stopped talking. Baxter and I sat in silence. I sipped the coffee. Baxter finished his cup in three gulps.

'David Waters was not what people thought,' Cass said softly.

'He ain't no pervert, not like people says. He was a nut job. Wacky in the brain pan.'

Baxter smiled. 'Cass, everybody thought David was nuts.'

'No!' she snarled. 'I mean he had something real wrong with him. Like one day he's mean as a snake and bopping people in the head, and the next day he don't remember doing it, and sweet as a lamb. You ever see that Spencer Tracy movie *Dr Jekyll and Mr Hyde*? Like that.'

There it was: a really hefty piece of the puzzle. If Cass's pronouncement was even partially accurate, David could have been both a vicious drug lord and a loving father.

I knew a little something about split personality. My father was a kind, loving man, but he was also a heater for The Combination. He taught me to play chess and told me I was a genius; he whacked people for money and didn't give it a second thought. It was just his job. After he was gone, and I found out what he was – thanks to a newspaper article about Murder, Inc., which is what the gentile press called his business – I asked my Aunt Shayna about it. She gave me the two-bit tour around Sigmund Freud. It piqued my interest and I read more. Aside from the fact that the Oedipal Complex has more to do with Freud than with most male children, I thought he was maybe the smartest Jew who ever lived. He replaced Lenny Bruce in my estimation. The point was that I understood how David Waters might have been two people.

'Yeah, thanks, Cass,' Baxter said, completely dismissing her observation. 'I'll have that lemon-filled.'

She caught my eye and read my mind: we were going to have a talk after Baxter left. She nodded once and was gone.

'You were saying that things got out of hand?' I encouraged Baxter.

'It used to be a little harmless pot passing through town on the way to Miami,' he said.

'Yudda,' I told him, so he'd realize I was in the know. 'Skip ahead.'

'Well.' He was uncomfortable that I was wise to Yudda, but he forged on. 'It all changed when the Columbians got into the picture. And then David Waters decided he was Mr Big Stuff. And then Ironstone turned on David. And then the Tribal Council got involved. I'm telling you, legalize drugs and open stores. Put the bastards out of business and let the little man make a living.'

'Not a proponent of the War on Drugs.' I said.

'It's not a war on drugs,' he said angrily. 'It's just something a politician can say so that it looks like he's doing something to help, which he is not.'

'And then Lena waded into all that mess,' I interrupted his observation.

'I knew what David did. Everybody knew.' He shook his head. 'I have to say I was pretty happy to see him dead.'

'But the mess is still very much in evidence,' I asserted.

'Yeah.'

'And you're afraid it might fall down on you,' I went on. 'You are at least tangentially involved in international drug trafficking. Plus, the aforementioned evidence tampering in a murder investigation.'

He reared back. 'Wait. Are you threatening me?'

I set down my coffee cup and swiveled my bar stool so that I could look him straight in the eye.

'No,' I said firmly. 'I meant it when I said I didn't care about your pocket money. I'm suggesting that we work together, you and me, for the benefit of the nation.'

'The nation?'

'Too grandiose?' I nodded. 'All right then, so we can maybe clear up a little of the mess in Fry's Bay. I need to get my kid out of trouble. And I need to get David's insurance policy to pay out to his progeny. Oh, and I need to make sure Yudda's not in trouble; he makes the best seafood in Florida.'

'Anything else?' Baxter asked, eyes wide.

'I need to get some new furniture for my office,' I said, 'but maybe that can wait.'

'Yeah, what happened to your office?'

That was a good question. What *had* happened to my office? I was only in a coma for a little while, but who in their right mind would take my ratty old furniture – and did it have anything to do with the rest of the mess? It seemed so unconnected that I shuffled it back into my pocket, saved for a rainy day reflection in favor of more pressing matters.

'First things first,' I told him. 'How do we clear Lena out of the legal system and get her into some kind of foster care and away from here?'

Baxter nodded. I could hear the gears in his little brain whirring.

'Let's say, hypothetically,' he began, 'that an officer of the law, by accident, discovered a syringe full of whatever underneath the booth where David Waters was killed.'

'Why,' I responded, 'that would lead such an officer to believe that maybe Lena fired in self-defense.'

'Say.' He nodded. 'It might at that.'

'And then the officer could examine the gun used by the terrified little girl,' I went on, 'and he might discover that it was a VP70, a 9mm machine pistol with the three shot burst system and a hair trigger. *Way* too much gun for a child. She only meant to wave it around, stop him from stabbing her with the syringe.'

'But this damned gun,' he added, 'it just went off – as guns will do in the hand of a child – and fired three bullets at once. Into David Waters.'

'After which he died and good riddance,' I concluded. 'The end.'

'Of course we'll need the DA on board, and a coroner's verdict,' Baxter said, 'but I think that's it.'

Cass breezed back in, gave me my English muffin and a box of half a dozen assorted.

Then she set down a white bag in front of Baxter.

'It's three,' she said softly. 'Two lemon and one chocolate. On the house.'

Baxter stared at the bag like it might explode.

'What's the occasion?' he asked.

'The occasion is I lost my temper for a minute there,' she answered. 'Sorry.'

He didn't take his eyes off the bag.

'Cass,' he said slowly.

'Plus which,' she interrupted, 'I heard what you said just now. It's a good plan. Let that little girl go.'

'You really do hear everything, don't you?' I said to her, smiling. 'You know everything that's going on.'

She didn't smile back.

'I do,' she mumbled. 'It's a fucking curse.'

TWENTY-TWO

Baxter headed back to his office to put his simple plan into action. I'd gulped down my English muffin and started toward that conversation I was going to have with Cass but was suddenly seized by an overwhelming desire to go to Abiaka Park. Could have been that I wanted to see Hachi and just hoped she'd be there. Could have been that there was something in the back of my brain that was trying to get my attention, some bit of information that I'd overlooked or hadn't noticed on a conscious level.

I was glad I'd driven to the donut shop instead of walking, the park was a couple miles away. I hopped into the T-Bird.

The morning was shaping up nicely. The sun was out and the clouds were moving faster than freight trains. The wind was coming in from the ocean, probably meant a storm was on the way.

The park was more crowded than usual. Five people were landscaping. Hachi wasn't one of them, but John Horse was. When I saw him I got the crazy notion that he'd summoned me to the park and that's what accounted for my odd impulse to visit.

He saw me drive up and he waved from where he was sitting in front of some purple fountain grass.

I got out of the car and he stood, brushing dirt off his hands and onto his jeans. He smiled and I suddenly felt calmer. About everything.

'Hello, Foggy,' he called out.

I headed his way. 'Morning.'

'I'm glad to see you,' he went on. 'I've got a few things to tell you.'

We repaired to the same bench where I'd sat with Hachi.

'You're probably confused about David Waters,' he began. 'I was too, at first.'

'You got Hachi to plant doubts in my mind,' I said, 'right here on this bench. I'm wise to your tricks, you know.'

'Good,' he said. 'I want you to be wise. I also want you to know that David Waters had trouble with dark spirits. Doesn't matter to me if you think of them in psychological terms or mystical terms; it amounts to the same thing.'

'Well this is weird,' I admitted. 'Cass, you know, over at the donut shop, she was just more or less saying the same thing.'

'I know.' He nodded.

And there was one of his tricks: to claim that he knew something like that. There was no way to prove or disprove his assertion. It made him seem like the shaman he wanted me to believe he was. But it was also evidence that he was pretty good as a con man. Maybe it didn't matter which he was. Maybe it was like he'd said: it amounts to the same thing.

'She told you,' he continued, as if he'd read my thoughts and wanted to prove his magic, 'that he had a split personality. That he was two people. At least.'

I nodded. I didn't want to speak because I knew that if I did I would give him more ammunition for his improvisational theatrics.

'Anyway.' He shrugged. 'I'm glad that Baxter is going to do the right thing.'

Now, how did he know that? Or was that sentence just bait? Was it supposed to make me reveal something? It was a vague enough pronouncement that it really might have applied to nearly anything.

'What I want you to know,' he said after a second of hesitation, 'is that your current client, Lena, did the right thing. She had to shoot him. He wanted to die. Since he was twelve or so, he was in trouble. I don't know what happened to him, but something broke him in half, and he never healed. If I'd known about it sooner, I might have helped him. But whatever it was that damaged him, it happened while I was incarcerated.'

His voice was very soothing, almost hypnotic. I felt dizzy for a moment. Then I had the sensation that everyone around me was an actor and I was in a movie. Lena lied as a matter of course – I didn't blame her, but she wasn't the most reliable person. John Horse routinely invented himself in deliberately confusing ways. And Cass from the donut shop: she was suddenly the fabled Cassandra who my Aunt Shayna said was a relative of hers in Russia but who I later found out was a Greek myth: gifted with knowing the truth, fated never to be believed.

I think I said, 'I feel funny.'

The next thing I knew I was lying on the ground in the park with two or three strangers staring down at me. John Horse was not among them.

I tried to sit up. It didn't work.

'Where's John Horse?' I asked.

They stared. They were all Seminoles. They were pretending that they didn't speak English.

'E-ah-kal-e-mas-cheh,' one of them mumbled.

'No,' I snapped, 'I'm not *very sick.*'

'Hocktoche,' another one said. 'Is-tah-chee.'

'Little girl?' I blinked. 'Do you mean Lena?'

'Yes,' the first one said. 'John Horse went to get the little girl.'

I rubbed my eyes, trying to clear my head.

'What happened to me? Why am I on the ground?' I looked at all the strange faces.

The first one knelt down and tried to hand me a pill. I stared at it.

'Hil-lis-wa,' he said.

'No.' I looked him in the eye. 'That's not *medicine.*'

'It's from John Horse,' he said. 'You need to take it.'

'Did he do this to me?' I asked. 'Did he knock me out with his voodoo?'

No one answered.

'Sorry,' the guy with the pill said.

And then he slapped me hard on the chest. I gasped. He popped the pill into my open mouth and then put his hand over my face.

All I could do was swallow. I was too weak to fight the guy off. I couldn't even stand up. So I chocked the pill down and started coughing. Then a couple of the guys got me to my feet.

'You'll be OK now, Foggy,' one of them said.

I tried to focus on him.

'Taft?' I mumbled.

He was dressed in a flannel shirt and jeans, his black hair loose and long.

'Come on,' he continued. 'You're going to throw up now.'

He was right. I spent a half an hour doubled over, eyes closed, convinced I'd be better off if I'd just go ahead and die.

When it was over I found myself sitting on the ground with all five Seminoles around me.

'What the hell?' I managed to croak.

'What's the last thing you ate?' Taft asked me.

I sniffed. 'Ate? I don't know. I haven't eaten anything in a while. I've been busy.'

'John Horse told me you were at the donut shop,' Taft countered.

'Wait.' I blinked. 'I had an English muffin.'

'Cass.' He pronounced her name like it was the answer to a difficult riddle.

'No,' I insisted. 'Cass did *not* poison me.'

But even as I said it I remembered something that John Horse had told me once. He'd said that every drug was a poison, and vice versa. And that the things you see under their influence are like little telegrams from your unconscious. If you can read them right, you can learn a lot about yourself. And my last thought before I whacked out was about Cass. Maybe I was trying to tell myself something.

'Why would Cass poison me?' I asked no one in particular.

Taft leaned forward. 'You know something you're not supposed to know. That would be my guess. You understand that Cass was involved with David's drug activities, right?'

'Cass?' I said, my voice a little shrill.

'Oh.' He nodded. 'You don't know about Cass.'

'She–she once told me she was a big band singer with, like, Benny Goodman or something,' I began, nearly to myself. 'And she hated Peggy Lee.'

'Yeah, that's not true.' He smiled. 'She runs half the bad stuff in Fry's Bay. It's small time, compared to Ironstone, but everybody in that world knows about her. She's got two houses and a nice local coke connection.'

'Houses?'

'Prostitutes. She tried to get some Seminole girls, that's how we first found out about her. She agreed to leave our girls out of it, and we agreed to live and let live.'

'And by *we* you mean Ironstone.'

He nodded. 'And the Tribal Council. Mister Redhawk knows about her too. As long as she sticks to white people, who cares what she does?'

I squeezed my eyes shut. 'Fry's Bay is turning out to be a much different little berg than I thought it was.'

'Even a pretty little rock can hide a scorpion underneath it.'

'I guess.' I took another stab at standing up on my own. 'So John Horse went where, now?'

Taft smiled. 'He took your car. He went to make sure Lena was all right. Cass tried to take you out for a reason. And Cass probably doesn't like the fact that Lena killed her best meal ticket.'

'Yeah,' I said, 'I'm going to have to find out a lot more about all that, but at the moment I feel very anxious to see Lena. And to get my car back. I've seen John Horse drive.'

Taft turned and walked toward the back of the park. 'Let's go.'

'You have a car here?' I asked him.

He nodded.

'Then why didn't John Horse take *your* car?' I pressed, irritated.

Taft looked at me over his shoulder and kept walking. 'Are you crazy? I've seen John Horse drive.'

Five minutes later we were in front of my apartment; so was my car, unharmed. A more religious person would have offered up a prayer of thanks.

But that little moment of relief was replaced by panic when I saw my front door wide open.

I jumped out of Taft's Ford pickup and ran a lot faster than I should have in my condition.

The apartment was empty. Some of the furniture was askew.

Taft showed up behind me and stood silent. I turned to him.

'So, about Cass?' I began. 'She was David's cohort? Did she have any muscle? Could she have overheard what Baxter and I were planning and sent someone here for Lena?'

'Could have,' he admitted, 'but why?'

'Don't know,' I agreed. 'Is she really that upset about David Waters? Almost everybody in the world is glad that David's dead.'

'Sad to say about a fellow Seminole,' Taft said, 'but yes.'

'So would Cass really try to dose me with a dicey muffin?'

'Do you realize how funny you talk?' he asked.

'It's only funny in Florida,' I answered. 'And it just occurs to me that if she did that to me, maybe Baxter got some bad donuts.'

I needed time to think. My head was still musty from the poison, if that's what it was – and the throwing up. I thought if I called Baxter to see if he was all right, it might give me a minute to clear my mind.

I made it to the phone in the kitchen and dialed his number. There was no answer. I hung up. I thought maybe I'd call the hospital, check in with Maggie to see if Baxter was there. But before I could dial that number, the phone rang.

'Moscowitz,' the voice said before I could even say *hello*.

'What?' I snarled.

'This is Fidestra. We got the kid. And the old man. You tell that to your friends in the DEA. You tell them we want to make a deal about their agent.'

I held my breath. 'Right. In the first place, I have no friends in the DEA. In the second place, I have no idea what kind of deal you're talking about. And finally, if you hurt Lena I'll kill you, it's just that simple. And if you hurt John Horse, the entire Seminole nation will kill you. Frankly, you'd be better off with me. I'll just put ten or twelve bullets in your head. But the Seminoles, they'll spend a couple of months, maybe longer. There you'll be, out in the swamp . . .'

'This is John Horse?' Fidestra sounded scared for the first time since I'd met him.

I wasn't surprised. It stood to reason that this old Cuban guy had somehow heard rumors or stories about John Horse. I hadn't been in Fry's Bay for two months before I got wind of his legend.

'Man, have you messed up good,' I went on, chiding him. 'You kidnapped a little girl and a spirit man. The former gets you twenty years in prison. The latter sends you straight to hell. I wouldn't be in your shoes for a million bucks. So long.'

I made as to hang up. It was a bluff, but it worked.

'Wait!' I heard him shout into the phone.

I put the receiver back up to my ear.

'You can't be far away,' I said. 'Just tell me where you are and I'll come get you; see if I can figure you a way out of this.

Why in hell did you think that taking the kid would get you anywhere?'

'Her sister is the DEA agent!' Fidestra growled.

I smiled at first; shook my head at his ignorance, but then something really spooky invaded my brain. What if Ellen Greenberg *was* the DEA agent? No double, no tricks – she actually was working for the Feds. And her new look was a disguise. And the letters weren't intended for David or even for Lena, they were coded communications to her DEA cohorts. It would explain some things, but it would also make some things weirder. Still, I had to convince Fidestra that he was wrong just to keep Lena safe.

'I don't mean to insult you,' I said to Fidestra, 'but you're a chump. The DEA agent was a substitute, a look-alike, a plant from the Feds after Ellen got next to David Waters.'

Silence reigned on his end.

I used those moments of golden repose to ask myself questions: where Fidestra might be, who had told him that Ellen was the DEA agent, what had made him snap enough to kidnap a kid?

'Listen,' he began, and I could actually hear him sweat. 'These Columbians, they're crazy. They don't care who they kill.'

'Meaning they're about finished with you,' I concluded. 'You want out. Or at least you want me to think that. But you realize that you suckered me twice before, and I'm not exactly disposed to believe you.'

'Well, you should believe that I'll kill the little girl and John Horse.'

'I believe that you're that stupid, yes. But it doesn't make any sense objectively. You kill them and then what?'

Again, silence.

'Here's an idea,' I said at length. 'You come on back to my place, I'll get in touch with the local law. You become an informant and get into the Witness Protection Program.'

'The *what*?'

'It's a new thing. You tell the Feds everything you know about the Colombian operation, and they hide you in, like, Oklahoma.'

'I don't want to go to Oklahoma.'

'Not the point.'

'No.' He was getting crazier; I could tell by the tone of his voice. 'If I find the DEA agent and kill her, the Columbians will back off.'

'No. They'll say thanks right before they fill you up with bullets. If they get to you before I do. If I get there first, I'll be the one with the lead.'

I was trying to sound as tough as the guys I knew back in Brooklyn. They could sling around a line of intimidation that could worry J. Edgar Hoover. I figured if I put up a tough enough front, he wouldn't hear how desperate I really was.

'Anyway,' I went on when he didn't respond, 'I already know where you are. Our Seminole friends are there now. That little scraping sound you heard a second ago, that was Holata. *Holata* means *Alligator*. He's coming for you.'

All bluff and no content. But my thinking was that every little sound might be amplified by fear. And Fidestra was afraid.

'You–you don't know where I am,' he stammered.

'Right,' I said confidently. 'Then what's that sound outside your door?'

Suddenly, like a shot of starlight, I heard Lena's voice in the background.

'He knows you're in the abandoned bakery, dumb ass,' she said.

Nice work, kid, I thought.

'Shut up!' Fidestra shouted. 'How could he know that?'

Very faintly I heard John Horse say, 'My tribe is helping him. They always know where I am.'

Good. That was playing right into my tactic: create enough paranoia in Fidestra to make him even stupider than he already was at that point.

'Buscar fuera de la ventana!' he shouted.

I laughed. 'You won't see them outside your window,' I told him. 'They're invisible.'

I glanced at Taft and put my hand over the phone.

'They're at the abandoned bakery around the corner from the donut shop,' I whispered.

He took off without a word.

'Listen,' I continued with Fidestra, 'your only play is to do what I said: work with the Feds. But you've got, like, five minutes before your entire situation goes all the way south.'

Fidestra was desperate, anyone could hear that in his voice. His brain had caught fire and driven him a little insane, enough so that he had raced to Fry's Bay to kidnap Lena in the hope of finding Ellen Greenberg, who may or may not have anything to do with anything.

Of course the coincidence of that action and my poisoning was too much to ignore. So I continued.

'And you know that Cass almost killed me,' I said evenly. 'If she had, you'd be completely screwed now. No way out. So if I were you, I'd back away from Cass.'

Again: all guesswork. Maybe this wasn't Cass's doing at all. But it was worth a shot. If I was wrong, he'd just be confused for a minute, which was to my advantage. And if I was right, he'd start thinking that I knew everything, which would really get me somewhere.

'She didn't try to kill you,' he said. 'She was just trying to take you out of the picture long enough for me to get the girl. You were supposed to be unconscious on the floor of your apartment by now.'

Of course that might have happened if I'd gone right home with the donuts for the kid instead of to the park. I'd be conked out, he'd bust into my place, grab Lena, and have her spirited away to God knows where. But John Horse somehow knew what was what and went in Lone Ranger style. It didn't keep Lena from getting nabbed, but it did slow down Fidestra.

And then I remembered Baxter's lemon-filled bombs.

'All right,' I said to Fidestra, 'you have the upper hand. I don't want anything to happen to the kid, or to John Horse. I'll tell you what I'm willing to do.'

And then I hung up. I thought that would scare him. But I also had to call Baxter, and I had to get to the bakery building.

I dialed the police. A bored voice answered.

'Fry's Bay Police—'

'Get Baxter now!' I barked. 'Someone's trying to poison him!'

'Who is this?'

'Can you see Baxter?' I shouted.

'He's right here,' the irritated voice answered.

A second later Baxter was on the phone.

'Who is this?'

'Foggy. Don't eat the donuts.'

'Foggy?'

'Did you eat the donuts that Cass gave you?'

'What?' He was really confused. 'Not yet. I was trying to take care of the business we discussed—'

'Cass tried to poison me,' I interrupted again, 'and she's probably done the same thing to your donuts that she did to my muffin.'

'Are you drunk?'

'And now we have to go over to the abandoned bakery around the corner from the donut shop because one of the guys involved with the Columbian Black Tuna bunch, he got Lena. He's there in the building. He also took John Horse.'

'What–what are you talking about?'

'Do you want to get out from under all this or not?' I shouted into the phone. 'If you do, you'll meet me at the bakery building five minutes ago!'

I slammed the phone down and charged out the door.

Thank God John Horse had left the keys in the ignition of the Thunderbird. I fired it up and made it to 70 mph before I came to the first intersection.

TWENTY-THREE

The alley behind the bakery building was dark even in the daytime. I still had Holata's gun, and I'd reloaded it, but I really didn't want to start shooting up the place with Lena and John Horse in the line of fire. I thought my best plan would be to talk.

So as I neared the creaky metal door that opened into the abandoned bakery, I called out, 'Fidestra, it's Foggy.'

Maybe I should have waited to see if Baxter was going to show up, but I really wanted to know that Lena was all right.

'If you have a gun,' Fidestra answered me, 'I'll start shooting the second you walk in.'

The gun was in my pocket, but why bother the guy with details?

'Nothing in my hands,' I assured him.

I peeked around the edge of the entrance. Nobody in sight. I stepped in – because idiots go where angels fear to tread.

The place was all shadows and patterns of light. It was a giant open space, and the industrial-sized bread making equipment was still in evidence, although it was significantly worse for wear. Dust motes ruled the air; rats had control of the floor. Pigeons had roosted in the high rafters, and their guttural murmuring was an oddly calming soundtrack to the otherwise horror-movie ambiance.

I stood in a slanted beam of light so that Fidestra could see me, see that I didn't have a gun in my hand.

'Fidestra,' I said in a normal tone of voice, 'I need to see that the kid's all right.'

'I'm OK,' Lena sang out, but her voice was a little mournful.

'What's wrong?' I asked.

'Shut up!' Fidestra shouted.

'I'm embarrassed,' she went on, ignoring the Cuban maniac with the gun. 'I let this guy nab me.'

'John Horse?' I called.

'I'm here,' he answered very calmly. 'This is a really interesting situation. I'm enjoying myself.'

'Good.' I took a few steps. 'Fidestra? Quit messing around and let's talk. Quick. I think the cops are on the way.'

'Cops?'

'That's probably my fault,' John Horse lied. 'I called them before I came barging into Foggy's apartment. I was afraid I wouldn't get there in time. Which I didn't. Sorry.'

'Everything happens to me!' Fidestra shouted. 'Everybody wants to kill me! I'm not that kind of person. I like to go fishing.'

What that had to do with things was a little vague, but I understood his gist. Nobody thinks he's the bad guy. Hitler didn't think, 'I know, I'll do things that will make my name synonymous with all things evil.' He probably thought he was doing what he needed to do to make his life better. Still. He was Hitler, so.

'Come on out,' I encouraged Fidestra. 'Let's figure this out.'

Suddenly there he was, in the corner of an angle of shadows, gun in hand, sweating like it was a hundred degrees.

'I was just explaining to Lena a while back,' I began, as if we were just continuing a conversation we'd already started, 'that the Witness Protection Program is a part of the Organized Crime Control Act. If you help out with the DEA investigation, you can be relocated, hidden by the federal government.'

'Relocated where?' he wanted to know.

'Don't know exactly,' I assured him, 'but it won't be the graveyard, which is where you're headed now.'

He measured those words, trying to size things up.

'No, but, why don't I just kill the DEA agent like I said?' he asked me at length. 'Get the Columbians off my back.'

'Because you're not a dumbass,' I said simply. 'I could tell at the Cherry Pocket that you were at the end of your rope. Who drinks all day in a crummy little place like that and then goes home to watch *Columbo* and fall asleep? A man in misery, that's who.'

He sighed. 'All my old friends are dead.'

'You said,' I answered him. 'So I'm giving you a second – or is it *third* – chance to do the right thing. Help us out. Let the kid and John Horse go, and let's talk to the DEA. It's your best play.'

He lowered his gun. 'Yeah. I guess.'

He inclined his head, and Lena and John Horse came into the light. John Horse was grinning like the village idiot. Lena just looked mad.

I headed their way.

'This is all going to work out,' I said, partly to myself. 'We're going to contact the DEA, they're going to tell us where Ellen Greenberg is, you get a new life; everybody lives happily ever after.'

That exact second a shot rang out. Fidestra went down. I ducked, trying to figure where the shooter was. Lena dove toward Fidestra, got his gun, rolled and came up behind one of the machines. John Horse didn't move or stop smiling.

'Foggy?' a voice called out.

'Baxter?' I answered. 'What the hell are you doing?'

'Doing?' he snapped. 'I'm saving your ass. I shot the man with the gun.'

'No, damn it.' I rushed to Fidestra.

He was lying on the floor with his eyes open, staring up at the high ceiling.

'Pigeons,' he said.

An ambulance came. Other policemen came. And then Ironstone Waters came, along with Crew Cut.

Fidestra probably wasn't going to live. Baxter had shot him in the heart.

Baxter sidled up to me after a while.

'Two of my guys ate those donuts you were afraid of, by the way,' he said. 'They're fine. What was that all about, with Cass?'

He looked at me like I was two kinds of stupid. Then he shook his head and walked away.

Of course Cass hadn't given Baxter anything wrong. Because they were on the same side. I felt a little stupid for telling him about the poison thing in the first place. So I wasn't about to say anything more to Baxter.

Something was way off. It wasn't a coincidence that he shot Fidestra right when we were on the verge of a deal to make things better. And he'd called Ironstone. And Cass hadn't dosed his donuts.

Unfortunately, that only made my paranoia itch in a different place. It was a little insane of me to think that Cass had tried to poison me. It was more likely that the butter she'd smeared on the English muffin was bad or some other God-awful germ was loose in the kitchen. Even if Cass was in league with David Waters, it was very hard to see her as a drug baroness and a small-town Borgia.

In the middle of such reverie, John Horse was suddenly beside me.

'Are we about finished here?' he asked.

I turned to look at him. 'I'm confused.'

He nodded. 'I understand. Let's go.'

'Go where?' I asked him.

He leaned close to me and whispered, 'Don't you think it's time for Lena to see her sister?'

My head snapped back. 'What?'

He shrugged. 'I thought we might go over to Mister Redhawk's digs, pay him a visit.'

That was all. But it was enough.

'Hey, Baxter?' I called out. 'The kid's had a rough day. Can I take her home now?'

He was standing close to the place where Fidestra went down, talking with Ironstone, and looked my way. Ironstone said something and then Baxter answered me.

'Sure. Just back to your place, though, right? No more trips. And come by my office after you drop her off. I got paperwork, you know.'

'I might get her something to eat first,' I said.

Lena heard. She had been standing alone, absenting herself from the hubbub. She wandered over.

'Where are we going?' she asked. 'I'm not really hungry.'

'John Horse thinks we ought to pay another visit to Mister Redhawk.' I looked her right in the eyes. 'It's about Ellen.'

She stared. She started to speak, but then she read my mind and stayed quiet instead.

We were in my car two minutes later, headed toward the fancy townhouse where Redhawk made his urban nest. It was the same seating arrangement as when we'd gone to see Ironstone, Lena in the other seat and John Horse contorted like a pretzel behind us.

'It's been a strange day,' he said, laughing.

'Tell the truth,' I concurred, 'I've felt strange since I came out of my coma.'

'Some people have hallucinations after they wake up from a long sleep like that,' John Horse said softly.

'What?' Lena asked, turning his way.

'Hallucinations,' he repeated. 'It's possible that Foggy has seen some things that weren't really there.'

'Because of the coma?' she asked.

'Because of the world,' I lamented. 'Maybe I'm a little off my game, but you have to admit that this entire situation has been discombobulating.'

'*Discombobulating?*' She stared at the side of my face as I drove. 'This is the word you want to use?'

'It's a perfectly good word,' I insisted.

John Horse laughed.

Moments later the three of us were in the elevator going up to Mister Redhawk's palatial penthouse.

'Are you going to tell me what this is about?' Lena whispered.

'I don't know what this is about,' I answered her. 'It was John Horse's idea.'

She turned to him. 'I would like for you to know that I don't think of you as a real person, exactly. I think of you more the way I thought about the characters I worked with at Disney's place – the fictional characters.'

He smiled. 'That's a great compliment.'

The elevator doors opened.

Mister Redhawk was standing right there. He'd known we were coming.

'John Horse,' he said.

'Is everything ready?' John Horse asked.

Redhawk nodded.

'Let's go, then,' John Horse said.

We all headed for his living room. There were three other Seminole men seated on the sofa. I figured them for tribal elders. One was in the typical blue jean jacket and flannel shirt; the other two were in business suits – expensive business suits.

John Horse sat down on the hearth, very close to the fire blazing in it.

Lena and I hung back. I wasn't certain what to do, and she was following my lead.

'It's time,' John Horse said.

All the Seminoles nodded.

John Horse looked at me.

'Ironstone Waters has been a problem for a long time,' he began. 'Come on in and sit down and let's talk about him.'

I took one of the overstuffed armchairs, Lena took the other one. Redhawk remained standing.

'Ironstone was always a wayward person,' John Horse went on. 'He built up his businesses without regard for the council and he took advantage of some of our young men. He indulged his broken child, David, and that became a problem too.'

'We let it go on too long,' Redhawk said plainly.

John Horse smiled. 'And then Lena came. I don't say that it was right for her to kill David, but killing him woke us up.'

'All right, first,' I interrupted, 'Lena didn't kill anybody. Lena's *gun* killed him. It's a special kind of weapon—'

'Relax, Foggy,' John Horse said, smiling. 'What I'm saying is that we're grateful to her for making our path clear. It's now inevitable that we will deal with Ironstone. Something we should have done years ago.'

'And I suppose you know that Ironstone has policemen on his payroll,' I said.

'Baxter,' Redhawk answered. 'And Porter, the other detective. He's in Miami right now. He's paying a visit to an insurance company there.'

'That wouldn't be the Escalante Insurance Agency, would it?' I asked, but I already knew the answer.

'I'm taking care of it,' Redhawk said.

I had no idea what that meant, but his voice was weirdly reassuring.

'Look,' Lena exploded, 'I've had a very difficult couple of days, including being kidnapped and witnessing a murder! I was promised that someone had news about my sister. So start talking!'

From the dark recesses of a room somewhere else in the house came a woman's voice.

'Quiet out there,' she said sweetly. 'I'm trying to put Ester to sleep.'

Lena shot out of her chair and screamed, 'Ellen?'

And suddenly there she was, the girl from the photo and *not* the girl from the photo: Ellen Greenberg, red hair, still carrying baby weight, but clearly kin to Lena.

Lena flew across the room and landed so hard in Ellen's arms that they both almost fell down. They were both crying and talking and laughing all at the same time, completely incoherent.

I was up too, staring at Redhawk. 'You had her here all this time?'

He was offended. 'No. I just found her.'

'Where?' I demanded.

'You were on the right path,' he answered me. 'We would never have found her if it hadn't been for you and the girl. Ellen was in Lake Wales.'

'You found her in Lake Wales?' I shook my head. 'I'm not sure that I believe that.'

'She disappeared from Fry's Bay about six months ago,' he said, as if it were an answer to my disbelief. 'She stayed at the Three Tee Pees for a while, then she moved to the Saddlebag Lake Resort. That's where we found her.'

'*What* resort, now?'

'It's new – two brothers bought up a bunch of land a couple of years ago so they could go fishing at the lake. Sold campsites. Ellen was hiding out there.'

I started to say about ten things, then turned to Ellen and Lena.

'So, Ellen,' I began, somewhat foolishly, 'you look different from your picture.'

'You dyed your hair,' Lena said softly.

'I also have some of the heft that Ester gave me,' Ellen said. 'Pregnancy makes you large, apparently. And I'd already put on a couple of dozen pounds since I left home.'

'Yeah,' I said, 'I need your story, Ellen Greenberg. We can talk about weight gain later. How about if you tell me and your sister where the hell you've been.'

'And what the hell's going on,' Lena added.

'Right,' Ellen said. 'Right. Let's sit down. It's really quite a story. May take some time.'

'No,' I complained, 'I'm not patient enough for your version of *War and Peace,* and I don't want the abbreviated story that Mister

Redhawk is trying to hand out. So let me tell *you* what happened, what I've figured out, and you can correct me if I go wrong.'

Lena stood back from her sister. 'I'm with Foggy. We've been through a lot, and I really need to get to a few punch lines.'

So I started.

'You blew into Fry's Bay about a year ago,' I began, directly to Ellen. 'You ran afoul of David Waters. He gave you a shot, gave you a boink, and, in the end, gave you a baby. Right so far?'

Ellen looked at Lena. 'Who is this?'

'Foggy Moscowitz,' Lena said. 'The Jewish Lone Ranger. From Brooklyn. Let him have his say, and I'll bet you he's ninety-eight percent right.'

'Well,' Ellen said, 'he's right so far.'

'I'm with Child Protective Services,' I assured Ellen. 'I've been watching out for your wayward sister.'

'Oh,' Ellen said. 'Well, somebody certainly needs to do that, apparently.'

'Not really,' Lena objected.

'To continue,' I interjected, 'You were in a daze for a while, part drug-induced, part devil-may-care attitude as described by Mister Redhawk. The hippie world is over, by the way. But I digress. Since you're Lena's sister, my guess is you have brains, so one morning you realized what was going on. You were in a world that was very wrong, you were pregnant, and things were about to get worse. I'm also guessing this is around the time that David began throwing his imaginary weight around and thinking he could take over the drug world from the Columbians.'

Ellen nodded her head. 'I have no idea how you know all this, but you're right. I took a break from David for a week or so, found out I was knocked up, kind of sobered up, and ultimately realized what had happened to me. David Waters got me into a drug thing that I couldn't get out of. *And* I was pregnant. I was scared. *Then* I got mad.'

'*Then* you went to the cops,' I surmised, 'but you're smart enough to realize, after you talked to them, that they weren't really going to help you.'

'Wrong.' She smiled. 'I went to the hospital. And because there's a special providence that watches over idiots, I was lucky enough to meet Maggie Redhawk. She got me straight.'

'Wait.' I turned to Redhawk. 'You said you didn't trust any governmental agency, but Maggie is a different story. Wait.'

I rubbed my forehead.

'What is it, Foggy?' Lena asked.

'Go on,' Ellen said, 'you're putting all of this together pretty well.'

'I've had all the pieces,' I said a little vaguely. 'I just now started putting them together a little. Maggie was mad about what David did to you.'

'*I* was mad about what David did to me,' Ellen said.

'You both decided to get even,' I went on. 'Maggie got in touch with the DEA. She put them onto you.'

Ellen looked at Lena again. 'He's really good at this.'

'He hasn't even started yet,' Lena assured her sister.

'They recruited you,' I said. 'The DEA convinced you to keep on with David, get all the information that you could. You became a DEA agent.'

'And it was working,' she said, 'until David got even more crazed and decided he could take over the world. We got a visit from a really bad Cuban named Fidestra.'

'We've met him,' Lena interrupted.

'David got his back up,' Ellen continued. 'I got scared because Fidestra – I don't know, I just had the intuition that he knew about the DEA.'

'So you took off,' I guessed. 'Went to the Three Tee Pees camp, then later to this Saddlebag place. How Redhawk found you there is still a mystery.'

'I told you,' Redhawk interjected. 'I followed your lead. But, as it happens, there's a Seminole busboy at the Cherry Pocket restaurant.'

That explained it. 'Ellen got next to him. Maybe even got him to mail her so-called love letters to David.'

'The Feds were already intercepting all of David's mail,' Ellen said. 'I knew they'd see the letters. I sent them as, like, a message in a bottle. I thought they'd come and get me. Only it turned out they were too stupid to figure out where I was.'

'But not me and Foggy,' Lena pipped up.

Ellen smiled just like a big sister. 'Yeah. You and Foggy.'

'And you've been hiding out all this time with a baby,' Lena said softly.

'I was really scared.' Ellen looked into the fire that was popping in the stone hearth. 'I think David would have killed me. But now that it's all coming down, I'll get him. He'll be sorry he ever messed with me, that son of a bitch.'

She didn't know. I looked at Lena. She nodded.

'Well,' Lena began slowly, 'that's kind of taken care of.'

Ellen looked back and forth between Lena and me. 'What do you mean?'

Lena steeled herself and said, 'I killed David. He's dead.'

'Just to be clear,' I interrupted, 'let me reiterate as I have several times before: the *gun* killed David. He could probably have survived one bullet. But the gun Lena had fires three at once. That's a lot tougher to come back from: three bullets in the chest.'

Ellen turned to Lena, wide-eyed. 'You had Mom's Heckler and Koch VP70?'

Lena nodded sheepishly.

'This is a family that knows its ordinance,' I whispered to John Horse, aside-style.

'David's dead?' Ellen went on, talking over me.

Lena nodded again.

'But,' Ellen began, and then her shoulders sagged. A great moaning sigh came out of her like some demon, long possessing her, had finally been forced out of her body.

'David's dead.'

Ellen began to cry. Lena, confused by all the emotion spilling around the room, joined her. The two sisters held onto each other.

'Ester's safe,' Ellen sobbed.

'We all are,' Lena assured her.

I let a little silence clarify the air before I spoke again.

'Ester's more than safe,' I said. 'She's also rich.'

Lena sniffed. 'Oh. Yeah. The insurance policy.'

'Which is a great puzzle now,' I said to no one in particular. 'David didn't give a damn about his baby or the baby's mother. Am I wrong?'

From the darker part of the sofa came the voice of John Horse, crisp and slow.

'Well, that's probably something I can explain,' he intoned. 'That insurance policy was taken out by a person pretending to be David's lawyer. She had all the necessary papers, this lawyer, and, at my instruction, took out the policy without David's knowledge.'

I was at a loss. 'What? And why?'

'First let me tell you the lawyer's name,' he said, grinning his most irritating grin. 'It's Hachi Tiger, a woman of the Snake clan.'

'Hachi?' I shook my head. 'She pretended to be a lawyer?'

'Oh, no,' he said at once. 'She's really a lawyer. Went to Duke. Works for her aunt, Betty Mae Jumper. Who was born Betty Mae Tiger.'

'Hachi is a lawyer and she's related to the only woman who's ever been on the Seminole council.' I blinked. 'And she – what exactly happened here?'

'When I found out about Ellen's baby, it was important to me that we take care of the child. I set the insurance plan in motion. I was going to take Ellen to a safe hiding place, but she disappeared. And then a little later, of course, David was killed. This has been a very confusing time.'

'So the insurance policy's not legal,' I objected.

'Oh, no, it's quite binding,' John Horse told me. 'Set up through the council. Very legal. Using David's ill-gotten money, of course.'

'Of course,' I answered.

'Mr Redhawk explained some of this to me when he found me at Saddlebag,' Ellen sniffed. 'I don't want David's money. I told him.'

'The thing is,' John Horse said, 'David needs to make restitution to you for what he did. And he needs to take care of his child. If he were alive, I would insist. Since he's dead, and it's already taken care of, you should take the money.'

Ellen looked confused.

'So, we're done,' Lena said. 'We're finished, right, Foggy?'

'If this insurance thing checks out, and everything else is level,' I said slowly, '*and* the Feds make good on their Witness Protection scheme, I'd say you're not just finished, you're sitting pretty. All three of you.'

Lena turned to Ellen. 'Can I see her? Can I see my niece?'

Ellen nodded, took Lena's hand and they went into some other room.

I nodded. 'It's not really finished, is it?' I asked John Horse.

'Not really.' He wouldn't look at me.

'You want to take down Ironstone Waters,' I said, looking between him and Mister Redhawk. 'That's not going to be easy.'

'You don't have to be involved,' John Horse said softly.

'Well,' I sighed, 'he *did* shoot me.'

'And Lena and Ellen won't ever be safe as long as he's left to his own devices,' John Horse said in a very convincing manner.

'I guess we have to get in touch with the Feds,' I mumbled, trying to sort it all out in my brain, 'to make sure Lena and her sister and the baby are all taken care of in this Witness Protection deal. I'm not quite certain how I should go about that.'

'We could talk to their primary agent on the case,' Mister Redhawk said. 'You've met him.'

'I have?'

'Seminole,' John Horse said. 'Cut his hair off. Posing as Ironstone's bodyguard.'

My head jutted forward. 'Crew Cut is a *Fed?*'

John Horse laughed. 'His name is Jim Cypress.'

'He's an inside man?' I couldn't believe it.

'It's a long story,' John Horse said. 'And wouldn't you rather make the world safe for Lena and her family and *then* ask questions?'

'By screwing with Ironstone Waters?' I asked. 'Absolutely.'

'Good.' John Horse stood up. 'What's your plan?'

'*My* plan?'

Mister Redhawk stepped forward. 'I've done my part. I don't want to have anything to do with whatever else happens. I don't want to be an accessory. So if you don't mind, plan your mayhem outside of this building. I'll make sure that my guests are well cared for.'

John Horse smiled and headed for the elevator. 'He's right. Let's go.'

I was a little reluctant, but I knew that Lena and her kin would be safe in Redhawk's care. And they were having family time. Best to let that be.

TWENTY-FOUR

We were out in the parking lot and almost to my car before we spoke again. The day was shaping up nicely, high clouds still blowing in from the sea, but the good kind of ocean smell, the one that reminds you of summer and suntan oil.

Unfortunately, my mind was distracted by our much more autumnal situation: dark skies and rain in the forecast.

'I want you to know that I've already thought up and discarded two plans to take down Ironstone,' I said as I opened the car door to my T-Bird. 'One involved a guy in Lake Wales named Tony. The other one involved Yudda. The problem with both those plans is that I like those guys and I wouldn't want to see them in the middle of this mess.'

John Horse climbed into the passenger seat.

'So where does that leave us?'

'I'm trying to think.' I cranked the car. 'A couple of things don't add up, to me, not the least of which is why Ironstone would go to a lot of trouble to nab Lena and then not really do anything with her; just let her go.'

'Yes,' he agreed, 'I wonder about that.'

I steered the car toward the police station.

'Baxter said to come by his office,' I muttered. 'That's a part of my third plan. The one where a cop is in league with the Seminole businessman who is, in turn, a part of a very large drug concern.'

'And you don't mind seeing Baxter get in the middle of the mess,' John Horse said.

'He's already in the middle of it; that's my point. He told me. But I think maybe he's looking for a way out.'

'That's where your third plan comes in,' he surmised. 'You want to give him a way out that includes bringing down Ironstone.'

'Yes,' I acknowledged, 'but it also involves you.'

'Me?' He smiled.

'I need your help with someone. Betty Mae Jumper to be specific.'

'Oh.' He nodded and stared for a minute.

'Hachi said something about David having molested one of Mrs Jumper's little girls, right?'

'Teresa,' he said softly. 'Not her daughter, her niece.'

'Nevertheless,' I went on, 'Mrs Jumper would be happy to see some sort of retribution, right?'

He nodded once.

'And it was clear to me that Ironstone didn't care for Mrs Jumper. He's a woman-hater, that's clear. Hard to believe in this modern day of *Ms.* Magazine and NOW, but that's who he is.'

'You always surprise me,' John Horse said. 'Would not have taken you for a feminist.'

'Are you kidding me?' I shook my head. 'I was raised by two women, either one of whom could kick Ironstone's ass all the way to Pittsburgh and have fun doing it. In fact, if my plan doesn't work out, I'll just call my Aunt Shayna. Then he'd *really* be in trouble.'

'Right,' he interjected, 'so what do you want me to say to Betty Mae?'

'The truth. Tell her that Ironstone knew what David was doing with little girls and didn't care. Even aided and abetted.'

'You think?' he asked.

'By knowing about a crime and not turning him in,' I assured him, 'he became an accessory after the fact, someone who had knowledge that a person committed a felony who also helped that person avoid arrest or punishment. Believe me, everybody in my neighborhood where I grew up was aware of the intricacies of that particular legal gestalt.'

'I believe you. But how does this help us, exactly?'

'Mrs Jumper puts the weight of the Tribal Council behind her request that Ironstone be arrested. We have all kinds of witnesses as to David's behavior, and I personally have knowledge that Ironstone knew all about it, found it disgusting, but didn't do a thing about it. See?'

'So when Baxter arrests Ironstone for this accessory after the fact charge,' he said slowly, 'he gets to say that he's bowing to the pressure from our council.'

'Which, in Fry's Bay, is no small statement. And then, with Ironstone under investigation for that, we coordinate with the DEA, and the walls come tumbling down.'

'I don't know,' he began.

'Hasn't it occurred to you that Ellen Greenberg knows a whole lot about the Waters family and their nefarious activities? Inside information? If she was clever enough to send coded letters that she thought the DEA would intercept and interpret, she probably has some very convincing proof about everything that's going down between Waters and the Columbians.'

'Yes, but that's really all we need, isn't it?' he said. 'Let the Feds handle this. Let Ellen turn over her information, testify, take care of the whole thing.'

'I would agree with that if the DEA had been able to decode Ellen's letters and help her out when she needed them most,' I grumbled. 'But apparently they aren't so bright. And who knows who else Ironstone has on his payroll. You say that Crew Cut is a Fed, but you'll excuse me if I'm cautious. Because, you know, Baxter's a *cop*, and he's on Ironstone's side. So much so that he's killed this guy Fidestra who I was about to convince to turn State's evidence.'

We were nearing the police station.

'Let me out here,' John Horse said abruptly.

I slowed the car. He opened the door.

'I'm going to make some calls,' he said. 'Betty Mae can call the mayor, a couple of the big guys in town, as well as the council. I'll make sure that they get moving this morning. Right away.'

He got out of the car and headed down the sidewalk in the direction of the ocean.

'Where are you going to use the phone?' I asked.

'Yudda's,' he said without looking back. 'I want a fish sandwich.'

That was that. I continued down the street to the police station. Then, out of nowhere, thunder.

I parked the car and got out, looked out toward the sea. Sure enough, way in the distance there were black clouds, and lightning was zigzagging the waves. I tried not to take it for a sign.

Instead, I put on a smile and motored through the front door of the police station. It was an exhausted place: too small, too much desperation in the stale air. Cigarette smoke and burnt coffee assaulted the nostrils. Florescent lights hurt my eyes; the sloppy demeanor hurt my feelings. Everything about the place, in fact, conspired to be depressing. But I felt the same way about every police station I'd ever been in.

There was Baxter behind his chaos of a desk, glaring at his Royal typewriter.

'You should go electric,' I said as I approached his havoc. 'IBM makes a very nice—'

'Shut up,' he said without looking at me, 'and sit down.'

I did both.

'Now this Fidestra character,' he began.

'No,' I interrupted. 'That's my opener: why did you kill the guy when I was just about to make a deal? And why did you call Ironstone? And how's our little gambit regarding Lena coming along? Have you added the syringe to the David Waters crime scene? See I keep asking questions without giving you time to answer because I know you don't have answers. Not for me. Because as I put two and two together, it adds up in your favor, doesn't it?'

The barrage-of-questions technique was one that Brooklyn cops had used on me a lot when I was younger. I got pretty good at ignoring it eventually, but the first couple of times it was used on me, I was very disconcerted. I was hoping the same might be said of Baxter.

He stopped what he was doing. He looked up. I didn't like the expression on his face.

'The thing is,' he said, barely above a whisper, 'the money's just too good.'

Which was a complete answer to all my questions: he wasn't ever going to be on my side. He was always going to play for cash, for Ironstone's cash in this case. And the fact that he wasn't even bothering to protest or hide was a real danger sign.

'It could be good for you too, Foggy,' he went on, even softer.

I chewed on my lower lip for a second before a couple of things came clear.

'I didn't really order an English muffin,' I said.

He blinked, momentarily confused by the non sequitur.

'Cass suggested it,' I said, staring him right in the eye. 'After I called you and said to meet at the donut shop, you called her, and she fixed up the mickey.'

He didn't say anything. He didn't have to.

'Cass is working with you,' I told him, 'for Ironstone. Of course your donuts were all right. All of your gab about helping with Lena, that was just an act. The only one you're really helping is yourself.'

'And I say it again,' he answered, 'it could be good for you too.'

'No, it couldn't,' I demurred. 'I don't really care about money all that much. I used to care about the kick. Now all I care about is atonement. I never really thought much about the pay. That's what gives me my devil-may-care attitude.'

I leaned forward and smiled to demonstrate the attitude.

Baxter leaned back in his chair. 'Well. I'm sorry, then. Sorry about the kid.'

At first I thought he meant that he was going to go ahead with criminal proceedings, charge Lena with murder. But a moment's meditation made me come to the conclusion that he wasn't so stupid. He was just going to get rid of Lena. And her sister.

I stood up. A small line of sweat turned my hairline. I had a flinty taste in my mouth.

'You've been tracking Lena this whole time,' I concluded. 'You were hoping she'd lead you to Ellen. And I helped her do that.'

'Yeah,' he laughed. 'Pretty neat, huh? Once we figured that Lena really was Ellen's sister and that Lena killed David on account of what he'd done to her, it was easy enough to let you do the leg work. That's your fault, really: you're too good at your job. I was positive you'd find Ellen. I told Ironstone to give you a long leash, and with a little help from the redskins, you came through. We would never have thought to look in Lake Wales and certainly not the Cherry Pocket. But once you were there, and Fidestra tipped us, the rest was just a kind of wait-and-see proposition.'

That flinty taste in my mouth turned out to be panic.

'You've had someone following me everywhere,' I managed to say.

'Even when you went to Redhawk's place just now,' he answered. 'Yes. Ironstone's probably there right now. We have Ellen, and all, as they say, is right with the world.'

If I'd been the kind of guy who prayed, I would have laid one down for Crew Cut, hoping that he was there with Ironstone and that he was really an honest Fed, watching out for the sisters.

I backed away from Baxter. He shook his head.

'It's too late, Foggy.'

'Ellen is a lot more than just a witness to all the stuff that the Waters family's done,' I finally realized. 'She has some sort of proof. Documentation. Something that could really bring down the whole operation.'

He just shook his head. 'Don't go back over to Redhawk's, Foggy. I actually like you. I wouldn't want to come to your funeral.'

'You wouldn't be invited,' I told him.

And then I ran.

TWENTY-FIVE

Everything was a blur: getting out of the station, into my car, back to Redhawk's. The next thing I knew I was parking in front of the building. I really didn't care for what I saw. The lobby lights were off. The day outside was very bright, and the relative black inside the building made it hard to see through the big glass windows.

Against my muscle instinct, I took it slow. I felt for the pistol in my suit coat pocket as I got out of my car, checked to make sure the gun was loaded, and eased open the front entrance to the building.

Right away I could see that somebody had dumped a load of laundry on the floor. Once my eyes adjusted to the lower light, I could see that the pile was Crew Cut, face down in a pool of blood, absolutely dead. I checked all my questions about what had happened to him for later reference. There were more pressing matters.

The elevator up to the penthouse was whirring. I looked around and found the stairs. Then I let my muscles have their way, and I flew up the stairs, working to beat the elevator up to the top floor. I made it to the stairway door just as the elevator doors were closing. I saw Ironstone's back. I also saw the Stoner 63 machine gun in his right hand. I didn't care for the gun myself, but some of the guys who went to Vietnam liked it, a few SEALS, some Marines. I couldn't help wondering where Ironstone had gotten it.

Didn't matter, of course, all I had to do was shoot him in the back before he could use it.

Unfortunately, the stairway door scraped behind me and he twirled around, spraying bullets. I barely had time to dive to the floor.

The next thing I knew there was more gunfire from inside Redhawk's living room. Ironstone hadn't come alone.

I rolled, fired the pistol, rolled again.

When I was able to glance over at Ironstone, I could see that I hadn't hit him, but at least I'd made him nervous. He was tucked behind one of the fancy art deco pillars that separated the foyer from the penthouse proper.

There was no place for me to hide, so I just aimed my gun at the shadow behind the pillar and fired again.

A second later, Lena appeared in the entranceway. She moved like a ghost right up to Ironstone and dug the muzzle of her Lilliput pistol into the back of his neck.

'I'm going to pop this gun four or five times,' she screamed like a banshee, 'and sever the part of your spine that leads to your brain!'

It was so shrill and hysterical that Ironstone dropped his machine gun.

I got up, pistol leveled at Ironstone's face, and walked up to him as fast as I could.

'And then when she's done,' I told him, burning my eyes into the back of his skull, 'I'm going to pull out your eyes, cut out your tongue, and shave your head clean!'

That was something I'd gotten from my friend Philip. If you were any sort of Seminole, you really didn't want your body to be mutilated like that because you'd have to go to the other side blind, dumb, and bald. I didn't know if it would work on Ironstone exactly, but I thought it sounded like a match for Lena's hysteria.

'Hi, Foggy,' she said, smiling. 'You weren't gone long.'

'I missed you,' I told her, my gun still pointed at Ironstone's chest. 'And a good thing too. Ironstone's not joking. He killed your friend Crew Cut.'

She ground the muzzle of her tiny pistol harder into Ironstone's neck.

'He *what*?' she growled.

'Yeah,' I assured her. 'Dead on the lobby floor.'

'Why?' she asked.

'That's right,' I remembered, 'you were out of the room when John Horse told me he was an undercover DEA agent. Got next to Ironstone after your sister took a powder.'

'*Took a powder?*' she mocked. 'You really are playing up the whole I'm-a-gangster-from-Brooklyn gestalt.'

'Look who's using the word *gestalt*,' I countered.

'Could we dispense with the cozy banter,' Ironstone interrupted. 'My neck is starting to get sore, and I really have to see Redhawk. As you know, I'm not here alone. I have a dozen men outside, and several more on their way up the stairs. The way you came up, Foggy.'

'I don't know if that's true or not,' I said, 'but I never took you for the especially brave type. I mean, you were surrounded by your guys when you decided to gun down a fourteen-year-old girl. Which is to say, I wouldn't doubt that you brought a small army with you now, since there are *two* scary girls involved.'

I was trying to get his goat, knowing his penchant for deriding the opposite sex.

He smiled. 'In a few minutes you'll be dead on some floor just like Cypress.'

Took me a minute to remember that *Cypress* was Crew Cut's real last name.

'Bold talk for an old man with two guns pointed at him,' Lena sneered.

Ironstone sipped in a single breath and then moved like lightning. He dropped, twisted, and wound up behind Lena with her gun in his hand. He had her in front of him like a shield and the gun was at her temple.

'I'm not an old man,' he corrected harshly. 'I'm a Seminole warrior.'

'Bullshit,' I told him. 'No respectable Seminole warrior would consider beating a little girl anything but an embarrassment.'

He shook his head, backing toward the living room area.

'I know you're trying to rattle me with that kind of talk,' he said calmly. 'It won't work because you're a Jew, and I know that all Jews are women. Of course you're on this little worm's side.'

'Well, see,' I responded, 'now I *have* to kill you. It's a matter of principle.'

He laughed. 'You know I won't hesitate to shoot her. And I already shot you once, so you *know* I wouldn't mind doing that again.'

'Foggy,' Lena began.

'Shut up,' Ironstone said, and then he smacked Lena hard in the side of her head with the gun.

I took an involuntary step toward him, and he fired the pistol.

A second later there was a jagged line of blood along Lena's forehead. It was just a graze, but it would have really hurt. She didn't make a sound, tough little biscuit that she was.

'That's just the beginning,' Ironstone said. 'I shoot her a couple more times like that, and she really starts to bleed – maybe her right hand, or the inside of her thigh. Wouldn't kill her. Just hurt like hell. So put your gun on the floor and walk around it. Follow me.'

He continued backing into the living room.

I locked eyes with Lena. She exhaled.

I set my gun on the floor and gave it a wide berth, moving very carefully into the living room.

It was empty.

Ironstone looked around. 'Where's Redhawk?'

'Went out the back with Ellen and Ester,' Lena said, 'when we heard you come in.'

The blood was down her face like a mask.

'At least put something on her forehead,' I said to Ironstone. 'Redhawk's going to be very upset if you ruin his floors.'

Ironstone glanced at her.

'Right. There's a bathroom over there. Get a towel.'

I dashed. It was a half bath, and the towels were snow white. I grabbed one, but something caught my eye. On the lid of the toilet there were several seashells. One was a large scallop shell with a nice sharp jagged edge. I scooped it up, wadded it into the towel, and headed back into the living room.

I motored up to Lena, but Ironstone backed away.

I sighed. 'This towel's only going to work if it actually touches her head. Let me—'

'Hand it to her very carefully,' he interrupted, 'with your arm stretched out. Not close to her.'

I nodded. Then I locked eyes with her again, glanced down at my hand, and then back at her. Before she had a chance to wonder too much about it, I held out the towel.

'Careful,' I said. 'Don't drop it. No telling what Ironstone might do.'

She was busy trying to read my mind when her hand felt the

shell in the towel. Her head only moved a half an inch back, but I could tell she got it.

'Just wipe your head right now,' I told her. 'Don't do anything else. I want to see how bad it is.'

'Head wounds bleed worse than they are,' she said. 'But I'm not going to lie, it really stings.'

She got the towel with both hands and wiped it across her face. The crease where the bullet had zinged was about three inches long, which, on her relatively dainty head looked pretty menacing. But it wasn't deep, and it was already starting to dry up a little.

'Better hold the towel up there right on it,' I said. 'Leave it there until I say, all right?'

She nodded and moved the towel to her forehead – right next to Ironstone's gun hand.

All of a sudden there was a male voice from the other room.

'You're really making a mistake, Ironstone,' Redhawk said softly.

Then he appeared at the other side of the living room. He didn't have a gun, and his hands were folded in front of him.

Ironstone stumbled backward a little and turned to face Redhawk.

'I'll kill her,' Ironstone snarled.

'I know you're willing to,' Redhawk said soothingly. 'But you won't have to. Not when I explain to you that you're operating under a false assumption.'

'What?' Ironstone snapped like he hadn't heard correctly.

'Ellen Greenberg does not possess documents of any kind,' Redhawk explained, 'that implicate you in the larger nefarious world of the Florida drug business.'

'The thing is,' Ironstone rejoined, 'she *does*. I don't know what she's told you, but when she left town, she took David's pocket calendar and several of his ledgers. I wouldn't mind except that my name is in all of those documents. The whole idea was to have David take the blame for the business and then get himself killed by the Cubans or the Columbians before anybody realized that I was really running things. That way the Federals would think their operation was over here in Fry's Bay and turn their attentions to Miami, where they'd do my work for me: exterminate the competition. It was a very nice plan.'

'Until Lena showed up,' I said.

'Yes,' Ironstone agreed. 'David was really more a disease than a son – I often told him that. I was happy to have him dead, just not that way.'

'Because *that way* meant *more* Federal attention in Fry's Bay,' I said. 'Not less.'

'Right.' He put his mouth next to Lena's ear. 'You and your sister are little vermin, you know that?'

Lena responded conversationally. 'Well, that's what our mother used to say. I didn't take it personally. She was pretty loaded most of the time.'

'I'm telling you, Ironstone,' Redhawk muscled in, 'Ellen Greenberg never had anything on you. She's not in possession of any documents. You know me. You know I only tell the truth.'

I was a little surprised to see that Redhawk's pronouncement gave Ironstone pause. His shoulders sagged a little, and his face contorted.

'You've lost your way,' Redhawk went on. 'You've fallen into the Caucasian trap of wanting money and power at the expense of spiritual awareness and peace of mind.'

'No.' Ironstone shook his head a little too vigorously. 'Look at all the money *you* have.'

Redhawk's voice remained steady. 'But not at the expense of my spirit.'

I sensed that Redhawk's argument might have taken hold, except for the fact that the entire condo was suddenly overtaken by burly men.

Two guys burst in from the stairs, and somehow one more came out of the guest bedroom shoving Ellen in front of them. She was clutching her baby tight as a drum. There were guns everywhere. Lena twitched, but I shook my head.

Redhawk didn't move a muscle.

'Ah,' Ironstone said, 'the fabled Ellen Greenberg.'

'Whatever you want,' she said fervently. 'Let my sister go, and leave my baby out of it.'

'It doesn't end well for you, I'm afraid,' Ironstone said, working his way closer to her, still clutching Lena in front of him. 'Moscowitz, get over there with Redhawk.'

I moved.

'Let Ellen give the baby to Mister Redhawk,' I said.

Ellen and Redhawk both started to object, but I got them both in my sights.

'He'll take care of the baby,' I said, willing them to read my mind, 'no matter what happens. He's a stand-up guy.'

'All right,' Ellen answered, taking the baby to Redhawk. 'What now?'

'You'll turn over any documents you have concerning my business,' Ironstone went on. 'And then you and your sister will come away with me. Understand?'

He jostled Lena.

'Ow!' Lena squirmed.

But I knew better. She wasn't hurting that bad and she wasn't bothered by a little roughhousing. She was working her way into position.

'Hey!' I objected a little too loudly. 'Leave the kid alone!'

I took a step forward.

Ironstone aimed the Lilliput at me, away from Lena's head – just like I wanted him to.

I smiled. 'You know,' I told Ironstone, 'Ellen Greenberg isn't her real name.'

'What?' he barked.

I looked at Lena. 'Well?'

'Oh,' she said.

Then she moved like a freight train. She dropped the towel, slashed Ironstone's inner wrist with the jagged edge of the scallop shell. He dropped her a little, and she stomped down hard on his instep.

The gun went off, but I was already on the floor barreling toward the goons who had come up the stairs.

Lena twisted her gun out of Ironstone's hand as he fell. Then she popped the henchman standing next to Ellen.

Ellen whirled like a dervish and wrenched the gun out of the wounded guy's hand.

I tackled one of the guys close to the stairs and he went down. Ellen shot the other one twice and he stumbled backward, confused.

Then I did a thing I had only done once before in my life: I put the palm of my hand against my guy's nose and leaned my whole weight onto it. The cartilage crunched, and the guy howled like a shot dog. If I'd leaned any harder, the busted gristle could have gone all the way to his brain and he'd be dead instead of unhappy.

I got to my feet.

Redhawk still hadn't moved much, except he was clutching the baby and turned so that his body protected hers.

Ironstone was on the floor groaning and bleeding. His man who had been beside Ellen was also on the floor; he wasn't moving at all. The other guy by the stairs was clutching his leg and trying not to cry; Ellen had popped him in the leg with both her shots.

I looked at Lena. 'Damn. The three of us, we're, like, the Musketeers.'

Without batting an eye Lena said, 'I work for Disney, that's *Mouseketeers*.'

I glanced at Redhawk. 'Everybody's a comedian.'

He offered up a very Jewish shrug. 'Depends on your definition of comedy, I guess.'

At that precise moment, the elevator doors opened and Baxter appeared, gun drawn.

He was momentarily knocked back by the tableau that presented itself, but he recovered right away.

'You've been busy,' he said to me, aiming his police issue right at my chest.

'Not just me,' I acknowledged. 'The sisters were pretty righteous.'

'You took long enough,' Ironstone groaned from his place on the floor.

His wrist was bleeding all over, and he couldn't quite seem to get to his feet.

'This is a pretty big mess to cover up,' I said to Baxter before he could answer Ironstone. 'It's Redhawk's home, and he's a citizen above reproach around here.'

'I responded to a report of shots being fired,' Baxter answered, 'and when I arrived – everybody was dead.'

I glanced in Ironstone's direction. 'Everyone?'

'Oh, Mr Waters wasn't here. You shot Redhawk and his men, but not before they killed you and the girls.'

'No, see,' I protested, 'somebody had to be alive to fire the last shot.'

'Yeah, that was you, apparently,' he told me. 'You got off a few shots before you succumbed to your wounds.'

'I *succumbed*?'

'You're tough,' he said, smiling, 'but you're not invincible.'

Ironstone struggled to his feet, then, and was lumbering toward the elevator.

'Just kill them and have done with it,' he mumbled to Baxter.

'It's not that simple,' Baxter snapped. 'This many people dead? It'll be a major investigation. And with Redhawk, it'll also be the Tribal Council. And Betty Jumper.'

'Betty Jumper,' Ironstone growled. 'I wouldn't mind if a bullet found its way into her brain. Twice.'

'So,' Baxter went on, ignoring Ironstone, 'I have to stage the scene, figure out which gun shoots who. You go on downstairs. Which, by the way, is a mess. Foggy killed your guy down there.'

'No,' I corrected, 'Ironstone did that.'

'Jim Cypress was a Fed,' Ironstone explained to Baxter.

'Jimmie's dead?' Ellen's voice was hollow.

'We were in the lobby,' Ironstone said, 'and he was stalling, saying we should wait to go upstairs. That's when I got my gun out and explained to him that I had already figured out he was a Fed. A Seminole Fed – there's a strange creature. Anyway, all that remains, really, is to say thanks to Foggy and the little girl for helping us find Ellen. All Cypress had to do was keep an eye on you two, and you brought us right to this stupid little DEA informer.'

But I was smiling.

Baxter noticed first, and he didn't like it.

'What's so amusing, Moscowitz?' he asked me. 'You're about to be very dead.'

'Maybe,' I conceded. 'But why do you think Crew Cut was stalling?'

'Who?' His head jutted back.

'Jim Cypress, the Fed. Why was he trying to keep Ironstone in the lobby?'

'Oooh, pick me!' Lena said, hand raised.

I turned to her. 'Yes? You, the cute one in the front row?'

'He'd already called his pals in the DEA,' Lena answered, grinning. 'He was waiting for them to show up.'

'That's what I think,' I said. 'Which means they're on the way here right now. Probably out in the parking lot, loading their guns. You'll never make it past the lobby.'

Baxter glanced at Ironstone.

'Could be,' Ironstone conceded.

But he was bleeding and starting to look a little dizzy. Baxter was momentarily unnerved by the possibility of Federal law enforcement agents in the parking lot. It seemed like a good time to move.

I lunged right for Baxter. Then, before he could react, I fell to my right. So when he fired his gun, the bullet sizzled past me and into Redhawk's wall.

In that same second Redhawk handed off the baby to Ellen, who twirled and ran for the bedroom.

Lena was on the floor, scrambling for a gun, any gun.

And then all of a sudden Redhawk had a knife in his hand. He threw it like he was flinging a dart at a target, and it hit Baxter in his gun arm just above the wrist.

The gun went off, and the bullet burrowed into Redhawk's thigh.

'Into the elevator!' Baxter bellowed.

He and Ironstone managed to scramble into the elevator before anyone could stop them. They pounded buttons until the door closed and the cab started down toward the lobby.

'Go!' Redhawk shouted, clutching his thigh.

I looked around, snatched up a gun that belonged to one of Ironstone's men, and threw myself toward the stairway. I hadn't hit the first step when I heard something behind me. I turned and there was Lena, a pistol in each hand, barreling toward the stairs along with me.

Before I could protest, she shot past me and it was all I could do to keep up. We ran, stumbling, falling slaves to gravity, until we hit the ground floor.

Ironstone and Baxter were already out the front door, headed toward some car. There were no Feds in the parking lot. There wasn't anybody in the parking lot.

I flew toward the entrance doorway, but again Lena was ahead of me. She blasted through the door like a grenade and started firing randomly.

Ironstone and Baxter weren't firing back. They were piling into Baxter's big black Buick, his detective car – the one with the bullet-proof glass.

Safe inside, doors locked, Baxter cranked the engine.

'Tires!' I shouted.

Lena and I both went for the front tires at the same time. One of us hit, and a tire exploded.

Baxter cracked his window just enough to stick the muzzle of his gun out and fire several rounds. Before I knew what was happening, Lena was flying. She sailed through the air right in front of me, blasting both pistols, hoping to get a bullet past the crack in the window.

But one of Baxter's bullets got to her instead.

I watched, like it was slow motion. The blood spit out from her side.

She took a bullet that would have gone right into my chest. I saw her crumple, midair. I watched her fall at my feet and lay there like a pile of dead leaves.

I realized that Baxter's car hadn't started. He was trying, but nothing was happening. I just didn't care.

I was crouched over Lena, at a loss for what to do.

Then, out of the corner of my eye, I saw John Horse and Hachi creeping up to the back of Baxter's car.

At the same time there were – I don't know – maybe a dozen Seminole citizens, all just standing in front of the car. No weapons. No words. Just cold eyes and stone faces.

'Foggy!' John Horse called. 'How's the girl?'

I fought panic. 'Shot, bleeding, unconscious!'

'Maggie!' he called.

The next thing I knew, Maggie Redhawk was beside me, holding something at the place in Lena's body where all the blood was coming out.

'Let's go,' Maggie said to me softly. 'We have to get her to the hospital right now. Is my brother all right?'

'He's shot in the thigh,' I said vacantly. 'But other than that . . .'

The rest of the scene was a blur. As Maggie and I were getting Lena into the ambulance that had been hidden just around the corner of the building, men in suits emerged from cars all over the parking lot. Anyone would have spotted them for Feds. They might as well have been wearing uniforms.

Ironstone and Baxter were hauled out of Baxter's car and put into handcuffs. I watched Ironstone scream at the Federal officers as the ambulance took Lena and me away to the hospital.

All the while the Seminoles stood silent and staring, like concrete statues.

And Baxter, the poor bastard, was crying like a little kid.

TWENTY-SIX

When Lena went into surgery, I was there. When she came out, completely still, I was there. I stared at her face, willing it to light up. The room was filled with that alcohol smell and depressing florescent lighting. Add in the crappy fake Scandinavian furniture and the busted blinds, it was pretty much a typical hospital room. And after a very long while, the machines hooked up to Lena started beeping and blinking a little differently.

And when she opened her eyes for the first time after that, there I was.

'You're awake,' I said.

'Maybe I am,' she responded, trying to get her bearings.

'You took a bullet for me.' I shook my head.

'Yeah,' she acknowledged.

'Nobody ever did that for me.' I smiled. 'And plenty of people have had the opportunity, believe me.'

'Oh, I believe you,' she answered.

'I guess this makes us even.'

She tried to sit up. 'Not by a long shot, buckaroo. You saved my life, like, ten times. Plus, you found my sister like you promised. Taking a bullet for somebody, sure, that's tough. But keeping a promise? Rare as hen's teeth in my experience. So I still owe you big.'

I shook my head. 'In the first place, it wasn't *ten* times; in the second place, *we* found your sister; third, who's counting?'

'OK.' She shifted in bed; it hurt to watch. 'Give me the news.'

'Ironstone's in Federal custody,' I began plainly. 'Baxter's in his own jail, and John Horse is everyone's favorite hero. Showed up like the cavalry at the last second.'

'Probably not the comparison he'd choose,' she mumbled. 'My side hurts.'

'The bullet went through, more or less,' I told her, 'but your hip bone deflected it and got chipped in the process.'

'Am I going to walk funny?'

'You mean funnier than you already do?' I asked, smiling.

'Where's Ellen?'

'Talking with the Feds,' I answered. 'I think she's trying to arrange the much vaunted Witness Protection scheme I told you about.'

'No.' She fussed a little, still trying to sit up. 'Don't trust those guys. They set my sister up, almost got her killed, didn't help when she was on the run, and their guy, that Crew Cut guy – some help *he* was.'

'Yeah,' I agreed, 'turns out that's on Baxter. He's the one who tipped Ironstone. He's the one, in fact, who's kind of the force behind the force.'

'Meaning that he was working for Ironstone all along, and finding out about the Feds as a so-called officer of the law.' She closed her eyes. 'Ratted out my sister.'

'That's about the size of it,' I agreed. 'You tired? You want me to shut up so you can sleep?'

'No,' she sighed, 'I'm trying to think where we can go – my sister, my niece, and me. If the Feds are that stupid, I don't want anything to do with them. Certainly don't want them to know where I am.'

I sat still for a second, pondering.

'I don't know your real name,' I said finally.

'Yes you do,' she scoffed. 'It's Lena. You got a head injury?'

'No, see,' I complained, 'you told me that your sister picked a name out of the obits when she split from your mother's house. Her last name's not Greenberg, neither is yours.'

'Oh, I see,' she began.

'So what I'm wondering, first, is why she chose *Greenberg*.'

'No idea, really, who our fathers were,' she said matter-of-factly. 'So we went with the maternal side of the family. Jews, as you probably know, dig matrilineal heritage.'

I blinked.

'Your mother is Jewish?'

'Ruthie Schmeltzer,' she sighed. 'The Whore of Rio, Florida.'

'Nice,' I said, 'very Biblical – but you're telling me you're Jewish?'

'I don't think I'm anything, really,' she answered. 'I'm a troubled youth. You know: Dead End Kid.'

'So.' I nodded. 'You get some sleep, now. I'm going to go shake a couple of trees.'

'I don't know what that means,' she mumbled, 'but I could use a little nap.'

She was asleep before I was out the door to her room.

My office, I found, had been put back together nicely. New furniture, better lighting – somebody'd even swept. The walls were still that sickening green, cracked and peeling, but at least it wasn't a disaster area. I wasn't quite sure what had happened.

I called the main office of Child Protective Services in Miami. They were happy to report the reinstatement of my little satellite in Fry's Bay – without so much as an apology or a thank you. They also told me that the rest of my paperwork on the case involving Lena Greenberg was overdue. Which brought up the problems with Lena's case. Baxter hadn't produced the all-important, child-exonerating syringe. He'd probably destroyed it. So in a very real sense, Lena was still up on a murder charge. I told Miami as little as I possibly could, although I did mention Mister Redhawk's name a couple of times. That seemed to help. Then, before they could ask me anything else, I thanked them for fixing up my office. Turned out they had no idea what I was talking about.

My guess then was that Hachi or John Horse had overseen its reconstruction. A Seminole had wrecked it; a Seminole had to fix it.

I sat down behind my desk and tried to wend my way through the labyrinth of ugly possibilities for Lena and her sister – and the baby. The Feds had not, in fact, done much of a job protecting Ellen so far. I saw no reason to trust that they'd do any better in the future. Local law was a weak sister to the DEA, not remotely to be taken seriously. The Seminoles might help, but it really wasn't their tribe.

It was my tribe.

So what else could I do but reach for the phone and call on *that* tribe?

It only rang once.

'Hello, Ma,' I sighed into the phone. 'Yes, it's Feibush. Yes, I'm still in Florida.'

The next few minutes were spent accepting her loving critique of everything that was wrong with me, but it ended with the phrase, 'I'm so glad you called.'

'All right listen, Ma,' I said as soon as I could get a word in edgewise. 'You're not going to believe what I found in Florida: a couple of nice Jewish girls names *Moscowitz*!'

A moment of profoundly stunned silence was followed by the sentence I was hoping to hear.

'Bring them to Brooklyn,' my mother said. 'What are they going to eat in Florida?'

'Well,' I told her, 'if you say so. Look. As long as they're coming anyway, how about if they stay with you and Aunt Shayna for a while?'

'No more than three years,' she said. 'That's my limit on company from Florida. They can stay in the second bedroom.'

'They have a baby.'

'I have a crib.'

'Don't you want to ask me,' I began.

'You know your business,' she interrupted. 'I'm assuming they're in some kind of trouble and they need to get out of town. So now can you tell me: are they really Jewish?'

'Jewish as you or me,' I assured her.

'Well.' It wasn't the sound of someone who believed me, necessarily – but it was the voice of compassion. 'I guess they'd better come right up. Shayna!'

And then I tried for the next thirty minutes to get off the phone. What with catching up on who died and who got married, I knew more than ever before about an extended family I had never met.

When it was all said and done, the Florida sisters with the flexible last names had a place in Brooklyn to stay for a while.

My next call was to Pan Pan.

'So,' I began as soon as he picked up the phone, 'I'm still alive.'

'Well, that's something, anyway,' he admitted.

'Here's the thing,' I went on. 'There are some people coming to live with my mother for a while and I'd like to see that they have protection.'

'Don't say anything more,' he interrupted, 'because I don't

want to have any more facts than I can divulge under duress. But I believe I understand and I'll see to it.'

'Get some of Red's old guys, I guess,' I suggested.

'Yeah,' he sneered, 'if I can spring them from whatever senior citizens' facility they live in. How about someone *under* a hundred?'

'Such as?'

'I had in mind Delbert Two Shoes and Mickey Miller.'

'Oh.' I sat back in my chair. 'Nice. How – why would they do it?'

'Maybe you don't quite understand the size of your rep,' Pan Pan said softly. 'You're a guy who boosted anything that wasn't nailed down, then absconded to Florida where he saves little kids. *And* sends money home. You're like a hoodlum saint.'

'Pan Pan,' I objected.

'Plus, you'll pay, right?'

'Of course.' I had no idea how I'd pay, but I would.

'So it's settled. I'll look in personally, the other guys will be like ghosts, but they'll be around.'

'Might not be any trouble at all,' I said.

'You kicked the Black Tuna in the ass, my friend,' he countered. 'If they find out about this, there's going to be trouble.'

'Yeah.' I rubbed my eyes. 'I'm going to worry about that, like, tomorrow.'

'Right,' he agreed. 'Be Here Now, man.'

'Absolutely.'

We hung up without *goodbye*.

Before I could muster my energy to head back to the hospital, John Horse and Hachi suddenly appeared in the doorway of my office.

John Horse was in a black business suit. I'd never seen him dressed like that, and it was unnerving. Hachi was equally decked out: sleek grey suit, knee-length skirt, low black heels.

'Is there a funeral I don't know about?' I asked them both.

'Come on,' Hachi said firmly.

'Where?' I stood. 'I want to go back to the hospital, see Lena.'

'It's about her,' Hachi said. 'Judge Arnett's having a look at a motion of mine. You should be there.'

'What's it about?'

She shook her head. 'I've seen you improvise. Better if I say nothing and you go with your instinct when we get there.'

They were both serious as a heart attack, so I acquiesced and followed them out the door.

Judge Arnett was a no-nonsense sort. He'd been a judge in Fry's Bay for twenty years, and no one I knew had ever complained about him, which was saying something. Somebody *always* hates a judge.

His office was like a movie set of a judge's chambers: lined with books, golden gavel on the desk, American flag in one corner; a window that looked out toward the sea. It smelled like pine and was more silent than a church.

The old man sat behind his desk adjusting his bifocals and reading over stacks of papers in front of him.

Hachi sat in one of the chairs opposite him; John Horse was in the other. I stood behind Hachi.

After about a half a century, Arnett looked up.

'This is without a doubt the strangest thing I have ever seen here in Fry's Bay,' he pronounced.

'Yes, sir,' Hachi said firmly. 'Who could have imagined that the police department in our town could be so thoroughly involved in so many illegal activities?'

He looked at her sternly. 'Detective Baxter does not comprise the entirety of our police department.'

'But his investigation does comprise the entirety of the case before you,' she countered.

'No murder weapon?' he asked.

'None that the police could produce,' she answered, 'no, your honor.'

'And this syringe that is in evidence was suppressed in the initial reports?'

'It was,' she confirmed.

He glanced up at me.

'You are the director of Child Protective Services for our area,' he began.

'In that I am the only one in the office,' I interjected, 'I suppose you could call me the director.'

'And you were on the scene the night of the David Waters murder.'

'I was.'

'Did you see a murder weapon in the bar that night?'

'No I did not,' I answered honestly.

'Did you see this syringe that counsel mentions?'

'I saw the agitated state of the child in question, the accused,' I said quickly, 'who later revealed the deceased's intention to assault her with the syringe. I realize that's hearsay, your honor, but we're talking about a child, the product of a terrible home life – a lost girl. Not exactly the sort of person to fabricate such an event, or wield the sort of weapon that killed David Waters. He was shot three times in a well-targeted burst. Is that the action of any little girl?'

He sighed.

'Maybe the drug dealers from Cuba and Columbia, they killed David Waters,' John Horse said. 'Doesn't that make a lot more sense?'

'Frankly,' the judge said, 'it does. Baxter fabricated this ridiculous murder charge against the child in order to protect his nefarious cohorts.'

'And you do understand that the girl, Lena Greenberg, is currently in the hospital,' I said, 'having jumped in front of me to shield me from a bullet fired by Ironstone Waters.'

Judge Arnett closed a folder on his desk. 'Yes.'

'I recommend,' Hachi began.

'Not necessary, Counselor,' the judge interrupted, waving his hands. 'These ridiculous charges against Elena Greenberg are dropped and we'll start a new investigation, from the beginning, into the death of David Waters. Although, confidentially, good riddance. Anything else?'

Hachi stood. 'No, thank you, your honor.'

'Might I just interject,' I began.

But Hachi took my arm and squeezed it hard.

'Thank you, your honor,' she said again, more emphatically.

'Exactly,' I said.

And we left the judge's chambers immediately. Hachi was locked onto my arm like a C-clamp, and John Horse was moving faster than I'd ever seen him walk before.

Once we were out of the courthouse, John Horse began to whisper.

'Do you have some place to take Lena and the other two?'
he asked.

'As a matter of fact,' I said.

But once more Hachi squeezed. 'Don't tell us. Don't tell
anyone. You understand that we still don't know who's working
for the Columbians or the Cubans or the Federal government.'

John Horse shook his head. 'It's all the same to me: dangerous
white men with no souls and lots of guns. I have to take off this
suit before it starts bonding with my skin.'

With that he was gone, off down the street headed God knows
where.

'It was a great thing you did in there,' I told Hachi, trying not
to enjoy how close she was standing to me. 'Getting Lena off,
I mean. You're really a remarkable person.'

She smiled. It affected me the same way jasmine always did:
I closed my eyes and sighed.

'I think I'd say the same thing about you,' she said, finally
releasing my arm.

'Me?' I blinked. 'The only thing remarkable about me is how
tired I am at this moment.'

'Well,' she acknowledged, 'you've been shot, beaten, pursued
by drug lords, betrayed by the boys in law enforcement, and
nearly killed by a certified Seminole demon.'

'And all on very little sleep and not enough good food,' I
added.

She patted me and inclined her head toward the docks.

'Maybe we could take care of one of those things,' she
suggested. 'Yudda's got blackened swordfish and hot chicory.'

TWENTY-SEVEN

The next morning, before the sun was up, I was yawning at the Greyhound bus station. Ellen and her baby were already on the bus. Ellen had dyed her hair again – black as a crow's wing. Lena was dolled up in her misleading child's apparel: a sensible black skirt, white blouse, hair pulled back into barrettes. She looked ten, and even I might not have recognized her in a crowd.

'Pan Pan Washington is meeting you at Port Authority,' I said for the third time. 'He'll have—'

'Foggy,' Lena said sweetly, putting her hand on my forearm, 'we'll be fine. I really don't have any way to thank you for – everything.'

'Good,' I said, 'because there's really no need. After about a week with my mother and my aunt, you'll start to regret the whole thing, what with the food and the cheek patting and the hovering.'

'Yeah,' she said softly, 'must have been tough growing up with that kind of motherly attention.'

I looked away. 'All right.'

'I'll never forget this,' she said with all the fervent conviction of the very young. 'You'll always be the most important man in my life.'

I nodded. I didn't say anything. I knew it wasn't true, but I didn't want to muddle her mind. Wouldn't be long before she met plenty of people who would mean more to her than a guy she knew for a couple of weeks in Fry's Bay, Florida. That's kids, though: you have to walk a very careful line between taking them seriously and not believing a thing they say.

Still, it was a nice thing to hear that morning.

The bus revved its engine and she sighed.

'Right.' She got up on her tiptoes and planted a little kiss on my left cheek.

And without further ado, she was gone.

Ten minutes later I was back in my apartment, but it wasn't really my apartment. It was a last impression of everything that had happened in the days preceding. The sofa was the last place Lena had slept while her sister and baby Ester had occupied my bed. The big chair, the one by the double glass doors that looked out onto the ocean, had been my restless nest. The sad, disheveled blanket was witness to my restless tossing and turning.

And the word *empty* had taken on a new meaning.

Just as I was about to slip into a very French melancholy, I heard the front door open behind me. I turned to see John Horse standing there, back in his usual flannel shirt and blue jeans. Only he was wearing some sort of necklace. That was new.

He just stared. He didn't say anything or move or indicate in any way that he saw me. He was staring out at the ocean.

I gave up trying to suss out the inscrutable and headed for the kitchen.

'Coffee?' I asked him softly.

'Look at the waves,' he answered.

I did. There were lots of them, hundreds of grey peaks rising and falling, some capped in white, others curling back into themselves. It would have been mesmerizing if I'd let it be, but I wasn't interested, not that morning. I went on into the kitchen.

'That's what we are,' he went on, still not moving. 'The universe is an ocean and we rise up, crest, and then go back to the salt and the water – become the sea again.'

'OK,' I said, plugging in the percolator.

'I only mention it,' he concluded, 'because it makes me feel better, when I've had a hard day, to know that we're only waves for a very short time. Mostly, we're the ocean.'

'So none of this is supposed to affect me,' I snapped, 'because I'm a *wave*?'

'No, as long as you're a wave, you're going to be affected by the agitation all around you: the other waves, the weeds, the tooth of the shark. It's just that you're not a wave for very long. After that, you're a part of everything else in the ocean.'

I shook my head. 'Enough with the wise-old-medicine-man shtick. Do you want coffee or not?'

He hesitated, then broke his stolid pose.

'All right.' He shrugged. 'It was worth a shot. Do you have English muffins?'

I swallowed. 'I'm off English muffins for a while.'

'Oh.' He nodded. 'Right.'

'I got bagels.'

'Perfect!'

The coffee finished percolating, the bagels were toasted, and John Horse and I sat at my kitchen table not talking, staring out the big glass doors.

And I didn't want to notice, but I couldn't help it: the waves were only waves close to the shore. Farther out to sea, it was calm. And on the shore, they were flat and thin, nearly transparent, running over the sand before they retreated.

'Damn it,' I said to him at length, 'now you got me thinking about these waves.'

He laughed. 'What about them?'

'I don't know exactly.'

He took another bite of his bagel. 'Our little lives in these temporary bodies, they only exist in a transitional realm, a place between two greater worlds.'

'I'm sorry I mentioned it.' I shook my head and finished my coffee.

I took in a breath. 'I won't say that all my problems are solved at this point, but I'm a little surprised that a certain latent depression doesn't appear to be settling in like I thought it was going to. In fact, I don't feel so bad after all. How do you do that?'

He knew what I was talking about. But instead of pressing his advantage, he went back to the more mundane world of Fry's Bay.

'I should probably remind you that there's a good bit of money in that safe deposit box. Lena left it for you.'

'I forgot about that.'

'And I guess it would also help to know that the insurance claim is paying off. Lena and her sister will have plenty of money – wherever they are.'

'Yeah,' I said, not looking at him. 'Wherever they are.'

'So.' He sat back, swallowing the last of his bagel. 'You want to go fishing? Like, deep sea fishing?'

'Sure.' I stood up. 'I was thinking of taking the day off anyway. Just let me change into something more sea-worthy.'

I shuffled off toward my bedroom. John Horse sat at the table and poured himself another cup of coffee, humming a familiar melody under his breath.

'What's that you're singing?' I called out.

'*Memories of You*,' he answered, 'the Benny Goodman version.'

An hour later we were both out on somebody's big boat in the middle of a calm ocean – no waves at all – angling for swordfish and drinking from a portable water cooler filled with gin and vermouth and some kind of bitter herb that John Horse said was supposed to prevent hangovers. That way, he said, we could drink as much as we wanted to. And we wanted to drink a lot.

Sometime that morning, out there in the middle of all that water, filled with Seminole martinis, I forgot everything and everyone. At least for a little while, I was just another part of the ocean.

Lightning Source UK Ltd.
Milton Keynes UK
UKOW04f0054081217
314069UK00002B/4/P